The Spirit's Apprentice

By
Pauline Maurer Larson

PublishAmerica
Baltimore

© 2007 by Pauline Maurer Larson.

All rights reserved. No part of this book may be reproduced, stored in a retrieval system or transmitted in any form or by any means without the prior written permission of the publishers, except by a reviewer who may quote brief passages in a review to be printed in a newspaper, magazine or journal.

First printing

All characters in this work are fictitious, and any resemblance to real persons, living or dead, is coincidental.

At the specific preference of the author, PublishAmerica allowed this work to remain exactly as the author intended, verbatim, without editorial input.

ISBN: 1-4241-9050-9
PUBLISHED BY PUBLISHAMERICA, LLLP
www.publishamerica.com
Baltimore

Printed in the United States of America

Dedication

To the millions who are tired of the status quo,
and who are yearning for the power to change their world
and to give meaning to their lives.

To the King eternal, immortal, my Lord, Jesus Christ—
may the readers of this book come to know him
and His resurrection power.

Acknowledgements

This book has taken many years to prepare and to write. Many people encouraged me during the process, even though there were times when it seemed like I would not finish it. In the words of the late Pastor John Osteen:

"Great it is to dream the dream
As you stand in youth
By the starry stream,
But a greater thing
Is to fight life through
And say at the end
The dream is true."

The dream is true…thanks to the countless individuals whose thoughts; ideas, perspectives, and ministries that gave me the inspiration and knowledge that is represented in this book.

I wish to thank my husband, AJ Larson, and my sons: Douglas and John Paul Gardiner, who believed in me and were such an encouragement.

I want to especially thank Hilda Johnston, Emma Johnston, and Arlene Dantin. These prayer warriors faithfully prayed and believed in this project. I also want to thank our church: The Chosen Generation, and the children of Metro Houston Ministries.

In addition there are several Bishops and Pastors that greatly impacted my life: the greatest influence has been that of Bishop La Donna Osborn. Other Pastors who have mentored me include the late John Osteen, Al Jandl, Clayton Shepherd, Bill Wilson, Benny Hinn, and Robert Dowdy.

I also want to thank Revs. Ken & Mary Bostrom, Pastors Aaron & Theresa Hrachovina, and Rev. Nancy Spicer for their support and friendship. In addition, there were so many other friends, and ministers whose prayers and encouragement made this possible. Unfortunately they are too many to list, but please know that you are all greatly appreciated.

CHAPTER ONE

It is written:
"So be careful how you live, not as fools but as those who are wise.
Make the most of every opportunity for doing good in these evil days."

The fog crept into the moonlight graveyard as four kids wove their way amongst the ancient tombstones. The wisps of fog muffled the sound of leaves crunching beneath their feet.

"Are we nearly there?" Myra said.

"Quiet!"

The four continued walking.

"What, afraid that you will awake the dead?" Myra asked. The others snickered at her joke. An owl hooted overhead, momentarily startling them. The night pulsed with the sounds of creatures that scurried in the moonlight.

"I suppose this will do," said June. Myra marveled at the mysterious shadows created by the headstones. The fog played with her imagination as she listened for sounds warning that they were being followed. They had found a small clearing to rest. June gently lowered the package that she had carried on to the ground, as the others gathered around it.

Myra eyed the area around the clearing. Not that she was afraid even though it was Halloween. She had told her parents that she was attending the church Hallelujah Night Celebration. The local church held its annual alternative to Halloween, which offered a safe alternative to Trick-Or-Treating. Safe, and yet how ironic, that she stood in the middle of a graveyard, with an Ouija board on Halloween night. She had heard that witches frequented this graveyard. Rumors abounded about how evil things happened in the graveyard during a full moon. Some said that they conducted human sacrifices in this graveyard. Yet she didn't really believe it, or did she?

Her thoughts turned to the plans that the group had for this night. They had dared each other to go to the graveyard and play the Ouija board on a tombstone. Although nervous, she longed for something supernatural to happen tonight, even if there was a full moon.

"Hey June, you look scared," said John Paul.

"Not me! I think that you are."

"Am not!"

"You are too!"

"Quiet, you are making too much noise." Doug said. "Let's play this and get out of here."

June sat cross-legged on the ground next to the board and placed the cursor on it. Doug sat across from her. "How do we play?" he asked.

"I don't know, but I think that you place your hands on the cursor and let it spell the words by itself. They say that the spirits move it and spell things that have to do with the future. You have to be real quiet." June lit the lantern and placed it next to the Ouija board so that they could see clearly what it would spell. The four watched the cursor for several minutes, and then it began to move.

"Are you moving it, June?" Doug asked.

"No, I am not. Look it is starting to spell out a word." The cursor glided over the words as it spelled out E-V-I-L. No one said a word, as they stared in disbelief. The damp air began to swirl as the wind made howling gusts around the clearing.

"Stop, I am scared, and I don't like this," said Myra. "I should have gone to the Hallelujah Celebration."

"Isn't it just like a girl to be scared?" "Let the wind blow and they are ready to quit," John Paul added.

THE SPIRIT'S APPRENTICE

"I am scared too!" said June, "let's try it again and then leave." They sighed with relief, as once again the two sat with their hands on the cursor and waited. Slowly the cursor began to move as it spelled out E-V-I-L.

"Do you think it is trying to warn us?" asked Myra. "Or does it think that you two are evil?"

"I don't know, but why don't we switch places and you can put your hands on the cursor?" said June.

"OK." John Paul and Myra sat on the ground and placed their hands on the cursor. Slowly it started to move. Myra felt it moving and asked, "Are you moving it?"

"No, honest I am not, it is moving by itself," John Paul replied. Once again the cursor spelled out the word E-V-I-L. A gust of wind knocked over the lantern, shattering the glass. At that precise moment, they heard footsteps approaching on the cobblestone path nearby.

"I think I see someone over there." Doug whispered to the group. Within seconds the four leaped to their feet and ran for the exit, abandoning the Ouija board. Myra's heart pounded as she listened for running footsteps. After running for several minutes the four slowed their pace as they tried to listen.

Myra's breath came in great gasps and her legs felt like rubber. They didn't hear anything so they continued toward the exit. With relief they saw the entrance gate fifty yards away. They had almost reached the towering wrought iron gates when they noticed a shadow moving near a sepulcher. The four quickened their pace, but so did the shadow. They dashed for the entrance, just as the gate mysteriously slammed shut in front of them. Terrified, they turned to face their pursuers. Several hooded figures moved in an arc formation behind them. Myra sensed that they were forming a human net behind them. She strained to see who they were, but the hoods obscured their faces. The gate loomed above them, as John Paul lunged against it forcing it to swing open. They scrambled through it and ran down the tree-lined road.

They ran for several blocks, fear propelling them forward. They raced into the night, hoping to place as much distance as possible between themselves and their pursuers. Myra noted with dismay that their pursuers were gaining momentum and closing the gap between them.

"Jesus help us!" Myra cried.

As they rounded the bend, they saw a church, standing like a lighthouse, its steeple reaching toward heaven. As if in answer to their prayers, the bells began to toll. The noise drowned the sound of the footsteps. With every toll of the bells their pursuers cringed, as though sensing the eternal judgment that they knew awaited them for their dark and evil deeds.

"Let's see if the church is open," said Doug. The four headed toward the building. As they neared the door of the church, their pursuers slackened their pace. Doug yanked at the door, hoping to find a safe refuge. The door opened without resistance, and they slipped inside. Candles illuminated the sanctuary, as a man knelt in prayer. They could hear him praying.

"Let's not disturb him, but let's find a place to hide. Whoever was chasing us will be waiting for us to leave the building." Myra said, "Besides, if we tell the man who we are and what we were doing we will be in trouble," the four whispered as they tiptoed down the hall. Doug tried a side door and it opened to a stairwell. The four tiptoed up the stairs and found themselves in the choir loft. They hid in the shadows, yet they could see the man near the altar.

"Do you think that he is the Pastor?" whispered John Paul.

"What if they lock us in here tonight?" June added, "I need to get home, I have a test tomorrow."

"What do you want me to do about it?" said John Paul. "It was your idea to go to the graveyard. Besides, my folks are going to be mad at me too."

The four gasped as the door to the sanctuary opened and a hooded figure walked down the aisle toward the kneeling man. The figure pulled a gun out of his cloak and aimed it at the kneeling man. The man rose to his feet, and faced the intruder. For the third time that night, Myra wished that she had gone to the Hallelujah Celebration.

One by one, they slid down the wall until they were below the choir railing. Staying in the shadows, they took great care not to make noise. With their backs pressed against the wall, they lowered themselves inch by inch until they were sitting on the floor. Peering between the rails, they watched the scene below them. Time seemed to stand still, as the two faced each other. The Pastor remained expressionless as he stood his ground. Not a muscle twitched in his face as he faced the intruder. Surely he knew that the gun spelled certain death at such close range.

Myra wanted to shout, "Run for your life!" If the Pastor was afraid he did not show it.

"Where are they, old man?"

The Pastor remained silent.

"I asked you a question," continued the figure.

"Are you looking for someone?" asked the Pastor.

"Don't play games with me. Where are the kids that ran into this place a few minutes ago?" The four flinched as they listened.

"What are you talking about? Why would you think that there are any children here?"

"Don't play games with me, old man."

"Why would I do that? I am a man of God."

"You have until the count of three to tell me where they are, or I'll splatter your blood all over this sanctuary." The intruder said as he pushed back his hood. His baldhead shone in the candlelight.

The Pastor still didn't move.

"One," he said as he cocked the gun and aimed it at the Pastor's head.

The Pastor remained silent.

"Two! You call yourself a man of God? The man laughed and added. "You'd better be right with God, because you are going to meet him soon." The man laughed.

"Three!" He pulled the trigger, and nothing happened. Frantically he pulled the trigger again and again, but each time nothing happened. Disgusted, the man threw the gun at the Pastor. The gun appeared to hit an invisible force field as the Pastor raised his hand to block it. The gun flipped into the air over the two men's heads and clattered to the floor.

"Now, it is my turn," said the Pastor. His eyes transformed before them to resemble those of an eagle with an unearthly glow in them. Even from the vantage point of the choir loft, they could see the Pastor transform, becoming bolder with the most piercing eyes that they had ever seen.

"You will never again raise that arm to harm another of God's creatures." No sooner had he spoken than the man grabbed his arm and began to scream, falling to his knees he doubled over and clutched his hand. Smoke rose from his hand and forearm, as the man writhed in pain upon the floor. Before their eyes, the man's arm shrank and withered to half its normal size. The arm aged to that of a ninety year old man.

"Are you ready to repent or do you want more?" asked the Pastor.

"No! Stop…please you have to make the pain stop."

"I will ask the Lord to have mercy on you." The Pastor kneeled beside the man, and placing his hands upon him began to pray. Immediately, the smoke stopped and the arm became its normal color but remained shrunken.

"The Lord is leaving your arm in a shrunken state as a reminder to stop your evil ways or a worse state will come upon you. Do you understand?"

"Yes!"

"Are you ready to live for the one true God? Are you ready to renounce your evil ways?"

"Yes!"

"Do you want power, real power?"

"Yes."

"Are you sure?"

The man nodded, "I believe!"

The Pastor produced a big book from his pulpit and showed the man various passages in it. The four couldn't hear all the words that were spoken, but they knew that the man was praying with the Pastor.

As soon as the man finished his prayer, his facial expression had changed. To their amazement, the Pastor hugged the man. They continued to talk for several minutes, after which the man left the church. The hooded man looked and walked differently. It was as if he had become a new person. Myra marveled again at what she had seen. Nothing ever happened like this in her church; in fact the services bored her so much that she almost hated church. The only reason that she attended was because her parents forced her to go on Sunday mornings.

The Pastor looked up at the choir loft, and addressed them. "Kids, I know that you are up there. You may come down now."

The four froze and didn't answer. "Let's let him think that we already left. He might do something to us too. I'll bet he knows that we weren't doing what we were supposed to do."

As if in answer to their thoughts, and sensing that they were frightened by what they had seen, he added, "You are safe, and I promise that I won't harm you." The Pastor waited for several minutes, then he left.

"Good, let's leave after we hear him drive away," whispered June.

"What if the others are waiting for us?" Asked John Paul.

"Let's just stay here until morning, and then leave." Said Doug. "Besides I have my cell phone and we can call our folks and let them know what happened."

"I will be in big trouble if I don't go home tonight." Said Myra.

"I think that he has already left, and if he has then we are in great danger if we walk out these doors. You know the hooded people will be waiting for us"

"Do you know anyone else that we could call who could pick us up?" Asked Doug.

"How are we going to explain what happened?" asked June.

"Let's go down and see if there is anything in the kitchen. I am hungry." Said John Paul,

They agreed and walked down the stairs. As they opened the door they came face to face with the Pastor.

"I have been waiting for you." He said. The four shrieked, and Myra almost fainted.

"It is OK, you are safe. By the way, I am Pastor Shepherd, and you are at New Life Christian Center. I will be happy to take you home in the church van."

"It is OK, I brought my car, " said Doug.

"Would you mind taking me home?" Myra asked.

"Can I ride with you too," June added.

"I might get in trouble if Doug brings me home late." Myra added.

"Pastor, would you mind if I called my Mom and had you talk to her? I know that she won't believe me if I try to explain what happened."

Myra waited several minutes before making her call. She lived with her mother and stepfather. Her real father had died when she was four years old. She missed his gentleness, and the fun that they had together. He addressed her as "Moola," and told her daily how much he loved her. Her stepfather, by contrast, who professed to be a deeply religious man, ruled their home with an iron fist. Literally beating her and her mother when they displeased him. He would justify his actions by the Bible, even though he didn't live what he preached. He often came home drunk, and in a rage. Myra anxiously dialed her home. Her stomach hurt, as it often did when she knew that her parents would be angry.

"Mom, I am at New Life Christian Center. I wanted to let you know that I am with Pastor Shepherd, and he is going to bring us home."

"What are you doing there?" her mother asked.

"John Paul, Doug, June and I got chased by some people that we think might have been witches. It was horrible, we were trying to outrun them, and saw the church. It was open and we hid in there. In fact, one of the hooded men followed us in…what?" Her mother had changed the subject and was obviously angry.

"No, I didn't go to the Hallelujah celebration, and I am sorry that I disobeyed you. Pastor Shepherd wants to talk to you." She handed the phone to him. But no matter how much he tried to reassure her mother, Myra could tell that she would be in trouble when she got home.

He asked them to come into the sanctuary. "Would you like to know God like I know Him?" he asked. "He is an awesome God."

"Yes." They all replied.

"There is a book that I hesitate to give you, because it isn't an ordinary book. It holds the keys to the universe, and has great power in it. No one who reads it with understanding will ever be the same."

"Can we read it?" they chimed.

"Many have tried to read it, but there is a secret to reading it. You must have spiritual ears and eyes to understand it. Otherwise it is just an ordinary book full of history lessons, and very dry to the reader. You must read it as though digging for ancient treasure. Those who seek to understand will be given the power to understand."

"Who gives us this power?"

He ignored the question and continued talking, "Do you know that there is a book in the library with the title, 'All I Want Is a Kind Word, a Warm Bed, and Unlimited Power'? Isn't that what everyone secretly wants?"

"Yes, that is what I want." Said June.

"Is that the title of this book?" asked Myra.

"No."

"Where can I get such a book?" Myra asked.

Pastor Shepherd took them to his office, and removed a large leather bound Bible from his library. Gently he held it and caressed it with his hands. "Be careful where you are when you read this. People may be angry and call you a religious fanatic. Don't use the sacred words as weapons to hurt people, but only to help people. When you speak the words audibly over your enemies it will change them and your situations. When you read the power passages aloud over yourself and others it will change them forever. Are you sure that you can handle such a book?"

"Do you only have one? John Paul asked.

"No, I am going to give you each a copy, and you may keep them." He said as he handed each one a copy.

"Thanks," they said.

"But this is just a Bible," June said. "I thought that you were talking about a magical book."

" That is what most people think, but it's not just a book, it is supernatural. It lives."

"Oh," Myra said.

"Do you know that it says that the word of God is full of living power? It is sharper than the sharpest knife, cutting deep into our innermost thoughts and desires. It exposes us for what we really are. Nothing in all creation can hide from it." He said.

" I had kept these Bibles for years waiting to give them to four special people. As you read these books, you must guard your hearts, and these words. These words contain the forces of life. You will literally feel yourself strengthened as you read the passages. Your health will even improve as you reach these words."

"Wow!"

"One of the translations says that the words are actually alive. Can you imagine a book that is a living thing?"

Each one carefully opened their Bibles, and thumbed through the gilt-edged pages. The books smelled of new leather. The soft black leather contrasted with the deeply embossed gold letters of the title. June rubbed her fingers over the letters. Doug stuck his nose inside the book, and said, "This book has a different smell to it, and the pages aren't like normal pages."

"That is because there is no other book on earth this like it, because it was not written by man."

"Who wrote it?" Doug asked.

"The Holy Ghost dictated it to men. In fact, you can't understand it without help."

"Where do we get the help, Pastor Shepherd?" asked June.

"Ghost? Wait a minute, I know tonight is Halloween, but a ghost? Are you kidding me?" asked Myra.

"No, He is part of the three that are one. The Father, the Son, and the Holy Spirit. He will be your helper and your guide." He looked at his watch and added, "Let's be going, it is getting late and you have school tomorrow."

As he drove June and Myra home, Pastor Shepherd shared more about the power of God. They listened eagerly as he talked about the power of God in such a personal way. Myra knew that no one had ever taught them such things.

"I have a theory about kids," he added. "All any kid wants is unlimited power to change their world. Isn't that right?" Myra nodded.

"I wish that I could change my stepfather, because he scares me when he gets drunk." Myra added.

"I can teach you how to use the unlimited power to change your world. By the way, please feel free to call me either Pastor Tom or Tom."

"Are you serious?" asked June. "I mean, not about calling you Tom, but that you can show us how to have unlimited power to change our world?"

"Absolutely," said Pastor Tom. Myra pondered all that she had heard. Could it really be true?

"I am starting an after school club at the school. Our first meeting will be next Friday at 4:00 pm. Listen to the announcements, because it will be called the BOC Club. The club aims to help with everyday problems in the life of the students. BOC means Blood of Christ; we chose that name because of the gangs. Anyone who lives in this town knows about the problem with the Bloods, so I wanted to start a gang that represented blood in a positive way. Besides our real gang leader is the best, he can walk on water. His name is Jesus."

"I like that, and I hope that I am able to come." Said Myra.

"I am coming!" said June.

He opened his copy of the book, and read a passage, "There was a small town with only a few people living in it, and a great king came with his army and besieged it. There was a poor, wise man living there that knew how to save the town, and so it was rescued. The man didn't do it with money or connections. He did it with wisdom. I can point you towards that wisdom. One poor man saved their city. Now I am not for being poor, but just in case you think that because you are a kid, that you can't do anything big. I wanted to show you that you could change your world. In fact, if the adults won't change it then the responsibility falls on your shoulders. The Holy Spirit awaits your decision to help him change the world. Are you willing?"

"Yes," They agreed.

"Are you sure? Because with this comes great responsibility, and once you commit to it there is no going back."

"Yes!"

"You will face many enemies and foes along your path. It won't be an easy task, and once you start this journey you won't be able to turn back. Your family may not understand. In fact, they may even disown you. Are you sure that you want to risk that?"

"Yes," They agreed.

"Tell the others to meet me at the BOC on Friday, and the journey will begin."

They dropped June at her home. However, the closer they got to Myra's home the more she became uneasy. Physically, she felt refreshed in spite of the evening's events. Yet she knew that she would have to face her parents in a few minutes. She said goodnight to Pastor Tom, swallowed hard and walked up the sidewalk to the house.

Myra rehearsed the night's events and how much had happened. She knew that she stood at the crossroads of her life. She couldn't help wondering if once again she would be discouraged from pursuing her dreams. What if her friends laughed at her or her parents disapproved? She didn't want to abandon the quest. Finally she had found something for which to fight, and no disapproval or lack of understanding was going to deter her. How ironic, she thought, that the normally quiet and shy Myra would even consider being involved in anything so radical. In the past, other people's opinions had affected her, and sometimes she had dropped out of activities because of a friend's disapproval. However, tonight had changed her life. For the first time, she had a purpose, a goal that really seemed to matter. Instinctively she knew that whether family or friends liked it or not she wasn't the same person. "This time I am not going to let other people talk me out of following my heart." She said to herself. With these thoughts, she opened the front door. Her parents were waiting for her.

CHAPTER TWO

It is written:
"Although my father and my mother have forsaken me,
yet the Lord will take me up (adopt me as His child)."

"You had better have a good explanation for your whereabouts," said George, Myra's stepfather. "You have upset your mother. Why she has been sick with worry."

Myra explained once again what had happened to her mother and stepfather.

"You are grounded for a week. You will come home after school and do your homework. No television and no phone calls will be allowed until next Friday night."

"But Mom..." Myra thought that this wasn't the time to ask if she could stay after school for the BOC. She decided to be the model daughter and hope that her parents would let her attend.

"No," her mother said interrupting her thoughts. Myra could tell by the tone of her voice that this was a time to keep quiet.

"Pastor Dowling will be most hurt that you didn't attend the Hallelujah Night Celebration. You need to apologize to him. Besides, you stay away from Pastor Shepherd; I have heard strange things about him."

"But Mom..." Myra protested.

"The answer is no." Her mother added. Myra hung her head, and turned to go to her room.

"That Pastor Shepherd does strange things, like speak in unknown languages. Tongues they call it. That stuff is of the devil."

"Now you take Pastor Dowling, that's a man who has a tough life. He struggles to provide a church for us, the least we can do is be loyal and supportive of him."

"I know that he works hard, but he is so boring, and he never talks about the Lord like Pastor Shepherd does. Mom I accepted Jesus tonight as my Lord."

"Don't you talk all that Jesus stuff to your mother." Her stepfather said, "Why you sound like one of those religious fanatics."

"I wasn't even saved."

"Nonsense child, you were saved when you were a child. You have been raised in a Christian home and in church all your life. You are just tired and confused, and don't understand what you are saying."

"Yes I do!" Myra protested.

"Your mother and I have a reputation to uphold. Why, if the church folks thought that you weren't a true Christian that would look very bad for us. So, I suggest that you don't mention this or all this Jesus stuff anymore."

"But Dad..." Myra protested. She had always called him Dad, even though he wasn't her natural father.

"Yes, Pastor Dowling would be terribly upset if he heard you talking like this." Her mother added.

After they had finished talking, Myra headed upstairs for her bedroom. She still carried her new Bible. Tearfully, she placed it upon her bed and slumped into her favorite chair. Baby, her Himalayan cat, nuzzled her and brushed against her legs. He even knows, she thought, that this is so unfair. After a few minutes she reached for the book, and held it to her chest. "Baby," she said to her cat, "Since they grounded me, I'll just spend my time reading this book." She remembered what Pastor Shepherd had said about asking the Holy Spirit to be her friend. She even sang the song that she had heard in the church van. "Welcome Holy Spirit...." She said. She listened and waited for something to happen.

Nothing happened, so she decided to go to bed.

Myra climbed into bed with a heavy heart. For what seemed hours, she stared at the ceiling, and cried herself to sleep.

Several hours later, she suddenly awakened. She didn't know what time it was, but she could see the moonlight streaming through her window. Her curtains were rustling in a soft breeze. Darn, she thought, I must have left the window open. She remembered her mother's lectures about catching cold from a window draught. "That is all I need on top of everything is a cold," she said to Baby. The cat sat on her bed, his attention focused on the moving curtains. She examined the window, and found that it was shut. The curtains still moved, but not from the wind.

"Holy Spirit?" she said.

An eerie silence filled the room, and she knew that she wasn't alone. The moonlight gave a surreal glow as it streamed through her window. She watched words form on shafts of light. Quickly, she rubbed her eyes. This must be a dream, she thought. She moved closer to the window and saw the ivory colored words forming a sentence, "For with God nothing shall be impossible. Luke 1:37."

Grabbing her Bible, she thumbed through it to the first chapter of Luke, and ran her finger down to verse thirty-seven. She hadn't known about the scripture.

"Holy Spirit, you are real!" No sooner had the words left her mouth, than a warm glow filled her body from head to toe, as though warm blankets had been placed upon her. Then she began to shake uncontrollably. She continued to shake, and shake. The warm glow turned into a feeling of pulsing electricity that ran up and down her legs, arms, face, and body. It didn't hurt, but tingled. She didn't understand what was happening, and she wished that she could call Pastor Tom. After what seemed hours, the shaking subsided enough for her to return to bed. She reached over to pet Baby. As her hands touched the animal, he flopped onto his side, and appeared to be asleep. "Oh no! Baby wake up!" The cat slowly roused itself and tried to jump off the bed, but his legs crumbled under him. She watched the animal stagger as though drunk.

"Oh Holy Spirit, I think that I hurt my cat." She said, tears streaming down her face as she cradled the animal in her arms. Instantly, she knew that the Lord had performed surgery on him, and was fixing something inside of him. She laid him gently onto the bed.

Myra fell asleep, and was again awakened. This time she knew that she had an unwelcome visitor. George, her stepfather, had entered her room. She could smell the alcohol on his breath as he lurched toward her. No, she thought I don't want him to touch me anymore. She pulled the covers up to her throat and waited for the inevitable.

George sat down beside her, and started to caress her arm. Her skin cringed at his touch. He continued to talk about her disobedience and her punishment, but she didn't even listen. She felt a boldness rise within her.

"Stop that!" she hissed. He slapped her across the face. Tears stung her eyes and her face smarted from the intensity of the slap. She hoped that she didn't have a black eye. Too many times she had gone to school and used excuses to explain the bruises. Then she remembered the written words, and thought about what had happened with the man in the church.

Slowly she sat up and faced her drunken stepfather. George's face leered inches from her face. She knew what was coming next, but tonight she placed her hands on his chest and pushed. George shrieked as he uttered foul language and said, "Your hands are like fire!" He lunged toward her again. She knew that he could be very dangerous; yet she heard the Holy Spirit telling her to blow upon him. Softly she blew at his face. George flew backwards into the air and slammed into the wall, before sliding onto the floor. Ouch that must have hurt, she thought. She tried not to laugh or smile, because she didn't want to make him even angrier. He didn't move. At first she thought that she might have killed him. She dismissed any thought of waking her mother. Her mother wouldn't have believed that George would do such things. Besides, George had threatened to beat her severely if she ever told of his night visits. Hate rose in her heart toward her stepfather, but she knew that the Lord would want her to forgive him. She found it hard to forgive someone who continually hurt her, and who wouldn't leave her alone. Then she remembered that Pastor Tom had told them how the battle wasn't theirs but the Lord's. George began to move, and slowly got to his feet. He glared at her for several minutes. Perhaps he was debating the wisdom of approaching her again, apparently deciding that he had had enough.

"I'll get you for this," he said as he left her room. She knew that someone greater than George would protect her. Just that evening, she had read in the sacred words, "But in that coming day, no weapon turned against you will succeed. And everyone who tells lies in court will be brought to justice. These benefits are enjoyed by the servants of the Lord; their vindication will come from me, I, the Lord have spoken!" That included people like George, or anyone who tried to harm her. Although she might have to face him again, she wouldn't have to face him alone. She opened the Bible and smiled as she read yet another promise, "they shall dwell with confidence, when I have executed judgments upon all those that despise them round about them; and they shall know that I am the Lord their God." She looked forward to the day that she would see that happen.

What she wanted more than anything was for his night visits to stop. She already felt dirty and used, even though she didn't want his advances. She feared him, and many times had wanted to run away from home. However, being a practical girl, she knew that supporting herself would be difficult until she finished school. Tonight, he had left her alone and she had won for the moment at least.

"What a night!" she said as she snuggled next to Baby. Soon she was asleep.

The next morning came too soon, as Myra slammed the knob on her snooze alarm. Ten minutes later, the alarm rang again. She groaned as she slipped out of bed and headed for the bathroom. Her normal morning routine consisted of a quick shower, and a breakfast of cereal before catching the bus that stopped at the end of her driveway. This morning, she took time to read more of the sacred words.

Her eyes devoured the words. Could these sayings be true? Did they literally mean what they said, and could they apply to her personally? Why hadn't anyone told her that such promises existed and that she could claim them? On the one hand, she felt cheated, but on the other, she was glad that she had found them now.

"Myra! Are you up yet?"

"Yes Mom." She continued reading, and wished that time would stand still for a few minutes.

"Whoa!" She said to herself. She had turned to a passage that said, "And now, O Lord, hear their threats, and give your servants great boldness in their preaching. Send your healing power; may miraculous signs and wonders be done through the name of your holy servant Jesus."

She stopped reading and prayed, "If you did it for them, please do this for me." She continued reading out loud, "After this prayer, the building where they were meeting shook, and they were all filled with the Holy Spirit."

Myra wondered what it meant to be filled with the Holy Spirit. Hurriedly, she laid the book down, and grabbed her schoolbooks before heading down the stairs to the kitchen. Although she had read for what seemed only a moment, the time had flown past. In fact if she didn't hurry she would miss the bus.

Just as she was pouring the milk into her cereal bowl her mother walked into the kitchen.

"You are going to be late if you don't hurry. By the way, George tells me that you were very rude to him last night, when he went to talk to you about your behavior yesterday. He says you even pushed him up against the wall. Not only that he says that you burned him with something very hot. He showed me two hand prints on his chest."

"Mom, I was tired and he startled me. I didn't do anything to him."

"That is not what he says. I didn't raise you to be disrespectful to your parents."

"I didn't mean to be, it's just that he woke me up and I had such a horrible evening. Do you remember me telling you about being chased by those men? Mom, can we talk later or I will miss the bus."

"Yes, of course, but you do need to apologize to him when he comes home from work." Myra sighed, how could she tell her mother that her stepfather was a perverted monster that made her life a living nightmare? She started to say something, but decided not to add fuel to fire that she had inadvertently started.

She kissed her mother goodbye and quickly ran down the driveway to the bus stop. Two other kids were already waiting, as the big yellow bus pulled to a stop. She sat next to Hilda who was a neighbor. "Hey, Myra did many kids come trick-or-treating to your house last night?"

"No, as a matter of fact I wasn't at home. How about you?" Hilda said, "Not many came, and my folks won't let my brother go. They say it is too dangerous. All kinds of weird people putting needles, or poison in the candy. It seems like they just like to spoil everyone's fun."

"Yeah, lots of sick people are out there, in fact we met some of them last night." She proceeded to tell Hilda about the Halloween outing, while omitting the details about her stepfather. When she finished Hilda seemed properly impressed. Myra had to admit that it made quite a story. "Wish that I could do show and tell, like we did in grade school. I'd love to see the teacher's face when I told the part about the gun." Myra added.

"No way, the teacher wouldn't believe you anyway. You know they would just say that you were a teen with an overactive imagination." Hilda said.

"You are probably right." Myra agreed. The two rode in silence, lost in their thoughts until they arrived at the next stop. Myra and Hilda sat on the left side of the bus two rows behind the driver. At the stop, a young man rode his bike up to the driver's window. He carried a paper sack.

The kids at Ball High knew him as Joseph, the leader of the Bloods, a dangerous teen from the Clayton Village Housing Projects. Rumor had it that he had killed several people in gang fights, and it was a well-known fact that he had been permanently banned from riding the school bus. He lived with his wheelchair bound grandmother and cousins. His uncle had shot a local jeweler at point blank range, after robbing the store and tying him in a chair with ropes and duct tape. He didn't know his father and his drug-dealing mother was in prison. Most students feared him. Now all eyes were riveted to him as he talked to the bus driver. "Can I get on the bus?" he asked.

"No, Joseph you can't. You know the rules."

Carmine, a young cousin of Joseph's leaned toward the driver and whispered, "That is a real gun in that paper sack."

Anita, the driver, shot back at Carmine, "How do you know?"

"Because...."

"Because what?"

"Because it is my gun."

"Your gun!" she whispered.

"Uh huh."

"Oh"

"It is actually my dad's. Joseph is my cousin and he must have gotten it out of our gun cabinet."

"Great, just what I needed to hear." Said Anita.

Meanwhile Joseph inched closer to the window as the last kids boarded the bus at the stop. All other eyes and ears continued to focus on him.

At that moment, one of the kids on the bus pushed down his window and made a face at Joseph. Joseph responded by pulling out his gun and aiming it at the bus. Myra nearly fainted. In the past two days, she had seen two guns. Her family didn't own a gun. In fact, they didn't even have a toy gun. Yet within forty-eight hours she had seen two people's lives threatened. Anita shifted gears, and stepped on the accelerator. The yellow bus lurched forward and nearly knocked Joseph off his bicycle. The sudden movement caused most of the passengers to lunge forward in their seats.

Anita floored the accelerator as she sped through the intersections. Meanwhile, Joseph followed on his bicycle, waving the gun in the air. Yet he managed to remain within shooting range of the bus. How ironic, Myra thought, last night hooded strangers chased us, and today a kid on a bicycle has us riding in a bus driven by a maniac. Several of the girls screamed, while the Anita tried to regain control of the careening bus. The panicking students added to the problem as they fell out of their seats when the bus swerved sharply to avoid oncoming vehicles. Anita had just gotten the bus around a corner, on what must have been two wheels judging by the angle of the seats, when they saw a large Mack truck barreling toward them. The sound of screeching metal filled the air, as the two mighty vehicles collided. The bus moved sideways, it seemed in slow motion as the students were thrown across the aisle and then forward.

Myra's last thoughts before she hit the seat in front of her were that all this had to be a very bad dream. Surely any minute I am going to wake up, she thought. However, when she regained consciousness, the burning sensation on her forehead was certainly real. She tried to move and found that Hilda had fallen on top of her. Slowly the others began to move, while some lay and moaned softly.

"Hilda? Are you OK?"

"I think so. Are you?"

"I don't know. I hurt my head."

"My side hurts." Hilda added.

As they were checking the other students, sirens approached. The police and two ambulances arrived on the scene. Quickly the ambulance workers and police assessed the injured. They unloaded stretchers and gurneys and prepared to load the injured into ambulances.

"You don't think that those witches put a curse on you, do you?" Hilda asked.

"I don't know." Said Myra. "I'll have to ask Pastor Tom if they do things like that."

Scott, one of the students, lay unnaturally still in one of the seats. One of the ambulance workers tried unsuccessfully to rouse him, as they carried him outside to a gurney. Myra and Hilda followed them, and watched as they put an oxygen mask over his mouth and nose, but the bag didn't seem to inflate.

"Look Hilda," said Myra. "Scott isn't breathing."

"They are breathing for him." Said Hilda.

"No, because the bag isn't inflating or deflating like it would if he was breathing." Said Myra.

"Let's ask them if he is OK." The two girls said, as they walked over to the gurney.

"Is he breathing?" Myra asked.

"You will have to ask your teachers about him." Said the attendant.

"Is he dead?" Hilda asked. The attendant frowned at her in answer.

"He is dead isn't he?" continued Hilda.

"What kind of question is that?" answered the attendant.

"Can we pray for him?" asked Myra.

"Sure, but right now we need to get him to the hospital. So you will have to step out of the way for now, while we attend to him." With that the attendant literally pushed them out of his way and wheeled the gurney toward the waiting ambulance.

"I think that he is dead," continued Hilda.

"What can we do? They won't let us touch him now or pray for him." Said Myra.

"I don't know, lets just hang around for a minute and see what happens."

"OK." Myra felt a nervousness rise in her stomach, as though little butterflies were flying on the inside of her. Her hands began to get hot.

"Wow, Myra, look at your hands! They are turning red." Hilda said.

"Yeah, they feel hot too." Myra noticed that her hands had turned a deep cherry red, and that they began to pulse with electricity. She wanted to lay hands on Scott and to impart the power that vibrated through her body.

The two girls started to walk away, when Myra turned and looked into the ambulance. As she watched, they covered Scott with a sheet. "He is dead!" she cried.

Without a word, the two turned and headed toward the ambulance. One of the attendants blocked the doorway and said, "I am sorry, but you can't ride in the ambulance."

"Can I just see him for a moment?" Myra asked.

"It is against our rules, but be quick." The attendant said.

"He is dead isn't he?" Hilda interjected.

"Yes, but do not tell the others, the family hasn't been notified." Quickly Myra and Hilda climbed into the ambulance. Myra placed her now pulsing hands upon Scott's lifeless chest. A sense of power and boldness arose in her as she felt power going from her body to the lifeless form. She swayed as she felt waves of what seemed to be an invisible electric current flowing through her body to his. "Scott, can you hear me?" she said. There was no response from Scott, not even the twitch of an eyelid. Myra had to admit that she felt intimidated as she stood next to Scott's dead body. Who was she to try to raise a dead person? After all, she didn't know anyone who had been able to raise the dead.

"Myra, do you think that if he does come back from the dead that he might be permanently brain dead?" asked Hilda.

"I don't know, I sure hope not."

"Maybe you should leave him alone?"

"What have we to lose?" Myra said.

"I guess that you are right."

"He was so cute, why don't you give him mouth-to-mouth resuscitation?" Hilda giggled.

"You are being bad!"

"You know what, I am told that the last sense to go is hearing. What if he hears you and he comes back to life?"

"Yeah right." Said Hilda.

Myra nervously eyed the attendants who were waiting for them to finish.

"Are you sure that you want to do this?" asked Hilda.

"No, I am not." Thoughts screamed through her mind telling her that she would be the joke of the school when people found out what she had tried to do.

"Excuse me, " she said to the attendant, but I just need a couple more minutes."

"OK but be quick, the other ambulance is ready to leave, and we don't want to draw attention to this one."

"OK," Myra said. As she spoke her mind searched frantically for a scripture. Pastor Tom had told her to pray the word of God over people, because they are God's words and they are full of life and power. Suddenly she remembered one, "The Spirit of God who raised Jesus from the dead, lives in you. And just as he raised Christ from the dead, he will give life to your mortal body by this same Spirit living within you." She wondered if she had quoted it correctly. Scott, I call your spirit back into your body, you will live and not die."

Time moved in slow motion after she finished her prayer. "Scott can you hear me? If you can would you move your little finger?" Myra watched as the little finger on his right hand twitched. "He is alive!" She shrieked.

The two attendants pushed her aside, and immediately began to work on Scott.

"I have a pulse!"

The second attendant attached wires for an EKG, and began to monitor his weak heartbeat. Meanwhile the first attendant continued to monitor his vital signs, and checked him for bleeding. Within minutes Scott's heart rate resumed a normal healthy rate. The attendants prepared to close the ambulance doors, just as a camera's flash startled them. The newspaper reporter quickly finished his business and left. Apparently, the onlookers had given him the necessary details.

Another bus arrived and loaded the rest of the students. They were taken to John Kemple Hospital. Several hours later they were released having had their wounds dressed and bandaged.

The next morning, George placed the newspaper on the breakfast table. "It seems that our daughter is a celebrity." He added sarcastically, "Our little Myra certainly seems to have adventure."

There on the front page was a photo of her laying hands on Scott. The photo bore the legend, "Student Comes Back from the Dead." The caption quoted her as saying, "He's alive!" Myra muttered under breath, "What next?"

CHAPTER THREE

It is written:
Even when I walk through the dark valley of death,
I will not be afraid, for you are close beside me.
Your rod and your staff protect and comfort me."

Myra yanked her locker open. She shared a locker with June, but today she must have missed her. June's coat hung on one side, providing evidence that she had already arrived. As usual there never seemed enough time, she sighed and hung her coat on the peg in the locker. After slamming her locker closed, and replacing the combination lock, she headed toward class.

No sooner had she sat at her desk, than a student placed a copy of the newspaper article on her desk.

"Look who's famous!"

"Way to go Myra." One by one, the other students expressed how happy that they were that Scott was alive. The teacher came into the room, and called the class to order.

"Myra seems to be a celebrity." She said. "I am so glad that you were able to help the Paramedics save Scott's life."

"What do you mean help?" said a student toward the back of the room. "He would be dead if it wasn't for Myra."

"Yes, I suppose…we do have much for which to be grateful." The teacher conceded.

"Now get out your homework, and bring it forward when I call your name." Evidently that was all that would be said. Myra didn't care. In fact, the rest of the morning floated past, as she was lost in her thoughts.

She had tasted the power of God. How awesome it had felt to feel the power flow into Scott's body, and then to know that he would live. It didn't matter who tried to explain away what had happened. Scott's return to life was totally supernatural, and she knew it. She had reached a point where she knew that someone greater had control of her life, and that he was real and lived inside of her. How incredible, that the God of the universe would choose to live inside of her. No matter how bad things might appear to be, her answer to any problem was only a heartbeat away. She felt like she had hidden treasure carried inside her human, "earthen vessel." In fact, that was a scripture, and now she knew what it meant.

Her teacher interrupted her thoughts by asking her to answer a question. Quickly she stumbled for an answer, as the others giggled. "You may be good at rousing a fellow student, but you someone to rouse you, now pay attention."

"Yes, I am sorry." She said. After the teacher had finished her lesson, a messenger came into the classroom bearing a note. The teacher called her to the front. What else can happen, she wondered.

" Someone is here to see you, it is in regards to yesterday's accident. You are to meet them in the office. You can go now if you like."

Myra hurried to the office. Pastor Shepherd was waiting for her. "Hello Myra" he said. "I am supposed to counsel all the students from the accident. However, I need to talk to you." Myra hugged him excitedly.

"Did you hear about Scott?" she asked.

"Yes, yes! That is one of the things of which I need to talk to you."

"I can't come to the BOC," she said interrupting. "My parents grounded me through Friday night."

"That is OK, but I do need to talk to you. Can you meet me in the cafeteria for lunch?" He asked.

"I guess so."

"I will bring you a hamburger and we can talk."

Myra returned to her class, puzzled and yet wondering what he had to say that was so important that he had interrupted her class. The bell rang, and the students headed for the door. She ran to the cafeteria. There, true to his word, sat Pastor Shepherd.

"Sit down, Myra and let's talk." He said as he handed her the hamburger.

"Do you remember the people that were chasing you?" he asked.

"Yes, how could I forget," she said.

"The man who attacked me with the gun, says that they are a coven of witches. They specialize in of the Dark Arts, and are even feared amongst other witches. Myra, I understand that they will be trying to abduct you, Doug, June, and John Paul. You need to be careful when you are walking home or to the store. However, I also need to teach you about breaking curses, and protecting yourself against evil in the spirit realm. You need to understand that there is a spiritual world out there that is very real."

"But isn't the Lord's power greater?" asked Myra.

"Yes, but in any warfare, you need to know your enemy. Myra you have enemies in high places."

"Oh...."

"Don't worry, nothing can harm you if you know the Bible, obey God, and if you use your head and act wisely."

Pastor Shepherd proceeded to explain about the origin of the war in the heavenlies. How there had been an ongoing battle between the devil, his fallen angels, and God with the entire heavenly host.

"Angels are real, in fact the Archangel Michael did battle with Lucifer. His name was Lucifer before he was cast out of heaven, now he is called the devil, or Satan. Of course you know that there are those who worship Satan. Perhaps you didn't know that Satan hates all mankind, because they took his place in heaven.

"The very god that they serve is out to destroy them. They don't know that and so are deceived. Satan will use them and then turn on them when he is done. Those same people that cast spells, and who think that they can control demons will one day find that they have no power and no control. By then it will be too late for them, and Satan will have no mercy on them. He knows that he will end up in Hell, and he wants to take as many people as possible with him. There is a real Hell, but it was never created for us. God never intended for people to inhabit that horrible place, instead it was reserved for Satan and his fallen angels."

"Why doesn't someone warn people about this?" she said.

"As a matter of fact, that is our job!" He said. Pastor Tom proceeded to explain some ways that she could protect herself from the tactics of the devil.

"One way is to have the baptism of the Holy Spirit and to speak with tongues."

"As a matter of fact, my parents told me to stay away from you, because you spoke in tongues." Myra said. He laughed when she told him. "Let me show you what it says in the Bible about that, 'these signs will accompany those who believe: They will cast out demons in my name, and they will speak new languages.'"

"Can I see that?" Myra asked. Sure enough the scripture read just as he said.

"There is a condition though."

"There is?"

"Yes, the scripture says in Acts. 'Each of you must turn from your sins and turn to God, and be baptized in the name of Jesus Christ for the forgiveness of our sins. Then you will receive the gift of the Holy Spirit. This promise is to you and to your children, and even to the Gentiles.'"

"You mean the Holy Spirit has been promised to all of us? What is this thing called tongues?"

"Myra, you ask so many questions, and time is short. The unknown tongue can be a sign for an unbeliever. For example, when you speak in a foreign language to someone who knows for a fact that you don't know his language. They know that only God could do that. Believers speak unknown tongues as their own prayer language to God. The good news is that no devil can interpret it and try to spoil the plan of God in your life. I call it praying in the spirit, and it helps to build your spirit. To make a simple analogy, when you buy a pair of shoes do you pay separately for the tongues?"

"No," she said.
"In the same way, when you receive the Holy Spirit you receive your own prayer language."
"I want that gift, I have been baptized."
"Just ask him for it."
"How?"
"When you are home and in the quiet of your room ask him for this gift. Begin to praise the Lord and you will hear words come that you don't know. Let them be spoken, they are the beginning of your prayer language."
"Can I be baptized again?" she asked. "When I was baptized a couple of years ago, I didn't know anything about receiving the Holy Spirit." She said.
"Yes, we can go to pool right here at the school and do it one afternoon. In fact, I am going to get special permission for the BOC. Of course, you can't do it this Friday, but maybe in the next few weeks we can do it."
"Yes! I do want to be baptized again."
Pastor Shepherd looked at his watch and said, "It is time for you to go to class. I will be in touch, and will see you next week. Remember, you can call me if you have questions."
That evening as she lay across her bed, she wondered if she should ask the Lord for the gift of the Holy Spirit. Baby rubbed against her arm. Finally she grabbed him and rolled him on his back so that she could rub his belly. He purred with delight.
"You are so spoiled." She said as she tossed him a treat, and returned to her reading. "Tomorrow I can sleep late," she told him, "Because we don't have school, because it is a holiday."
The next morning, after she had read for a couple of hours, she played one of the songs that she had downloaded on her MP3 player and began to worship the Lord. No sooner had she started singing than she wondered when she would receive her prayer language. She remembered that the Bible said that the Holy Spirit would be given to those who ask him.
"Holy Spirit would you baptize me with your Spirit, and give me a prayer language that is all my own?" she asked.

No sooner had she done that than she felt words rising up in her from her stomach. That is weird she thought, but nevertheless she continued to sing. Suddenly out of her mouth flowed words that she had never heard. A beautiful language flowed out of her lips. Her voice sounded different too. She continued to let the words flow from her lips. A feeling of power and happiness overwhelmed her. Happy that is, until she heard a loud knock at her bedroom door.

"Myra?" her mother called.

At first, she didn't want to answer the door, and ruin the wonderful atmosphere that filled her room.

"Myra? Answer me when I call you."

Myra reluctantly opened the door. Her mother entered her room, and looked around. "To whom were you talking?" she demanded. "Do you have someone else in your room?"

"No, Mom…just me and Baby."

"Nonsense, I heard another voice, and I demand to know who you have sneaked into your bedroom. I suppose that you had a friend stay overnight. Don't you remember that you were grounded?"

No matter what she said, Myra knew that she would be in trouble with her Mom.

"As a matter of fact, I was singing. There is no one else in this room."

"You were singing, but you don't sound like that. Don't lie to me!"

"I am not, Mom."

"But it wasn't in English. In fact, you were singing in a language of which I never heard. You haven't been hanging around with Pastor Shepherd have you?"

"Mom, I…."

"That stuff is of the devil. You have a devil in you!" her mother shrieked. With that she grabbed Myra by the arm, nearly yanking her shoulder out of the socket and dragged her out the door and down the stairs. "Come with me, we are going to get you delivered of this devil."

Myra knew better than to protest. Her mother made her get into the car.

"Mom, where are we going?"

"To Pastor Dowling, he will get you straightened out in no time." Myra knew that she should be scared, but a strange peace filled her. In fact, she felt sorry for her mother, because she felt such compassion for her.

They arrived at the church, and Myra's mother led them down the hall to the church office. Just as her mother was reaching for the doorknob to the office, Pastor Dowling opened the door.

"Mrs. Wright, what a surprise. Why, I haven't seen you in several weeks."

"Yes, I know. But thank heavens I found you in time."

"Time? Is something wrong? What can I do for you?" He seemed genuinely concerned. Myra noticed for the first time that there was the hint of a twinkle in his eyes. Myra admired his distinguished looks, even though he was elderly, and slightly gaunt with wisps of white hair. His eyes shone with wisdom and love.

"It's Myra!"

"What is wrong with her? Is she ill?"

"Yes, I mean no. She has a devil!"

"A devil?" He looked closely at Myra.

"Myra, have you been disrespectful to your parents?"

"No." said Myra.

"She sings in the devil's language! She speaks in tongues!"

"Oh?" asked Pastor Dowling, the twinkle increasing in his eyes. "Really? And how long has she been doing this?"

"She just started, that's why I rushed her here so that you can cast that devil out of her."

"Let's go into my office, shall we?" he asked. Myra followed them into his office and found a seat in the corner.

"First, speaking in tongues doesn't mean that she has a devil in her." Myra noticed that the elegant office had a large desk and leather chairs, which added an air of authority to his words.

"But I thought that you said that tongues were of the devil." Her mother asked.

"Did I? Oh yes, I suppose I did feel that way at one time."

"You mean you don't think that it is now?" Her mother rasped.

"No, as a matter of fact, I speak in tongues."
"You do?"
"Yes, it is marvelous in fact I suggest that you try it."
"Nonsense!" her mother said as she stood up and prepared to leave. "Come Myra, we will find another minister to solve this problem."
"Mrs. Wright, you have a lovely daughter. In fact, you should be glad that she spends her time reading her Bible and singing to the Lord."
"Even if she is full of the devil?"
"Now, now, Mrs. Wright, you haven't given me reason to believe that your daughter is demon possessed. She certainly seems to be in her right mind."
"I can't believe that you would take her side in this." Her mother angrily replied. Myra watched as Pastor Dowling sighed and shrugged his shoulders.
"How ironic, that so many people look for a minister who agrees with them. Then they get mad when they hear truth that they don't want to accept."
"Truth? You call this the truth? Don't worry we will find a church that preaches the truth." Once again Pastor Dowling sighed and shook his head.
I just want you to know that we will miss you, and that you will be welcome if you decide to return." He said.
"After all we have done for you and this church! Is that all that you can say?" she said.
"Please know that we certainly appreciated the twenty dollars that you placed in the benevolent fund last Christmas."
Myra and her mother left the church building. Myra tried not to laugh or even smile. Her opinion of Pastor Dowling had improved dramatically. Of course, now they would have to find a minister who didn't share her views. She hoped that she wouldn't be made a spectacle by someone who thought that she was demon possessed. Or that she would be forced to attend a lifeless church that bored her. Of course, any church was better than not attending at all. In recent

weeks, her parents had quit attending church. At first, she felt relief and enjoyed sleeping later on Sunday mornings. Now however, she longed to be in church and listen to the teachings about her wonderful Lord.

They drove home in silence, but as they entered the house, Myra's mother turned to her and said, "I'm going to get to the bottom of this. I know that you are desperately evil. So in the meantime, you will be confined to your room except for meals."

A tear fell from Myra's right eye, how had she gotten herself into such a mess? What would her life be like if only she had attended the Hallelujah Night Celebration? Then she shrugged, well I wouldn't have met the Holy Spirit and Scott would be dead. Suddenly she knew that this was part of receiving power to change her world. Everything in life has a price. She knew that the more time that she remained locked in her room the more time that she had to spend with the Holy Spirit and the Bible.

Later that night, she climbed wearily into bed and fell into a disturbed sleep. Tossing and turning, she awakened hours later, gripped by a sensation that something or someone was watching her. Her eyes strained to see what might lurk in the shadows that the nightlight cast over her bed. Funny she thought, but I could have sworn that one shadow moved. She continued to peer into the darkness to catch even the slightest hint of movement. Her attention remained focused on a shadow that she thought looked kind of like a bird. It must be one of the stuffed toys making such a strange shadow.

As she watched, the shadow shifted a tiny bit. She rubbed her eyes and continued to stare at the shadow, but it remained still.

"I guess I am just nervous, because of all the strange things that have been happening since Hallelujah Night," she said to Baby.

However, tonight this would not be the case.

How odd, Baby seems to be ignoring me, in fact he seems to be watching something at the foot of my bed.

"What do you see?" Oh how she wished that he could talk. The hair on the back of his neck had risen, and his back arched. Surely this wasn't a moth or a cricket that caused such a reaction from her usually friendly cat. Although she couldn't see anything, she sensed that something or someone was in her room. Her ears strained for the slightest sound. Perhaps a burglar had gotten into her room, should I call my parents? Finally, she decided to try to go to sleep, after studying the shadows and listening for sounds for what seemed to be hours. There was no way that she would get out of bed and explore her room and surroundings. After debating what she should do, she turned over and drifted into an uneasy sleep. "Craaa-h."

"What?" She said as she sat bolt upright. Drawing the covers close to her, she shivered; the temperature in the room had plummeted. Great, she thought the heater must have broken. She still couldn't shake the sensation that she was being watched. Her eyes turned toward the foot of her bed. Two glowing amber eyes stared back at her. Myra jumped, and slowly pulled the covers up to her neck, Baby sat next to her, she could feel the warmth of his body as he pressed against her. A growl rose in his throat as he faced the creature. Myra had to admit that the creature terrified her. Her mind desperately searched for a scripture or an idea of how to deal with the creature that perched at the foot of her bed. The thing leered at her with a malicious grin.

Slowly, she extended her arm sideways toward the lamp on her bedside table. She didn't want to startle the creature. The creature fluttered its wings and shifted, perhaps it was preparing to attack. Was this a spirit or some sort of living creature from the woods? Pastor Shepherd had talked about the reality of demonic spirits; maybe this was one of them. He had said that they were sent on assignment for evil.

She felt the stem of the lamp, as she inched her hand upward toward the switch. Meanwhile she kept her eyes focused on the glowing amber eyes. They continued to stare at her without blinking. Maybe this is a dream; she had just read Edgar Allen Poe's poem entitled "The Raven" in school last week. Except that was an ordinary bird, and it didn't look like any species of bird that she had studied in biology.

She felt better as she snapped on the lamp. Hoping that the light would reveal only her collection of books and her computer. Light flooded the room, illuminating all but the corners. Sitting on one of the bedposts was the largest raven-like creature that she had ever seen. However, its feathers seemed to be more like hair, and instead of a bird's foot it had long curved talons. The eyes glowed crimson in the light, portraying a picture of pure evil. Myra gasped and realized that this wasn't a dream. It raised a wickedly sharp talon and extended it toward her.

"You will die!" it croaked. The creature's talon again wrapped around the wood on the bedpost. Great, an English speaking bird that is telling me that I am going to die. What is going to happen next? I must have left a window unlocked, she thought, how else did it get into my room.

"Craaa-h!" It croaked again.

"What are you?" Myra asked.

"You will die!" It retorted.

"Nonsense, I will live and not die."

The horrible beast remained silent.

"In the name of Jesus you will go from this place!" she commanded. The creature flinched but didn't move. Apparently it didn't like that name. She nudged the cat, but he didn't move. So much for catching this bird she thought. Of course she had to admit that the cat wasn't stupid. Who could ignore the creature's long talons, or notice that it was bigger than he.

She remembered how she had worked with horses. The strength of a horse far exceeded her own, and yet they obeyed her because she knew her authority with them. They feared her riding crop or lunging whip. Even though the crop and whip were made of leather, and so little and fragile compared to their mighty power, weight and strength. Perhaps this creature would respond like her mare. She remembered how she had trembled with fear when the animal tried to rear to buck. Pastor Shepherd had told her that she had authority as a believer over anything in the spirit world. Mustering her courage, she faced the evil creature and said boldly, "In the name of Jesus, I command you to flee, now!" She didn't have to wait long for the creature to respond.

"Caah," it croaked as it flapped its enormous wings. At first it continued to eye her warily. As she stepped towards it, her eyes scanned the room for something to use as a weapon. It flapped its wings again and rose into the air, looming overhead as it circled her room. Then it landed on the windowsill and glared at her. Myra's confidence rose as she faced the creature. What if it doesn't leave she wondered. Should I try to grab it? Surely her parents must be wondering about the noise. The long talons clattered on the windowsill, interrupting her thoughts. Gathering her courage, she took a step toward it. The ebony creature's hair gleamed in the light. Eyes blazing, it snarled as it took a step toward her, opening its mouth to reveal rows of razor, sharp, ivory teeth.

"Craah! You will die!"

"In name of Jesus, you are commanded to leave this place, now!"

The thing flinched and shrank at the words, and then with a whimper it vanished before her. Baby leaped toward the foot of the bed, and placed his paws on the bedpost. He sniffed the place where the creature had sat.

"Now you decide to be bold, now that it has gone. I suppose you think that you scared him off?" She said. She reached over and grabbed him and held him tightly as she rubbed his chin. His eyes shown with gratitude as he purred. Whatever the thing had been, her cat had been properly impressed. Evidently animals can see into the spirit world.

Miraculously the room temperature returned to normal, and Myra settled into an uneasy sleep.

CHAPTER FOUR

It is written:
"...How can goodness be a partner with wickedness?
How can light live with darkness? What harmony
can there be between Christ and the Devil?"

Myra slammed her locker shut, and twirled around to face Doug. She sighed as she looked deeply into his big brown eyes. To her knowledge, he had never shown any interest in any of the girls at the school or at her church. She wished that he liked her as a girl, and not just as a friend. He proudly told everyone that they were best friends. Ironically, girls sought her friendship, thinking that through her they could get to know him. It wasn't that he was so handsome, although he definitely had a charisma and of course those big brown eyes. She had suffered through many a girl's confession of undying love for Doug. What is it about him; she wondered that made him so irresistible to women? Even older women catered to him. He was a legend at never having to spend money, because others were usually treating him to anything from meals, clothes, and even trips to ski resorts. Of course, he would smile, flashing his white teeth, exerting all his charm while batting those wonderful brown eyes as he expressed his gratitude.

Immediately, girl's hearts seem to melt and their pocketbooks would open. Myra knew this all to well. She had been a friend with him since he was seven. Doug's charisma caused him to be ushered into the presence of more than one famous person.

"You be careful of Doug," Myra's stepfather had warned. "He is a con-artist and a darn good one." Of course Myra didn't want to believe that. She assumed that her stepfather didn't like Doug because of his popularity. Deep inside though, she wondered if he might be right about him, especially since Doug had a nasty habit of not being truthful. Yet, he would explain each situation, and then talk about how he wanted to be a minister, and live his life for the lord. She found it impossible to stay angry with him, no matter what happened.

In fact, he knew the Holy Spirit, and had a relationship with the Lord that amazed her. Perhaps the Lord loved his big brown eyes as much as she did. The Lord answered his prayers too. One day they were walking down the road and it started to rain. Myra liked the rain and enjoyed the light drizzle, but Doug did not.

"I am going to pray that it doesn't rain." Said Doug.

"I want it to rain." She said.

"I don't."

"I do."

"I am still going to pray that it doesn't rain. You'll see, God always answers my prayers."

"He answers mine too!" she said.

"We will see." Said Doug. They continued walking and sure enough it had quit raining. Myra thought, doesn't it just figure, the Lord can't resist him either. Personally, Myra had been more than a little jealous of Doug's relationship with the Lord. He told her how he would get up at three am to pray before school. Unfortunately, Myra found that praying in a horizontal position was very conducive to sleep.

I am going to know the Holy Spirit like he knows him, she thought. She remembered how he would lay hands on sick people and they would get healed. One time he visited the Veteran's Hospital with a friend, and a paralyzed man got healed. So, she sighed, I am going to continue being friends with him, even if it means that I have to tolerate all the girls who chase him. What irritated her the most though, was that these girls didn't consider her a threat for Doug's affections. What is wrong with me she wondered,

I am cute and yet he doesn't seem interested in me as a girl.

Myra's biggest challenge was a mutual friend named Maureen. Maureen's love for Doug knew neither boundaries nor any scruples. She had befriended Myra and talked incessantly about how she planned to marry him and bear his children. She had to admit that Maureen's petite youthful looks made her a candidate for him. Of course her youthful appearance hid the fact that she was several years older than him. One day in prayer, she told the Lord, " I hate to admit that I am jealous of Maureen, but Lord, please don't let him like her more than me."

Of course, she couldn't resist asking Doug how he felt about Maureen. Although, he swore to her that he didn't like her, he did accept her expensive gifts. One day, he showed her a stack of love letters that she had sent him. So many letters, that Doug's mother had asked her about Maureen. Once again, she marveled about his charisma.

"Are you going to class?" Doug joked. "Or are you going to continue leaning against your locker?"

"Of course, I am going to class. I have Miss Amanda J Anderson and you know what she does if you are late! She makes you walk the hall," she said. Miss Anderson's build reminded her of a Brahma bull and she had a personality to match. Although the student's joked about her, everyone knew and respected her for being an excellent teacher.

"Then we had better get going, because the bell is about to ring." With that they hurried down the hall to their classes.

"See you at the BOC this afternoon." He yelled over his shoulder as he continued down the hall to his class.

She knew that he hated school, and often talked about quitting. Myra loved school, although she didn't like Geometry. Maybe the Lord could help her with her schoolwork. She certainly needed it.

Myra doodled in her notebook as she listened half-heartedly to the class. How I can't wait for class to be over, she thought. The students seemed to take forever giving their book reports. She had presented hers last week. Her thoughts focused on the meeting after school. A week ago, she had sat alone in her room, miserable as she fought thoughts of envy over her friends being able to attend the club. Life is not fair, she thought, they hadn't been grounded like she had. Of course, the next day they had excitedly told her about the meeting and how great it was. But this week, nothing short of a national disaster would stop her from going. Because she would miss the bus, her mother had arranged to pick her up after school. She had been relieved that her mother had let her attend, especially after the humiliating incident in Pastor Dowling's office. She sure hoped that her mother didn't know that Pastor Shepherd would be at the meeting, especially since she thought that anyone who spoke in tongues was possessed by the devil. She had told her mother that Dr. Norton had organized the meeting. Which was true, however, she omitted to tell her mother that he always invited a minister to speak, and that minister was none other than Pastor Shepherd. Tremendous things happened when he spoke, rumor had it that he had even raised someone from the dead.

"Dear Lord, don't let my mother come to the meeting," she whispered under her breath. "Don't let her embarrass me again." Her mother had been known to embarrass her more than once. In fact, many an adult had come to her rescue because of the harsh treatment and scolding of her mother. A few years ago, her mother had driven to the elementary school, a horsewhip in hand, because she had stayed too late playing with her friends. Although short in stature, the legend of her fiery temperament preceded her. She seemed to grow before one's eyes. Myra had been told that her friends referred to her mother as "The Dragon Lady." She had learned the hard way, that it was best not to argue and incur her mother's wrath.

She loved her mother, but secretly wondered if her mother hated her. She even wondered if her mother blamed her for her divorce. She couldn't imagine why though. However, since the divorce, her relationship with her mother seemed to be strained. Especially since she had married George.

"Myra, what do you think of Jill's report?" asked Miss Anderson.

"Umm..." Myra didn't know what to say, and she didn't want to lie. The class tittered and snickered as Myra stammered for an answer.

"Just as I thought, you weren't paying attention."

"I am sorry."

"Don't let it happen again or you will be staying after school to scrub the blackboards."

Great, she thought, just what I want is to stay after school, and clean a bunch of dusty old blackboards. Especially today, with the BOC, she had missed it once and she didn't plan to miss it again.

Finally, the bell rang; she scooped up her books and joined the crowd of students as the class emptied into the hall. All around her, students hurried to their lockers and the waiting buses. Myra hastily got her coat out of the locker and waited for Doug. He arrived a few minutes after her, and gathered his things. The two of them headed for the meeting. The school stretched before them like an octopus with tentacles of halls. How I wish that I had wings on my feet, she thought, as they hurried towards the cafeteria.

Dr. Norton greeted them and handed Myra an information packet about the club. John Paul and June joined them at a table near the front. Other friends continued to arrive, and Doug excused himself. He returned a few minutes with both hands loaded with plates of pizza.

"Trust Doug to find the food," said June.

"Did you bring any for us?" Myra asked.

"Get your own, it's over there." He laughed as he pointed to a nearby table. As usual, Myra was amazed at Doug's ability to find free food.

"How do you always find so much free stuff?" Myra asked.

"God always blesses me, " he laughed. Myra rolled her eyes; his lack of humility was amazing.

Other students joined them and filled the tables. The meeting swelled in size, and soon more chairs were being added.

Pastor Shepherd strolled into the room. His distinguished looks and very presence energized the group. He looks so much like the pictures of Jesus, and he seems ageless. She had heard the rumors that he was almost seventy years old. She couldn't imagine that he was that old, he certainly didn't look or act it. A hush fell over the group as Pastor Shepherd started to speak.

"Jesus told Peter to come, and that word equipped him to walk on water." He taught like no other, such wisdom and power filled his words. Why he teaches the Bible like we should believe it literally.

"Do you mean that I could walk on water if I believed that I could?" she asked.

"Yes, Peter was an ordinary man who believed, and although he doubted and started to sink. He still holds the world's record for water walking."

"Oh," she said.

"Starting in a couple of weeks, we will go into the Housing Projects for our outreaches. We will be doing "Street Side Sunday School." We are asking for volunteers for our teams. As a team member we will train you how to do games, skits, visitation, and to pray for kids. If you would like to do this, be sure to take a permission slip home and have your parents sign them. Bring them next week, and we will set up a time to train you. Raise your hand if you think that you would like to be a part of our outreach team." Pastor Shepherd asked.

Several students including Myra, Doug, June and John Paul raised their hands as he handed out permission slips. She couldn't wait to join the teams on New Life Christian Center's colorful outreach trucks. Pastor Shepherd showed pictures and a video of the existing teams in action. The teams worked on converted trucks that opened into mobile stages. The trucks did after school programs in the high drug and crime areas. They played games, and then preached a hard-hitting lesson. He explained that miracles happened out on location, and that they would be helping kids stay out of crime, sex, drugs, and gangs. They would help kids learn to make right choices in their lives.

The meeting drew to a close, and one of the students played "Amazing Grace" on his guitar. Myra closed her eyes and sang. Meanwhile Pastor Shepherd asked if anyone needed healing. Kids were crying and Myra felt like she had been clothed from head to toe with liquid love.

Charlie, a student with Cerebral Palsy, limped to the front. Talk about a tough case, Myra thought. Charlie's handicap was well known, and to everyone's knowledge he had been born with Palsy. His whole body would shake continuously. In fact it made Myra tired just to watch him. She wondered if he shook while he slept. However, even before Pastor Shepherd's touch, he had begun to tremble and shake even more violently. The shaking was different than that of the Cerebral Palsy. Charlie fell backwards, dropping like a stone and landed with a loud impact. He had collapsed onto the concrete floor, because no one caught him as he fell. Myra waited for him to move, but he didn't. Shouldn't someone see if he was OK? Howver, no one moved toward him.

Just at that moment, the cafeteria door opened, and Myra's mother entered. Talk about timing, for several minutes she pretended that she didn't see her mother. Why had she arrived early, she wondered. This is not fair! How could she come at such a time?

She shut her eyes and fought back the tears, afraid that her mother would now stop her from attending the club, or worse yet write a letter of complaint to the school. Surely she had noticed Charlie, and probably wondered what had happened to him. On the other hand, she had to admit that it was going to be interesting to see what happened when her mother met Pastor Shepherd.

Charlie continued to lie on the floor, yet neither Pastor Shepherd nor Dr. Norton seemed concerned. Myra's mother remained near the door.

After a few minutes, Charlie began to move, and a couple of students helped him get to his feet. Charlie walked with an unsteady gait. How incredible, he didn't shake! He walked in front of the chairs, looking at his limbs and laughing. Then he would cry as he walked. Suddenly, he began to run, and ran a lap around the cafeteria. Everyone knew that it was against the rules for anyone to run in the cafeteria, yet no one said anything. Charlie slowed and came back to the front.

"Charlie received his healing." Pastor Shepherd said. Of course it was obvious that he had been healed, because he no longer shook from the Palsy and could run.

"Yes! I am healed!" Charlie danced and cried in front of the students. People stood to their feet shouting and cheering. Even Myra's mother looked happy and relieved.

Once again, Myra marveled at how the Lord seemed to work things out perfectly. Her mother had seen that Pastor Shepherd used God's power to help people. Surely no one could think that someone possessed by the devil could do this. No one could deny that this was a mighty miracle. No doctor or medicine had been able to cure Charlie's Palsy. Only God could have done this. Best of all, she knew that he would be able to function as a normal teen.

The meeting ended, the people dispersed. Myra's mother greeted Pastor Shepherd shyly and they exchanged pleasantries. Even as Myra and her mother walked to the car, they chatted about the day's events. However, no mention was made about the club or the healing. In fact, during the long ride home her mother became unusually quiet. Myra didn't know whether her mother's quietness was a sign of trouble, or whether she had been thinking about what she had seen. However, knowing her mother's personality, her quiet behavior seemed ominous. Once again, she cried herself to sleep.

The smell of bacon frying in a skillet filled her nostrils awakening her. She knew that her mother was preparing for their weekly pilgrimage to the Mall. Every other week she would shop with a friend while her mother had her nails done and a pedicure. This week, her mother was taking Doug with them. Afterwards, they would eat lunch and see a movie. She showered, dressed and joined her mother for breakfast, while they waited for Doug.

He arrived on time, and the three of them drove to the Old Kerrville Mall. Myra marveled that Doug loved to shop, something that she detested. He would literally run in and out of the shops, while begging her to try on dresses. Going to the mall with Doug was like going with one of the girls. Still, she enjoyed his company, even if they were just friends.

The lavish window displays attracted their attention. Myra saw a

THE SPIRIT'S APPRENTICE

dark figure move out of the corner of her eye.

"I just love these Saturdays," he said, "But I hate school." Myra turned to see what it was that caught her eye, but didn't see anything. She continued walking beside Doug.

"I wish that I didn't ever have to go to school again." Something scurried along behind them. Myra strained to see what it was.

"What are you looking at?" he asked. "Pay attention, I am talking and it's rude to ignore me." He laughed.

"I am not ignoring you. I thought that I saw something over there." She pointed to the recessed entryway of a shop.

"I don't see anything." He said and shrugged. Myra turned again and was horrified to see a small creature that looked almost reptilian in appearance. In fact, it seemed to absorb light, and to be a kind of hole in space. She knew that it moved unseen and immaterial to the people around her. It drifted along propelled by its swirling, quivering wings, which made a grayish blur. It reminded her of the gargoyle on one of the historical houses that lined the esplanade into the city. The creature's spider like body appeared part human and part animal. Two huge cat-like yellow eyes bulged out of its face. The eyes darted to and fro, and it emitted a smell like rotten eggs.

"Do you smell that?" she asked.

"Smell what?" he asked, "You mean the cinnamon rolls in the mall courtyard?"

"No, this smells like rotten eggs!" she recoiled at the thought.

"I am wasting my time going to school, and I want to quit," continued Doug. At that moment, the little demon slithered closer to him, its taloned feet scraping the floor. Myra watched it in disgust. She looked around, but noticed that no one else appeared to see the creature. It glared at her revealing a row of sharp yellow teeth. Then it turned its attention back to Doug as it crept along behind him. Like a leech looking for an opportunity to latch onto a body, its hideous eyes watched his every move.

"Doug don't you see the thing that is following you?" she asked. He turned around and looked.

"I don't see anything except lots of people in the mall." He shrugged.

"You don't see that black thing?"
"No."
"What?"
"You are funny."
"I am not trying to be funny."
"OK, anyway I was telling you that I want to quit school. I am never going to pass my math class. Besides I could be making lots of money working for my uncle. He said that he didn't care if I finished high school or not. I am not going to need math to be a minister either."

As Doug spoke the demon crept closer, until it was reaching its taloned fingers towards his leg. The yellow eyes focused on Doug. Myra noticed the leer on its gnarled face. The thing made her angry as every time Doug spoke negative words of defeat it came closer.

"Doug there is an evil spirit following you, and every time you talk about quitting school it comes closer to you."

The two walked in silence, Doug's discouragement grew with each passing step. Like a blanket of despair, the atmosphere grew somber. The gray color of the mall corridors added an impersonal and cold touch to the mood. She could feel his heart get heavier with each passing step. So much so that she fought discouragement as well. This must be a spirit of heaviness, just like the Bible talks about in the book of Isaiah.

"I need to talk to someone though, I know that you understand, because you are my best friend. You know that I can't tell my parents these things. They would never understand." He continued. With each step, the demon closed in on his prey until its hands were clinging to Doug's leg.

"It is not that I do not want you to share your feelings, it is just that I can see this horrible creature that is clinging to your leg."

"That is funny, I have a pain in my leg right about my knee. I must have sprained it when I played soccer yesterday." He said.

"That pain might be from the talon on the demon's finger." She said.

"What do you want me to do?" he asked.

"Pastor Shepherd says that the scriptures tell us that we have authority over these spirits. If we command it to go in the name of Jesus, it has to flee."

"You want me to do that here?" he asked. "People will think that we are crazy."

"Let's go into the parking lot then" she said.

The two walked into the parking lot. With each step, the demon dragged along behind him, its taloned hands still holding on to his knee. Myra could see the creature's eyes fill with fury and rage. She wanted to kick it, but knew that it wouldn't do any good. How do you kick a spirit she wondered? What a nerve, here I am a child of God and this thing doesn't seem intimidated by my presence. She wondered if she would be able to get it off Doug.

They found a secluded spot in the parking lot near a light. She turned to face Doug and the demon.

"In the name of Jesus I command you to go!" Myra commanded. Suddenly from the nearby shrubs came a blinding flash of bluish-white light. The demon trembled and released its grip on Doug. Glaring at them, it flew into the air, and landed some distance away. It didn't move but waited and listened to their conversation. This reminded her of the raven like creature that came into her bedroom.

"Hey, the pain is gone! I feel better, and I don't even feel discouraged. Maybe I can graduate." He said.

"Evidently when you talked about quitting school that spirit heard you and came after you."

They returned to the mall. The demon stalked them, but followed at a respectful distance. Myra wondered what the blinding flash of light had been. She imagined that the flash of light had most likely been a heavenly sword wielded by an angel. Could it have been their guardian angels? She had read in the sacred words where one angel had defeated 185,000 men.

How exciting to know that the sacred words were true. She had read that even the demons trembled at the name of Jesus. Pastor Shepherd had said that the spirit world was more real than the natural world. She longed to see an angel. Those who had seen them said that they towered over people, being of great stature.

CHAPTER FIVE

It is written:
Better is a poor and a wise child than
an old and foolish king, who will no
more be admonished.

Myra bowed her head and closed her eyes, for the second time that morning she fought the urge to scream. Earlier that morning in prayer, the Lord had impressed her to go into the attic and to search for something that would reveal her destiny. She had searched and found a prophecy in an old trunk in the attic. At first the trunk's lock had refused to open. She had persisted, and her efforts were rewarded when it opened revealing a treasure trove of old photos and family albums. Her eyes had been drawn to a piece of paper, attached to a yellowed photo of her, and a newspaper article. They were held together by a paper clip. The photo showed her being christened as a baby. She had worn a long flowing white christening gown, with a ribbon in her hair. The photo showed her parents standing near her, while Bishop AJ Pearson held her in his arms.

Myra gently unfolded the yellowed paper. She read what evidently was a typed copy of the prophecy that the Bishop had spoken over her during the christening. As she read the prophecy, she wondered why no one had told her about it. She read the following words, " The Spirit of the Sovereign Lord is upon her, because the Lord has appointed her to bring good news to the poor. He has sent her to comfort the brokenhearted and to announce that captives will be released and prisoners will be freed. He has sent her to tell those who mourn that the time of the Lord's favor has come and with it, the day of God's anger against their enemies. Mighty, mighty will be this handmaiden of the Lord. She will impact a city, a nation, and even the world. For the glory of the Lord is shining upon her. Darkness as black as night will cover all the nations of the earth, but the glory of the Lord will shine over her. All nations will come to see the light that shines through her. Mighty kings will come to see her radiance."

Why hadn't anyone told her of her destiny? What did it all mean? Perhaps this was one of the reasons that she had so many problems. The dark forces didn't want her to discover her destiny.

Later that morning she decided to ask her mother about the prophecy. She found her sewing in the kitchen.

"Mom, I found this in the attic." She asked.

"What is it?" her mother asked.

"It seems to be an article about my christening."

"Oh."

"What does this prophecy mean?" she asked.

"I don't know. I do remember Bishop Pearson muttering something about your destiny. But, you know he was probably just being nice."

"You mean you don't think that he meant it?" Myra asked.

"Oh I am sure that he thought that you are a splendid young lady and that you will do some young man proud. You will surely affect the world by having children."

"You mean that's it? I will be a wife and mother? That is all?" she asked.

"Motherhood is a calling, my dear."

"I didn't mean that, but it isn't like you will affect the world being a wife and mother."

"Oh, but of course you can through your children, and by being an encouragement and support to your husband."

" I just think that Bishop Pearson was trying to say nice things." She added. "Everyone knows that girls have their hands full being wives, mothers and sometimes having to work too."

Myra knew that being a mother and a wife was very important and honorable. However, she also knew that the prophecy went beyond being a wife and mother. She wisely chose to drop the matter. She could tell that her mother did not understand the significance of the prophecy. Either that or she didn't want her daughter to pursue such dreams. She determined to pray and find out the truth.

Could the Lord use someone like her, an insignificant schoolgirl to change a city, a nation, and even the world? Why not, she thought, and why not me? Evidently, people didn't see her the way that the Lord saw her. Still, if her parents and other adults were so smart, then how come our world is such a mess? Obviously, they didn't have all the answers. Perhaps they had given up their dreams because they hadn't seen them come to pass. That didn't mean that hers wouldn't. She knew of at least one person who had made a difference. Jesus did when he walked the earth.

There was no school today due to a teacher's In-Service. Myra decided to visit New Life Christian Center and talk to Pastor Shepherd. She called the church, and he agreed to meet her at the church's Youth Center downtown, which had been an old YMCA building. The church had purchased the building for its youth activities, in addition to having a traditional church building located on the edge of town. Her mother had agreed to let her ride the bus downtown. Of course, she hadn't told her mother that in addition to going to the Neiman Library, she planned to walk the three blocks to New Life Christian Center.

Pastor Shepherd stood outside the Youth Center arguing with a City official, who stood beside a tow truck. Evidently the City planned to tow one of the outreach vehicles. Upon arriving, she listened to their conversation for several minutes.

"This vehicle is not an abandoned vehicle and is legally parked, with current tags and stickers," said Shepherd.

"We can't allow you to park this vehicle here anymore," said the official. Myra noticed that his name badge said Collins.

"You need to move it, because people are complaining about it," Collins continued. "They don't like looking out their windows to see this big yellow truck, or the other truck either. Besides you need to move it more than a few inches each day."

"We have been moving it, and we are using it. In fact, we are trying to help this city reduce its crime rate." Shepherd said.

"You aren't moving it enough, we have a new ordinance that says that a one and a half ton truck can't be parked on the street between 7 am and 7pm. We really want you to move it out of the area." Collins added. Myra listened and then walked down the street a few yards to wait until the dispute was settled. She shook her head. Why do people persecute those who were trying to help people? Can't they see that the crime rate in this town is terrible, and juvenile delinquency is at an all-time high? The City was renowned for its gangs, and drive-by shootings. Juvenile crime between 3pm and 6pm ranked one of the highest in the state and nation. Once again, she resolved to do something about it.

After the City official left, Pastor Shepherd walked over to her. "The trucks can be left here for now." He said. "Believe me this has been an ongoing battle with the City. It started ten years ago when we began busing children into a historical house on Main Street. It seemed that the neighbors didn't like it, being afraid of the children from the housing projects. Especially since they were of a different race. The City has some convenient zoning laws that enable the local residents to stop anything new that they don't like."

"That is not fair!" she said.

"No, it isn't, but the Lord has allowed us to continue."

"Why don't they see that you are trying to help the City?" she asked.

"Because we face an enemy, not the City, but the devil who doesn't want us to help people." He said. "Of course the devil uses people to come against God's work. He convinces them that we are a menace and a danger to the city instead of a help."

"The kids never created problems for the neighbors, but they did call the local TV station and told them that the city was trying to shut down their church."

"Really? How funny that they would do that. Then what happened?" she asked.

"The TV station came out and interviewed the kids. Of course the newspapers came too. You see the kids wanted change. They didn't like the way things were."

"Too bad the adults don't want change as much as the kids do," she said.

"I agree, it would sure make my job easier." Shepherd added. "Let me show you some photos and the building." They entered the old building. Myra marveled at the soft mauve and teal carpet, the Olympic-sized indoor swimming pool. The beautiful gymnasium, locker rooms, and racquet ball courts.

"What a wonderful building," she said.

"Yes, and the Lord has given it to us. It is debt free." Shepherd showed her the photos of thousands of children seated on the tarps as they listened to one of New Life Christian Center's staff present a lesson. She thumbed through albums showing photos of the kids playing games and having fun. One photo showed a girl who was walking who hadn't been able to walk.

"What happened to this girl?" she asked

"That girl had a mighty miracle, she was carried into one of our Nuneaton crusades. Apparently she hadn't been able to walk in over a year. She had an immunity disorder that resembled AIDS. Do you see the other kids standing beside her in the photo?"

"Yes."

"They prayed for her, and she was totally healed by the power of God."

"I want to go on the outreaches, but I haven't had the courage to ask my Mom to sign the permission slip. Would you pray with me that she would allow me to go?"

"Certainly, did you know the scriptures tell us that he will give his people favor with others?" Shepherd grabbed Myra's hands and together they prayed:

"Lord, give Myra favor with her parents, and let them sign the slip so that she can be a participant of the Street Side Sunday School outreaches. It is written in the Bible, 'for thou, Lord will bless the righteous; with favor wilt thou encircle him as with a shield.'"

"I feel better about it now." She said.

"Great, then I will expect the signed forms on Friday," he said. His eyes shone as he spoke.

She resolved to present her mother with the permission slip, as soon as her mother came home. She would start by cleaning her room. Once she finished her room, she started cooking dinner. She wanted to be sure that her mother had no reason to complain about her behavior.

When her mother came home she seemed tired and disturbed. Myra waited until she had sat with her coffee and relaxed for a few minutes.

"How was your day?" her mother asked.

"Great, I had a great time." She replied.

"Did you go to the library?"

"Yes, and I also saw Pastor Shepherd. He asked me if I had gotten my permission slip signed yet." Myra held her breath as she waited for her mother's response.

"I suppose that it would be OK for you to go. Your stepfather wants you to work; he thinks that you should be helping with the bills. Do you suppose that they will pay you?

If not, I don't suppose that you will have time to be a part of that club."

Myra's heart sank; she hadn't planned on this response. Maybe she could ask Pastor Shepherd if he needed anyone for a part-time job. Unfortunately, she knew that the ministry stretched to pay the staff and provide for the food, prizes and expense of the outreach. They used volunteers whenever possible. She doubted that he would agree to pay her. Still, she would ask.

"I will ask Pastor." She said.

"Good, and I will have George talk to you tonight about it." Great she thought. She hated it when George came into her bedroom late at night. Why couldn't her mother see what a monster that he was?

They ate dinner in silence. I wonder why George can't talk to me about it now instead of having to come into my bedroom late at night? She almost asked him about it, but didn't want a family quarrel to result. Also she wanted to delay talking about it as long as possible.

She needed time to figure what she had to do. She certainly didn't want a job that would prevent her attending the BOC meetings. Her grades were good, but she struggled with math, and a job would make it even more difficult for her to maintain her grades. She knew that it was a household rule that if her grades slipped then she would be banned from attending any after school activities. She knew that the first on the list would be the BOC, because they knew that she liked it so much. Life just didn't seem fair. One day she would be grown and wouldn't have to be subject to their rules. Oh, how she longed for that day when she would be free to make her own choices about her life.

Later that evening, she laid out her clothes for the morning. Just as she finished, the door opened and her stepfather came into the room. How typical she thought, he didn't even knock. She knew that he hoped to see her undressed.

"Your mother tells me that you were asking permission to attend that BOC outreach program."

"That's right, I do want to be a part of the outreaches." She said.

"Your mother and I have discussed it, and we think that you need to buckle down to helping with the household expenses. After all, you aren't a baby and you shouldn't expect to live here for free."

"But, I am in school." She protested.

"You have not contributed to your support here, and it is time that you did."

Myra resisted the urge to cry in front of her stepfather. At that moment, she almost hated him, but knew that she had to forgive him instead.

"Other kids work and so can you. You will be expecting to go to college, and you need to start saving for that as well." She knew that college was expensive, but still she didn't want to compromise her chances of a scholarship. She knew that it would be hard to keep a good grade point average and work full time.

"How much do you want me to work? I do have to maintain my grades, and I go to school full-time." She asked.

"We think that you should work several evenings a week." He

said. Myra gasped; there certainly was no way that she could do the outreaches and work that much.

"Maybe Pastor Shepherd will pay me to do the outreaches."

"That's right I forgot that you are such a good little girl." He snarled sarcastically. Myra knew what was coming next. "You sure have become religious all of a sudden." He added.

"I wonder what the dear Reverend would say if he knew what we did at night?" he laughed. "Of course, I will tell him that it is all your fault for seducing me."

"That is not true!" she hissed. "You wouldn't dare."

"Oh yes I would tell him. Men understand these things, bet he wouldn't have much more to do with you. Especially when I told him how you throw yourself at me, and how I have to fight your advances." He laughed sadistically.

Something snapped in Myra's mind. She had had enough of his night visits. Feeling dirty and used, while hating both her and him for what he did to her. With anger burning within her, she lunged at him.

"I will show you what it is like when I throw myself at you." She shrieked. She shoved him as hard as she could. George pushed her aside. Doubling his fist, he slammed it into her face forcing her backwards and against the mirror on the wall. It shattered and Myra fell to the floor. Tears flowed from her eyes caused by the trauma of the blow. Her nose throbbed and bled. Blood covered her T-shirt; the pain seemed almost unbearable as she lay on the floor. She heard her bedroom door slam shut as George left the room.

She lay for what seemed hours, thinking. Here I am lying on the floor with what feels like a shattered nose. How ironic, my nose may be shattered, and my mirror and dreams are certainly shattered. No man will want a girl that has been messed up like I have, especially with a deformed nose. After several more minutes she remembered, the world might think that she was ugly but Jesus still saw her as beautiful. With those thoughts she got to her feet and went into the bathroom to clean the blood from her face.

Horrified, she noticed her misshapen nose; she wondered if it had been broken. She had heard of others breaking their noses, and knew that in time she would mend. Her clothes would wash, and life would return to normal. Gingerly, she slipped the T-Shirt over her head and soaked it in the sink in cold water. It had been her favorite T-Shirt and she hadn't wanted to ruin it. After washing the tears and blood from her face, she took a couple of aspirins for the pain. Next, she tried to brush her teeth, but her mouth hurt, so she decided to go to bed. She sure hoped that her mouth didn't hurt as much in the morning. She slipped into her pajamas and headed down the hall to her room.

When she returned, her mother was in her room holding pieces of the broken mirror in her hands.

"George tells me that you threw a book at him, and broke the mirror. He said that you were mad because he asked you to help with the family finances."

"George is a monster, and I hate him!" She said. In her heart, she knew that this wasn't the way that she should feel. She hoped that God would forgive her angry outburst, and help her forgive the man who tormented her so much.

"George and I forbid you from going on any of the outreaches. Ever since that you have met Pastor Shepherd, your behavior has been intolerable."

"Mom don't you see my nose? Don't you care?"

"George says that you ran into a door knob and hurt your nose."

"Mom, do you believe that?" Several minutes of silence followed, while Myra waited for her mother's answer.

"No. I don't believe it." She said at last.

"What have I done that has been so bad?" Myra asked.

"George says that you have been acting very strangely. He wonders if you are doing drugs, either that or that you are a manic-depressive. He says that you have mood swings and that you are totally unpredictable. He even says that you pushed him against the wall a couple of weeks ago. He says that you did that for no reason or provocation."

"George comes into my bedroom at night, and does terrible things to me, Mom. I am tired of his threats."

"That doesn't mean that you should be disrespectful."

"I am not."

"Don't lie to me!"

"I am not lying, Mom. He threatened to tell Pastor Shepherd some things about me that weren't true. I did push him, because I was so mad. But he didn't need to slug me with his fist. The mirror broke because I fell against it, knocking it off the wall. That is the truth."

Her mother stared at her in stunned silence. Myra wondered what would happen next. She watched her mother to determine her reaction to what she had said. She knew that this was the moment of truth.

"Mom you have got to believe me." Myra sobbed. "Besides, he threatened to beat me and maybe even kill me if I ever told you." Her mother ran to her side, and put her arm around her.

"I...do...believe you." She said.

"You do?"

"Yes. I am sorry that I doubted you."

"I don't want to have to work and go to school. I will work in the summer, but it is too hard to go to school, work, and maintain good grades. I love the BOC, and it is just one afternoon a week."

"I will sign the permission slip." Her mother said.

"You will?"

"Yes." Her mother said. "Do you think that you need to go to the emergency room and get your nose X-rayed?"

"Mom, I am afraid to do that, because George might really hurt me if I tell anyone else the truth about what happened to me. What am I supposed to say? That I ran into a door knob?"

"You are right." Her mother said. "As a matter of fact, I was shocked when I saw you walk into the room with a misshapen nose." Then her mother surprised her by saying. "Why don't we pray about what to do?" The pain in her nose, and the shattered mirror were almost worth it now. What had been intended for evil, the Lord had turned for good. She had never prayed with her mother. Her mother went to church, but told her that she didn't believe that God intervened in the affairs of men. She had even said that "God might as well be a fence post in the sky" as far as she was concerned.

Obviously she didn't know her Lord like she did. Myra bowed her head and prayed a simple prayer with her mother. While her head was bowed she felt heat streaming over and through her nose. Her mother's mouth fell open as she watched Myra's nose straighten.

"Myra, God just straightened your nose! It looked like someone with invisible hands grabbed it and moved it back in place."

Myra grabbed a piece of the broken mirror and looked in amazement. Sure enough the nose was restored. In fact, all swelling had gone and her nose was even prettier than before.

"I always wanted my nose to be shorter and slightly pixie like. Look Mom, I have a perfect nose now!"

"Now we just need to keep George away from it." Her mother said. They both laughed. Myra handed the permission slip for her mother to sign.

"Don't worry about working, if you will work this summer that will be enough."

"Thanks Mom, and Mom, I do love you."

"I love you too." Her mother said. Her mother hugged her and left. That was the first time that she could remember having been hugged or told that she was loved. She knew that other families constantly hugged, and told each other how much they loved each other. At first, she resisted the hug, because it felt funny to hug her mother.

Kneeling beside her bed, she said her prayers and thanked the Lord for his intervention. "Dear Lord, please stop George from touching me ever again." Somehow she knew that she could trust Jesus, and that he would take care of her. She knew that there were no guarantees in this life, except for one: God's love would never fail her. Then she remembered a song telling about how the Lord's eyes were on the sparrows and how he watched over his children too. How wonderful to be a child of God.

Maybe I will cause Mom to divorce George? She laughed softly to herself, she had been afraid that she had caused her mother's divorce, and now she wanted to cause her to get divorced again. She remembered how much fun she had had with her mother. How they had gone to the zoo, and rode the small train in Lincoln Park.

How could Mom continue to live with George knowing that he had molested her daughter? She prayed that her mother would have the courage to do what needed to be done. Somehow she sensed that her mother was afraid of George. Perhaps she feared that he would beat her. Maybe she feared being alone, and thought that it was better to be married to a monster than to face life as a divorced, lonely woman.

Myra decided to prepare for the possibility of running away. I guess I will stay, but pack a suitcase just in case I need to leave. I don't want to hurt my Mom, but I can't let this man hurt me like this again. If my Mom won't protect me then I need to protect myself. After she finished praying, she pulled her suitcase from the top shelf of her closet and packed it with some emergency items.

Baby tried to climb into the suitcase, and she gently lifted him out and set him on the bed. "I sure don't want to have to leave you." She said. She shoved the suitcase under her bed. She didn't want to leave her beautiful home, but she feared George's revenge for telling her mother the truth. She knew that her nose had been broken, and only the supernatural power of God had restored it. She knew that he might make good his threats to beat her severely, or to even kill her. How ironic that he had accused her of being "Manic-Depressive." Surely if anyone in this family had that disorder it had to be him.

School counselors had advised the students that if they were being abused by a stepparent or relative that they needed to let it be known. She resolved to tell Pastor Shepherd at the first opportunity. He would know what she should do. She wouldn't run away until she had talked to Shepherd, unless of course, George attacked her again.

After she had put away the suitcase she reached into her dresser and found a small piggy bank. She counted the money and pulled out her saving account passbook. She didn't have much, but if necessary she would use it.

Where would she go? What would she do? She prayed that the Lord would lead her to the right people who could help her.

Baby snuggled next to her. Jokingly she said, "Baby do you know Jesus? The scriptures tell us to go into all the world and tell every creature about him." The cat purred and rubbed against her. She ran her fingers through his long fur. Playfully, he pawed at her while rolling onto his back. Sometimes she wished that she could be like this animal and not have to worry about anything. Oh how she would miss his soft fur, and loving presence. It sounded funny to say that her cat seemed the only sane and normal thing in her life, but it was true. Having said her prayers, she climbed into bed and fell into a troubled sleep.

The next morning she ate her breakfast hurriedly, avoiding the steely gaze of her stepfather. Tension filled the room as her mother and stepfather answered her questions with exaggerated politeness. Yet whenever she could, she avoided eye contact with George. She had already caught one of his glares from across the table. It seemed as if the very walls wanted to scream.

Breakfast over, she grabbed her backpack and headed out the door after quickly kissing her mother's cheek. A lump rose in her throat, as she fought the tears. She didn't want to run away. She still hoped for what she knew could only be a miracle. It would take a miracle for her to stay. She stopped in the doorway, remembering that she needed to talk to Pastor Shepherd, and would need to explain why she wasn't coming home on the school bus.

"Oh, I forgot to mention that I need to stay after school today. Don't worry, I have a bus pass, and can catch the Number 9 bus." She said.

"OK, but be home before 7:30 pm." Her mother answered. She was so relieved that her mother didn't question why she needed to stay after school.

She ran toward the bus stop, and almost missed the bus. Although the bus was full, Hilda had saved her a seat. She sank down in the seat relieved that one more crisis had been averted. She knew that Miss Anderson had no sympathy for those who were late, and had instituted a new policy that all homework received a zero if it was received after the announcements, and roll was taken. I am going to have quit living like this. My life is too much of a roller coaster ride. Sometimes I just wish that I could make this crazy ride stop. Not for the first time, she considered what it would be like if she committed suicide. No I couldn't do that to Baby or my Mom.

Still, she had gotten permission to come home later. That was the first miracle of the day, now if she could just be able to talk to Pastor Shepherd. She decided to call the church at the first opportunity.

At the break, she called his office and arranged to meet him after school. He offered to come get her and take her to a nearby park where they could talk.

The rest of the day passed uneventfully. Nobody even noticed the remains of the bruises around her eyes, and her nose didn't even hurt.

She met Shepherd in front of the school, and gratefully climbed into the church van.

"What is up?" he asked. "What happened to your face? It looks different."

"That is what I want to talk to you about." She said. She quickly recounted the previous evening's events. She also told him about her stepfather's night visits. He listened thoughtfully.

They strolled around the park's jogging path, and talked. Pastor Shepherd had brought her a sandwich, which she ate quickly. She had skipped lunch, because she had been too upset to eat. Now however, her hunger had returned. Somehow she knew that tonight she would get the help that she needed.

While she ate, Shepherd remained silent. It was obvious that he was weighing the situation, and pondering what to say. Finally he broke the silence.

"If you report this, Child Protection Services will intervene." He said. "I don't know what they will do, but they might place you in a foster home."

"I was thinking about running away." She said.

"Don't do that, it will only compound your problems. How do you think that Jesus would handle the situation?" He said.

She didn't have any idea how he would handle it. "I don't know. He wouldn't run away, but I don't think that he would allow himself to be abused either."

"I agree."

"So, don't you think that Jesus wants this situation to stop?"
"Yes, but how?"
"I don't know what he is going to do, but I do know that one option would be that you could stay with my wife and I." He said. "In fact, we could use you at the church, and maybe give you a little pocket money."
"Really?"
"However, I doubt that your mother would agree to it. I also don't know whether CPS would agree to it either. Why don't we pray about this?" The two of them prayed that the Lord would intervene.
"What do I do right now?" she asked.
"I don't like the fact that you will have to spend another night in that house, but I am feeling that the Lord is going to do something. Let's not do anything about this tonight. I will continue to pray, and see what the Lord wants in this situation." She felt a little disappointed, and yet relieved too. After the walk, he drove her home.
"I don't know what the Lord is going to do, but he will do something, just wait and see. In fact, I believe that you will call me with some sort of news." He said.
When they arrived at her house, she noticed with mixed feelings that George's car wasn't in the driveway. He usually came home around 6:30 pm. Perhaps he had needed to work late, something he did occasionally. Unfortunately, his lateness often resulted from having stopped at a local bar. Then he would come home drunk. Myra shivered, maybe I can stay in my room and he will leave me alone.
"Lord, help me I don't know what he might do to me if he comes home drunk." She prayed as she walked in the front door.

CHAPTER SIX

It is written:
"For I know the thoughts that I think toward you,
saith the Lord, thoughts of peace, and not of evil,
to give you an expected end."

"Mom, I am home." Myra called as she walked through the front door. The emptiness of the house stunned her. Baby walked toward her crying, bewilderment on his face. The room was empty. Myra stared in disbelief. All the furniture was gone. She ran through the house, searching for something to tell her that this was just a bad dream. What had happened to her family? She had thought that she would be the one who ran away, and yet here she had found that her family had left her! She knew that Pastor Shepherd had felt that her situation would change, but surely this had to be a cruel joke. She ran up the stairs and found her room intact. How ironic she thought, her room remained undisturbed, a cruel contrast to the emptiness of the rest of the house. She walked through the house, her feet echoing as she walked. What should she do? She went back up to her room and sat on her bed. She moved her pillow, causing an envelope to fall onto the bed. It contained a note, which read:

Dear Myra,

George left us this morning. I didn't want to tell you this at breakfast, but he had told me that he was leaving. He hired a moving van and took the furniture. He gave me only enough money for one bus ticket. So I have gone back to Alvin to live with my mother. You may call me collect when you get home. If I get the money I will send you a bus ticket if you decide to join me in Alvin. I am sorry that you have been left with this, but I just can't handle any more problems right now. I am sure that Pastor Shepherd will help you find a place to live, and help you with school. The rent is due on the house, and George closed the bank account without paying the rent. I hope that the landlord lets you stay a few days until you can make other arrangements. There isn't any more money; in fact I was tempted to borrow some from your piggy bank. You will be glad to know that I didn't. George took the car too. I didn't want to pull you out of school. I left a message on the Shepherd's answering machine telling them that you would need their help.

At least you won't have to worry about George's nighttime visits anymore.

I know that this is hard, but I do love you. Believe me, I feel that this is for the best.

Love,
Mom

Myra sat in stunned disbelief and unable to move. The only furniture in the house was her bedroom suite. Even the refrigerator had been removed, and all her things apart from her bedroom were in a box in the kitchen. At least her mother had left her a few days worth of dried groceries including cat food. She didn't like dried milk, but knew that she would manage somehow with the Lord's help. Her mind couldn't comprehend what had happened. Shocked beyond measure and too numb to even call Pastor Shepherd, she sat on her bed until the early hours of morning.

She heard the phone and the doorbell ring, but ignored both. Somehow she couldn't move. Finally, she climbed into bed at 5 am, and slept until noon. Her first thoughts were that she had missed school, and that no one was going to write her an excuse. What will I tell the teachers? Should I call Pastor Shepherd, or my Mom? No, she would wait. Baby rubbed against her legs, obviously wondering when he would be fed. She decided to feed him.

"At least you didn't leave me." She told him. She counted the cans, and found that she had enough for five days. Carefully she poured the dry biscuit into his bowl, and opened the can into his second bowl. Tears smarted in her blue eyes, as her strawberry blonde hair cascaded over her face. What a mess I am, with tear stained hair! I had better get myself together, before I allow myself to see anyone.

The doorbell rang, but she still didn't want to answer it. What could she say? The doorbell persisted, but she wouldn't answer it. She didn't want anyone to see her like this.

She could see that Pastor Shepherd and a lady who was most likely his wife were on the porch. At least they cared enough to come, but she still couldn't face them.

"Lord forgive me, I just don't want them to see me like this." She said as she ran up the stairs to her room.

The doorbell rang again. Myra pressed her hands against her ears to block out the sound, and buried her face in her pillow. What am I going to do? Pastor Shepherd had been a friend to her, and he only wanted to help. Why can't I face him?

She listened to the sound of retreating footsteps. Relieved that he had left, but at the same time she wanted to run after him and say, "Wait!"

"Lord, I don't know what to do?" She raised her head toward heaven and cried, "Help me, Jesus!" Peace descended like a warm blanket, as she rocked herself to sleep. How odd, it was as though for one second in eternity, all heaven had stopped to hear her plea.

That evening she checked the pantry and found that her food supply was limited to a nearly empty box of cereal, and a carton of out-of-date powdered milk. She had no refrigerator, but at least she had cat food. No matter what happened, she didn't want Baby to be hungry.

A loud knock at the door disturbed her thoughts. Peering through the window was none other than Mary, the landlord. The neighborhood kids called her a witch, because of her pointed nose, peeked forehead and wart on her chin. Mary 's reputation for being a gossip and possessing a caustic tongue preceded her. The kids joked that her tongue was so long that she could sit in the living room and lick a spoon in the kitchen. Now here she was on her front porch. I suppose that she is here to collect the rent, and of course to find out all the gossip. Quickly she ducked out of sight, hoping that Mary hadn't seen her dart out of the hallway.

Although she had evaded Mary, the reality of her situation hadn't changed. She couldn't pay the rent; in fact she only had a little money. Speaking of money, I sure hope that George and Mom hadn't raided my piggy bank. However, when she emptied it onto her bed, she knew that one of them had taken most of the money. Great, I have nowhere to live, no money, no family, no food, and no job. The only money that I have would be barely enough for bus fare, even if someone bought me a ticket to Alvin.

Myra sank to her knees beside her bed and prayed. Baby rubbed around her legs, and she pushed him aside. "Sorry, Baby, but right now I need to hear from God."

She spent the next few hours in prayer and searching her Bible for answers. Funny she thought, I usually read my Bible because that is something that a Christian is supposed to do. Now it is like every word of it is speaking directly to me, and I can't seem to get enough. How can a book written thousands of years ago speak to my situation today? Then she remembered that the sacred words said, " For the word of God is full of living power, it is alive, and is sharper than the sharpest knife, cutting deep into our innermost thoughts and desires. It exposes us for what we really are. Nothing in all creation can hide from him." After several hours, she fell asleep on the floor.

She awakened in the early hours of the morning. Her limbs ached, and her neck hurt. Stretching, she groaned and headed for the bedroom. Baby lay curled by her pillow. Trust a cat to find the one comfortable spot in the house. In the morning she showered feeling grateful that George hadn't been able to dismantle the bathroom. At least she could close the commode lid and use it as a chair. She proceeded to polish her toenails, and brush her hair. There were no chairs in the house, only her bed and her bureau. After showering, and dressing she ate the rest of the cereal. I need to get help, maybe now I can face people.

She had to admit that her prayers had been answered, but not in the way that she had expected. The Lord did remove George from her life. She would never have to fear his night visits again.

I do need to call the Shepherds; they will wonder why I am being so rude, and not answering the door. No sooner had she decided to call them, than she heard another loud knock at the front door.

"Open up, this is the police." Myra heard the police bullhorn and knew that she must obey the law. Reluctantly she opened the door. A policeman and the Shepherds stood on her front porch. Although she had never met Mrs. Shepherd, her incredible beauty amazed her.

"Hello, I am Virginia Shepherd, and I am sorry that your parents left you," she said. Her eyes resembled those of an eagle and yet were filled with kindness. Myra remained speechless.

"Are you OK?" asked the officer.

"Yes." Myra answered.

"We understand that your parents left you, but they had requested that the Shepherds take you into their home until something can be resolved with the family."

"Yes." Myra replied. How humiliating that everyone would know that her parents had abandoned her.

"Myra will be fine with us officer, and should there be any change in her family situation we will help her reconnect with her parents." Pastor Shepherd said.

"They aren't my parents." Myra said harshly. The three on the porch stared at her.

"Actually my mother and stepfather are separated, and I hope that they stay that way." She couldn't believe how angry she sounded. No wonder, it wasn't every day that her parents had dumped her into the care of people she hardly knew.

"Don't worry time has a way of healing situations. For now, you will be safe with the Shepherds." Replied the policeman.

The Shepherds helped her load her things into the trunk of their car. Myra grabbed the reluctant cat, and carefully climbed into the back seat of their car. Baby's claws latched on to everything within range. She had several scratches from her normally gentle cat. He was terrified, even though she whispered soothing words to him. "I hope that I can hold onto Baby, and that he doesn't jump out of my arms. He is really scared."

"He will like it at our house, we have one cat, and she is very gentle. In fact, she looks a lot like him only smaller." Virginia said.

Myra had to admit that she liked Mrs. Shepherd. She seemed so elegant and kind. Maybe living with them would work out for the best, just like her mother's note had said. At least they cared enough about her to see if she was all right. Which was more than her mother had done.

"Do you want to call your mother?" Virginia asked.

"No, I would rather not." She answered. She knew that she needed to forgive her mother. She expected a sermon on that from the Shepherds, and braced herself for the inevitable comments. However, they surprised her by not saying anything more on the subject. In fact, they changed the subject totally.

She wanted to stay with the Shepherds and let her broken heart mend. Hadn't she read last night how Jesus came to heal the brokenhearted?

How ironic that only a week ago, she had wished that she didn't have to live with her mother and George. She had longed to live with someone like the Shepherds. Now here she was in the backseat of their car, with all her worldly belongings in the trunk.

I feel like such an emotional freak. I hurt so much because they abandoned me. Yet another part of my heart is leaping for joy because I no longer have to live with George. I don't want to live with my Mom either, because she doesn't believe the way I do and we argue a lot. I especially don't want to live with her if she gets reconciled with George. I hope that I won't be made to live with them again. I know that it isn't Mom's entire fault, and I do hope that in time that I can visit her. But in the meantime, I would rather live near the church and be able to help with the ministry, she thought.

Myra settled into her new home, and was delighted that Baby and Blessing, the Shepherd's cat, seemed to like each other. That is after an initial hissing and spitting which resulted in a lamp being overturned as Blessing careened through the house in hot pursuit of Baby. The Shepherds prayed that the two would become friends. Indeed, their prayers were speedily answered. Only an hour later, Blessing lay on her back on the living room rug, while playfully pawing at her new four legged companion.

Myra's new room featured white carpet, and of course a bouquet of fresh pink roses. Pastor Shepherd raised wonderful roses and every day he brought a bouquet from the garden for the home. This he did as a display of love for his wife and family. The words "I love you" were said often and with sincerity. A sign in her room bore the legend, "Love only spoken here." What a contrast, to her family who at best exchanged only pleasantries. She had lived for so long with an angry undercurrent in the home that she didn't know how to react to so much love and kindness.

Myra steadfastly refused to call her mother. One evening, her mother called, Myra handled herself well in spite of their short and stilted conversation. Myra told her mother that she wanted to continue to live with the Shepherds. Her mother seemed to have so many problems that if anything she was relieved about not having another mouth to feed.

"Perhaps this is for the best," Her mother said.

"Mom, I…love you." Myra flinched as she made herself say the words. Why was saying "I love you, so hard, she wondered. She missed her mom in some ways, and ironically couldn't imagine that she wouldn't be living with her anymore. Sometimes she wished that this was a dream or that she was on vacation, and soon it would end and she would wake up at the old house. Yet the reality was that her mother had abandoned her. The only good thing was that she didn't have to see George anymore.

After she finished talking to her mom, Virginia Shepherd held her, while Myra wept bitter tears.

"I feel like such a cry baby. That seems to be all that I do."

"Nonsense, to Pastor and I, you are such a refreshing change from some of the students in school." Virginia said

"How do you mean?" Myra asked.

"So many kids have problems. Like the students at your school who use magic to bring curses on their enemies, family, neighbors. They do it because they are told that they can stop anyone who gets in the way of what they want to do. "

"I know. I have heard them talk."

"Yes, but the sad part of it is, that although it sometimes works, they don't know that those same demons have them in a deadly grasp. When they decide to get free they can't. The same sorcery that they use will eventually turn on them and destroy them. The devil has played them for fools, using them as pawns in an evil game that ultimately seeks their destruction."

"True."

"What is funny is that they laugh at us, but when they need help, guess to whom they turn? They come, or at least their family brings them. They call it counseling. We call it deliverance. You ought to see what happens during the deliverance. Just last week, one girl slithered on the floor like a snake. Her body moved in ways that a normal human can't move. Then there was another girl who spoke with a man's voice. The voice said 'I am not coming out of her.' That sounded so bizarre, and yet once that girl got free she was so happy. She fell on the floor, and rolled, cried, and laughed for an hour."

"I would like to have seen that." Myra said.

"Don't worry, if you stay around here you will. Sometimes those spirits try to get them to commit suicide. That is why we are glad that you are here. You are their age, and you have been given great power. We believe that you will be able to help some of these kids get free. They are so miserable, and then some of the covens pledge to kill them if they decide to leave."

"That is terrible."

"Yes indeed it is. Sometimes the families will have the kids stay with us for a time. Because they know that no dark witchcraft can get to them while they are here."

"Really?"

"Yes, we believe that you are destined to be a world changer."

"I don't know. My life seems to be such a mess."

"I believe that in the regions of Hell you are famous. In fact, you are famous in heaven too."

How ironic, she felt anything but special and/or famous. She felt used and abused.

"What about the fact...you know...what happened with George and I? Wouldn't people be disgusted if they knew what had happened to me? I mean it isn't like I wanted it to happen. I was afraid of what he would do to me if I said no."

"Nonsense, besides the Lord has restored your purity. As though nothing ever happened. It is a matter of the heart. Didn't you say that after your conversion, George wasn't able to touch you?"

"He did break my nose."

"But God healed it. Besides the sacred words say, '.... that those who become Christians become new persons. They are not the same anymore, for the old life is gone. A new life has begun!' So you have begun a new life here, and I know that there are great things in store for you."

That night Myra knelt beside her bed, exhausted and yet she couldn't sleep. The cuckoo crowed twelve times letting her know that it must be midnight. Tomorrow is a school day, and I need to sleep and yet I can't stop thinking about what has happened. She reached over to pet Baby, both cats vied for her attention. Now she had two beautiful pets. Stretching and yawning, she opened her Bible and began to read. Maybe if I read my Bible I will get sleepy.

She looked up from reading, and saw the largest person that she had ever seen in her life, standing at the foot of her bed. He remained standing perfectly still as he gazed upon her. This must be an angel of the Lord.

He stood nearly seven feet tall, with long blonde hair. She had longed to see an angel and yet here she was, scared of his presence. She didn't know that they were that tall, and unsmiling too.

"I am a messenger of the Lord. You must sleep. The Lord has sent me to tell you that you need to cast the cares of the last few days onto him, for he cares for you." The angel said and vanished before her eyes.

No wonder I am having a hard time sleeping, I get the most amazing visitors into my bedroom. Still, having my guardian angel for a nighttime visitor is better than most of the other visitors that I have had.

She slept peacefully until morning. Baby slept in the corner with his new companion, Blessing. So much for my cuddly companion, guess he has a new life too. The next morning she felt totally refreshed. Her heart knew such peace and joy. It had to be another miracle.

The Shepherds had given her an excuse for her two-day absence. Fortunately her teachers didn't ask questions, and even gave her extra time to complete her homework. Of course her friends all wanted to know the details. She hated telling them anything, and found herself answering their questions with either a yes or a no. After all, she reasoned, it really wasn't any of their business to know her family's problems. Some kids could be so cruel and nosey too.

Gratefully, the day ended and she rode the bus to New Life Christian Center's Youth building. Pastor Shepherd planned to take her home after he finished work. In the meantime, she decided to go for a swim in the pool. She jumped into the shallow end and swam. The water felt so refreshing, as she swam several laps. Hoping that she would be allowed to swim for the rest of the afternoon.

Pastor Shepherd had told her that many people received a healing while in the pool. After swimming several more laps, she climbed out of the pool and sat on the edge. How marvelous to have the whole pool to herself. As she sat there, she began to sing a song to the Lord. Suddenly, she felt like something was suctioning her toward the ceiling. As though a giant vacuum cleaner was drawing her out of her body. She heard a "Whoosh!" instantly she felt herself being pulled out of the room. She didn't know if she was in her body, or was in the spirit.

She was being carried in something at an incredible speed. They zoomed through the subdivision and beyond. She saw that she was riding in something that resembled a horseless chariot. However, it also resembled a cable car in that it was completely enclosed. Looking up, she saw the same angel that had visited her bedroom.

"You must be my guardian angel."

"Yes." He answered.

"Where are we going?" she asked.

"You have an appointment with Lord God Jehovah." Myra rode in silence for several minutes. I can't believe that I am talking to an angel. I hope that he doesn't mind if I ask him some questions.

"Am I dead?" she asked cautiously.

"No." Obviously the angel wasn't one for casual conversation. The chariot slowed and came to a stop. The door opened and Myra received the shock of her life. She knew that she was in heaven. She stepped onto the greenest grass that she had ever seen. The streets were gold, a transparent gold unlike anything that she had seen in earth.

Myra fell to the ground and began to praise the Lord; the angel fell to the ground and worshipped beside her. Together they cried, "Glory to God in the highest, Hosanna to His Holy Name." Even the flowers around her seemed to be singing praises to the Lord. Myra carefully stepped around them, but they were everywhere. The flowers looked like little faces ringed with petals. There were so many, that she accidentally stepped on one. When she stooped down to look at it, she saw that it had bounced back unharmed. The angel told her that there was no death in heaven. In the distance, she saw hills and beautiful lush valleys. The fragrance and the colors were beyond description. She never wanted to leave.

"Oh angel where are we going next?" she cried.

"You have an appointment, but first we must go over to those trees. You will need to eat the fruit in order to maintain your strength." Said the angel pointing to a grove of trees. The landscape reminded her of earth with its lush valleys, majestic mountains, and clear steams of water. The mountains had snow and yet it wasn't cold.

Flowers abounded everywhere, and the fragrances defied earthly description. Trees lined the River of Life as it flowed throughout what must be Paradise. Hundreds, perhaps, thousands of people stood under the trees.

"These are the people who accepted Jesus, but who never lived for him. They will need to build their strength before they can go before the heavenly throne."

The angel showed the river that flowed through heaven. He told her that it proceeded out of the throne of God. On either side of the river, were the Trees of life, which the angel told her bore twelve manner of fruits. They yielded their fruit every month: and the leaves of the tree were for the healing of the nations. People gathered under them to recover from the wounds of their earth life.

The River of Life sparkled as it flowed. The angel noticed her watching the flowing water.

"You can swim in the River of Life and can even breathe under water."

"Do you know that no one will be cursed in this place? You will live in perfect peace. Gathering around the throne of God, and all His servants shall serve Him, and you shall see his face; and his name shall be in your forehead. And there shall be no night there; and you won't need a candle, neither any sunlight. Because the Lord God gives us light, and we shall reign for ever and ever." Said the angel.

Once again Myra marveled at her surroundings, everything had light. She also saw children and animals. A gorgeous white tiger walked passed them, and an Orangutan peered out of the bushes at them.

"Can I pet the tiger?" Asked Myra.

"There will be time for that later. Now let's go over to those trees, I need to give you some of the fruit." He said as they walked. He plucked a copper colored fruit from one of the trees and handed it to her. She ate it, noticing that it didn't taste like any fruit on earth.

"You will need to eat this fruit so that you can maintain your strength. You will need it to have strength to keep your appointment." She ate more of the fruit and smelled the fragrance of the leaves. The angel picked several more fruit and told her to carry them for their journey.

"What is that fragrance?" she asked.

"It is the fragrance of God. He is in everything here. The fragrance of the leaves sends strength into your body."

As she walked she noticed that although the light was so bright, there were no shadows. She turned and watched for a shadow to follow as they moved. Then she noticed that even the trees did not cast a shadow.

"I don't see any shadows." She said.

"God is light and in Him is no darkness. The sacred words say, every good gift and every perfect gift is from above, and cometh down from the Father of lights, with whom is no variableness, neither shadow of turning. That is what that means; you will not find a shadow in this place."

The sound of children singing filled the air. Children carrying harps were running and praising God.

"I didn't know that there were children in heaven."

"These are the children that the earth didn't want."

"Are they children of abortion?"

"Yes, they are excited about meeting their parents."

"They want to meet them?"

"Oh yes, they can't wait to see their mothers. God brought them here, because they needed to learn the oracles of God. People teach the children here in special services. "

" There is someone I want you to meet." The angel continued, "Do you remember the stories about Abraham and his son Isaac?"

"Oh yes, we used to sing a song about Father Abraham in Sunday school. I never liked the song, but I knew that he had many sons."

"That is correct. By the way, are you thirsty?"

"Yes, I wouldn't mind something to drink."

Coming toward them was a large, barrel-chested man whose youthful appearance hid the fact that he was thousands of years old. He stopped to dip a golden goblet into the river. The river resembled a bayou or a creek, and yet it sparkled with crystal intensity. The light shone like diamonds upon the river as it flowed. The angel explained that it originated at the throne of God and flowed out as a River of Life.

"Meet Abraham," said the angel. Myra felt as though she had known him all her life. As though he had been her own father. She knew that the sacred words said that if you belong to Christ, then you are Abraham's seed, and heirs according to the promise.

"Myra, drink this!" Abraham said. How amazing that he knew who she was.

"Are you…um…are you…."?

"Abraham, that's right. Paradise is where I meet the newcomers and visitors."

"Praise God," Myra said. Immediately a wave of praise moved through the crowd of people gathered by the river and under the trees.

"I thought that Paradise no longer existed after Jesus ascended into heaven."

"No, God brought it to heaven so we might enjoy it."

"Drink the water, it will refresh and help you." Myra carefully held the golden goblet. She had never held a real gold goblet. She quickly drained the cup and handed it back to Abraham. Heavenly water had a unique taste that refreshed unlike any water on earth.

How impressive that he had handed her a golden goblet instead of a paper cup. She wanted ask him about the story in Genesis, telling how he prepared to offer his son Isaac as a sacrifice. Did he know ahead of time that the Lord was going to prevent him from slaying Isaac? Of course, the scriptures tell, how a ram was caught by its horns nearby. Abraham and Isaac had killed it instead.

"I need to be going. I have to meet others who are just arriving."

"I must take you to the city where you will have your appointment. Let us make haste." Said the angel. They continued toward the city.

Once again, she saw children singing, and playing. Suddenly, they began to whisper excitedly. "Hosanna to the Highest, He is coming."

"Whom are they talking about?"

"You will see."

A light came out of the city, far away from them. The children ran toward the Light. Myra knew that this must be Jesus. She remembered how the children had run to him when he walked on earth with his disciples.

Myra walked her attention focused on His hands, which reached for the children as they played, sang, and hugged Him. She heard Him speak, "Suffer the little children to come unto me for of such is the kingdom of God."

"Angel, I feel kind of weak." Myra said.

"Eat some more of the fruit," he said as he handed a piece to her. They continued on their journey. Myra slowed as they approached a huge wall. The closer they came to it, the larger it became. This must be the wall in the Bible, the book of Revelation.

"Yes," said the angel in answer to her thoughts, "It is 72 yards tall. The city is about 1500 miles, and its length, width, and height are the same." Myra marveled at the gorgeous jasper, and the city resembled clear glass but was pure gold. Different precious stones made the foundation of the wall of the city. The stones gleamed in the light. The light remained so intense that there was no need of the sun, nor moon in it."

"Does the Lord light everything, or is there another source of light?"

"The glory of God lightens everything." The angel answered. He took Myra by the hand, "We need to go to the chariot so that we can complete the journey."

Myra saw the Book of Life. A huge book, that has the names of all those who will have chosen to make heaven their eternal home. It stood five feet five inches tall, and had a thickness of a couple of inches. The gold binding bore the legend, 'Book of Life' etched deeply upon it.

"Angel can we stop and see it?"

"No, that is not permitted." He said. The chariot continued its journey before slowing to a stop.

"Kneel, he is here." The angel commanded. Myra fell to her knees, feeling weak. The angel handed her another piece of fruit.

"I see Jesus," Myra whispered. He walked directly towards her. Suddenly, she longed to be held in his arms, and yet she felt so worthless. As he walked, the children continued to run up to him and he just hugged them.

"I am a kid, can I go hug him?" she asked the angel. His look told her to stay on her knees and wait.

Jesus' countenance glowed like the sun, resembling a shaft of golden light. How glorious he looked. Immediately Myra fell on her face at his feet. The first thing she wanted to do was to tell him how sorry she was for everything that she had ever done wrong. I wonder if I should say hello, or ask him to forgive me. Immediately, she knew that he knew every good and bad thing that she ever done, even her problems with George. She knew that he knew all about how hurt and angry she felt towards George, and her mother for abandoning her.

"Oh, my Lord! "

"I am here."

Myra remained at his feet. His feet resembled burnished brass. She had often wondered if he had nail prints in his feet. Now she lay with her face inches from His feet, face to face with the reality of the crucifixion. Not only did he have a mark, he had a hole in each foot the size of a coin. Shafts of light radiated from the holes. His clothes resembled diamonds and a rainbow surrounded his presence. The crucifixion had to be more horrifying than she could imagine.

"Jesus?"

"You may get up. What do you think of heaven?"

"It is so glorious. Can I stay now?"

"No, I need you to go back and tell your generation that I am coming back soon. Tell them to quit playing with sorcery and black magic. They need to know that the same Holy Spirit that was with me during my earth walk, will lead and guide them to do even greater things, if they will just yield to His direction in their lives. Tell them that I love them, that I have plans for them, plans for good and not evil. I need you to tell my people that I am coming soon." He spoke urgently.

"But who will believe me, I am just a kid, just a girl."

"I believed in you, enough to bring you here. Besides, Solomon was just a boy when he became king."

"But..." Myra started to say something and decided to be quiet. Yet she knew that he could read her mind.

"With me all things are possible. You will affect your city and your world if you serve me with all of your heart."

"I have nothing to offer you."

"Nothing? When you team with me you have everything. You feel foolish, and yet I choose the foolish in order to shame those who think they are wise. And I choose those who are powerless to astound those who are powerful."

"I know some think that I am foolish, because I love you so much." Myra said.

"Daughter, I love you very much. You are not foolish in my eyes. Although the world may think differently." He said. Myra had never felt so special and honored.

"Many times I have chosen things despised by the world, things counted as nothing at all, and used them to bring to nothing what the world considers important, so that no one can ever boast in my presence.'

Jesus put his arms around Myra. She felt totally loved for the first time in her life. With his arm around her he motioned toward a man wearing a crown that approached them.

"Myra, I want you to meet another king. Do you remember reading about king David?"

"He has red hair, just like the scriptures say." Myra said marveling.

"To the King of Kings I extend my crown," David said as he bowed before Jesus and extended his crown toward him.

"I want you to take Myra for a tour of her home and neighborhood." Myra didn't know what to say, she wished that she could talk longer with Jesus.

"Are you King David, the father of Solomon?" she felt stupid for asking. She had never met anyone as old as Abraham and David. Yet they looked so young.

"Should I bow?" Myra asked. King David laughed softly.

"No, the only king who you should bow to is the King of Kings. I am your tour guide."

"Really? That is too awesome, to have King David as a tour guide."

"The greatest privilege that we have here is to be a servant. We are here to serve you."

"Yes. In answer to your question, my son, Solomon, was just a boy when he became king. He was smart, because he asked for wisdom. I suggest that you do the same." Myra knew that he had read her mind.

"Come, let me show you your house."

"My house? You mean I have a whole house just for me?"

"Yes."

"Does it have an indoor pool?"

"Yes."

"Does it have a Christmas tree?"

"Yes."

"Really?"

"Of course, it was built with your desires in mind."

"Does it have a stable and a horse?"

"You have a wonderful horse that is yours to ride."

"What about a cat?"

"Of course, young lady, you have so many questions." King David laughed, and so did her angel. Myra noticed that it was the first time that she had seen her angel laugh.

CHAPTER SEVEN

It is written:
"And I saw heaven opened, and behold a white horse;
and he that sat on him was called
Faithful and True, and in righteousness
he doth judge and make war."

King David took Myra to her house. Myra rubbed her eyes in disbelief. She shut her eyes and opened them again to see if what she saw was true. There before her was a replica of a gorgeous home that she had seen in a magazine. She had cut out the picture and kept it in her Bible. The only differences were that the spacious house seemed larger and sat on huge sweeping grounds. A water fountain graced the manicured front yard. Gorgeous trees and shrubs provided the landscaping.

"How do you like it?" David asked.

"Oh its wonderful!" Myra answered.

"Would you like to go inside?" he asked.

"May I?" Myra leaped with joy. She walked into the expansive foyer. The floors gleamed. Marble and the precious stones formed a wonderful mosaic pattern of the Lord and a girl riding double on a beautiful white stallion. Then she noticed the marvelous floral wallpaper. She loved roses, and here the wallpaper was made of roses. Only the roses were real.

"Look at the roses on the wallpaper."

"Everything here is real."

In the center of the house was a huge kidney shaped pool and spa, built of marble in colors that she had never seen on earth. No words could describe the beauty of the house.

"I wasn't expecting anything like this. It is so beautiful, and the furniture is exactly the kind that I dreamed of having one day in my home. That is when I grow up and have a family."

"Yes, the Lord knew that you would like it, so we put it in your home. God gives you the desires of your heart. All desires are fulfilled here. All the desires that you have, and a few that you couldn't imagine having."

"I want to stay here!" she cried.

"It is not time for you to stay." Replied the angel. At that point David led her outside to a grove of trees behind her house and whistled. Out of the trees emerged the most beautiful horse that she had ever seen.

"Behold a white horse," said the angel. "Did you know that the scriptures tell about a white horse riding forth to conquer on the earth. On the horse is someone carrying a bow, and a crown was given to that person to conquer. Do you know who that is? He is a counterfeit of the real King of Kings who will also ride a white horse. Soon the counterfeit king will go forth into the earth."

"Oh," Myra answered.

"There are many white horses that go with the Lord at that time for the last battle. You will have a part in this. In the meantime, this is your horse."

"Oh, this is too wonderful!"

The horse stood several hands taller than most earth horses. His magnificent, arched neck rose out of his powerful shoulders. The neck being trimmed with a long mane that hung nearly a foot below his neck. His hips were straight, and his tail arched into the air forming a plume that cascaded to the ground. Never had she seen such a breathtaking creature. The horse lowered its head toward Myra, as she extended her hand to pet his velvety nose. He nuzzled her. Its huge gentle eyes radiated light. Obviously this animal was a fiery warhorse.

The stallion's forehead dished like an Arabian horse, revealing its exquisite bone structure that was exotic in appearance. The nostrils flared gently as it sniffed her hand.

"You may ride him if you like."

"With no saddle or bridle?"

"He is yours to ride, you don't need a bridle or saddle."

"I haven't ridden in awhile, I hope that I won't fall." Myra wanted to ride him, but she had to admit that although she had ridden horses on earth, she hadn't ridden such a mighty creature as this one.

"Don't be afraid," said David reading her mind. "You won't fall."

"What is his name?"

"Shekinah Fire." Said David as he gave her a leg up onto the horse's back. Shekinah Fire craned his neck toward her and said, "Are you ready?" What next? Here she was astride a talking horse. Then she remembered having watched animated movies that featured talking horses, but they were computer-generated images and not real horses. This horse talked because he understood her language.

"I am ready." She felt stupid talking to a horse. She grasped his mane, and gulped.

"Careful, you don't have to pull my mane, or kick my sides, just ask or think what you want me to do. I can fly too." Shekinah Fire said. Great I just got a lecture from a horse. The horse shook his head, in response to her thoughts.

Shekinah Fire began to walk, slowly at first and then he eased into a gallop. Myra felt strangely secure, almost as though she was attached to the animal. No matter how high he leaped or how fast he turned she moved in total harmony with him. He took her past waterfalls, and into a forest. Soon they were flying through the sky and around the clouds. After several minutes they returned, and she dismounted. She threw her arms around his neck and hugged him.

"Next time, bring a carrot." He whinnied in what sounded like a horselaugh. The ride ended all too soon. David left and the angel continued showing her the streets of heaven.

"Did you know that the Lord has a Royal Riding Academy and that every believer has their own white horse?" said the angel.

"I can't wait to take riding lessons with Shekinah Fire." Myra said.

"The time is drawing to a close and it is time that we returned." Said the angel. "However, there is one more stop that we need to make." They continued to walk down a street lined with enormous mansions. This street reminded her of a heavenly version of homes and famous estates of the rich and famous, that had been featured in magazines.

"Whose houses are these?" she asked.

"They are the patriarchs." Myra noticed that the flowers were exquisite.

"These flowers are different, each one has a little face that looks like a person." Myra marveled at a meadow that was filled with white flowers. The flowers edged in purple showed the face of a person.

"Yes, these are different. Did you know that every time someone accepts Jesus as their Lord, a flower is made with their face etched in purple upon it?"

"Angel, on earth when you walk through the graveyards there are tombstones of people who have died. Here it is like a field of living memorials."

"That is right, there is no death here. Just like there are no shadows because if you notice everything is transparent."

"Oh angel, do I have to go back? My parents don't care, and I have to live with the Shepherds. Can't I stay here?" Myra asked.

"No, as a matter of fact, our next stop will show you why you must return." They entered the chariot and were soon zooming through the streets of heaven. All around them throngs of people walked. Their faces appeared so carefree and happy as they went about their travels. They arrived at the Book of Life.

"Now it will be permitted for you to see the Book." Explained the angel. Myra marveled at the book. The cover reminded her of gold lame' cloth. The names were written in silver and underlined in red.

"Why are they underlined in red?" she asked.

"That is the blood of Christ."

"Oh!" Myra scanned the book, looking for names. Turning the pages, she searched, but in her heart she knew that her mother's name wouldn't be found. She also knew that George's name wouldn't be found. I don't care if George makes heaven or not, she thought.

"The Lord cares." The angel spoke to her mind. "Did you notice that some names are not in this book?"

"Yes," Myra answered sadly.

"That is why you must return. There are many who need to hear your testimony. In the coming weeks, you will be taken to the lower regions and visit the damned."

"Must I?" Myra said horrified.

"It is the Lord's will that you see. It is time for you to return." The angel said. Myra and the angel entered the chariot. Immediately they gained momentum as they flew through the heavens and the sky. The earth rose to meet them, appearing as a ball, growing closer and closer until they were descending through the roof of New Life Christian Youth Center. Myra found herself sitting by the pool alone. She glanced at the clock and saw that she had only been gone an hour. At that moment, Pastor Shepherd entered the pool area.

"Are you ready to go home?" He asked.

"Give me a few minutes to shower and change." Myra answered. How marvelous that the Lord had timed everything so perfectly. She hadn't even been missed. She arrived just in time to change and head to the Shepherds house in time for dinner. She wondered if Pastor Shepherd had noticed anything different about her. She decided to ask him.

"Do I seem different to you?" she asked.

"As a matter of fact, you are glowing." He said.

"I just visited heaven." She proceeded to tell him all about her visit to heaven. He seemed so excited.

"What you are telling me has been confirmed by other believers who have shared similar stories." He said.

Myra finished dinner, and helped Victoria with the dishes.

"I wonder when the Lord will take me to the lower region?"

"I don't know, but I should think that it will be soon." Victoria answered.

"But I don't want to see that awful place." Myra protested.

"You are special, my dear. You have been chosen as one of God's special messengers, and it is necessary that you see these things." Victoria replied.

"Have you ever been to heaven or to Hell?" Myra asked.

"No, I haven't been privileged to visit either realm. Although many have shared their testimonies in the church."

After the dishes had been finished, Myra hurried to her room and did her homework. Christmas break would begin next week. Already her homework load had increased as finals approached. Myra faced the Christmas holidays with mixed feelings. She loved Christmas trees, and the decorations. However, this would be her first Christmas apart from her family. Baby rubbed up against her, and pushed against her with his head. She petted him absentmindedly as she prayed.

"Maybe I will go to Hell tonight," she said to Baby. "So many wild things happen to me at night, I suppose that would be the obvious time that I would make such a visit."

That night, she drifted into an uneasy sleep, waking during the night to make an unscheduled trip to the bathroom to quench her thirst. Baby and Blessing remained curled up beside her on the bed. Morning came, and the alarm awakened her. At first, she felt disappointment that nothing out of the ordinary had happened. Then she remembered that she didn't really want to visit that terrible place anyway. Maybe the Lord changed his mind, she thought wistfully.

Pastor Shepherd drove her to school. "Don't forget after school today, I will pick you up and we will go to the church to continue helping with the Christmas stocking project." Every day that week, apart from the day she visited heaven, they had spent hours sorting the newly arrived boxes of stockings.

Although the stockings wouldn't be given out until next week, thousands had to be made, sorted, and assembled. Even though churches from around the country sent hundreds of boxes of red and green stockings, volunteers worked for days sewing and stuffing hundreds of stockings a day in order to meet the quota for the thousands of kids who attended the Street Side Sunday sites in Atherstone and Nuneaton. Every year the ministry formed an assembly line to stuff the stockings with toys, candy, and prizes. The stockings were bagged in fifties and placed in readiness to be loaded onto the ministry trucks. Already some of the church classrooms were filled with boxes, and bags of red and green stockings. Myra had heard the stories of the needy children who didn't have any Christmas presents except for these stockings. The Shepherds loved this time of year, even though they worked long hours preparing over 5,000 stockings for these children. After school, they headed toward the church and joined the numerous volunteers.

"I think that if I close my eyes I will still see a sea of green and red for all those stockings," Myra had said as they sorted some of the boxes as they arrived. "Since the green stockings are for the boys, and the red ones are for the girls, what happens if they get mixed up?" Myra asked.

"Oh it does happen, so we try to make the stockings as generic as possible," Victoria answered.

"I feel like Santa Claus," joked Pastor Shepherd. Indeed the church reminded her of movies about the North Pole and Santa's workshop. However, helping with the stockings eased Myra's pain.

"It is funny, but somehow when I work on the stockings I don't hurt inside," she told Victoria.

"When you forget about yourself and help others, it helps heal a broken heart," she replied. "God makes sure that someone takes care of your needs too."

Work progressed on the stocking project, and over the next few days Myra completed the last of her tests. School would soon be out for the holidays. They decorated the house after setting up a white-flocked Christmas tree that they trimmed in purple and gold. Nativity scene ornaments, cascading bows, lights, birds, and sparkling ornaments trimmed the tree and the living room. Beautiful packages filled the space under the tree, waiting for Christmas morning. Christmas was approaching, and yet in spite of all the festivities, Myra wondered when she would visit hell, the home of the damned. She tried not to think about it, since she found even the thought of the trip to be very disturbing. What a horrible contrast it made to the joy of Christmas.

Brushing aside the thoughts of visiting hell, Myra sank into bed after completing another busy day. Myra awakened to find her angel at the foot of her bed.

"Fear not, the Lord is with you, and blessed are you among women."

Myra remained silent as she wondered what the angel had meant by such a strange greeting.

"Fear not, Myra, you have found favor with God," the angel continued.

"Angel, is it time?"

"Yes, please take my hand." Myra placed her hand in the angel's hand and together they rose high into the heavens. She looked down to see the earth below, and wondered since she had thought that Hell's location was in the center of the earth.

Protruding out of the earth, and scattered across the earth's landscape were funnels that spun to a center point and then outward again. Resembling giant dirty coils, they moved continuously, and sprang up from all points of the earth.

"These are the entranceways to Hell," explained the angel as they entered one of them. The smell made her gag. Never had she smelled an odor like it. It reminded her of the smell of decaying flesh. The odor overwhelmed them from every direction. The lower they descended the more they heard screams and cries. They passed forms that appeared to be attached to the walls. The imprisoned wall creatures screeched at them as they passed. Only the presence of the angel prevented her from screaming in terror.

"Oh, I can hear, smell, see, and feel the evil in this place. Angel must we go, can't we turn back?"

Something moved in front of them, slithering and casting gray shadows against the walls. Myra recoiled in horror; the creature was an enormous wide-mouthed snake. Looking closer she saw that snakes slithered everywhere along the path.

"The things that you are about to see are given to you as a warning. You must tell others. The human soul lives forever somewhere. Heaven or Hell, every person must choose one for his or her eternal home. When a person fails to choose, then Hell is automatically their eternal destination. Hell is real, and no one should go to that place. The torments and excruciating pain last for all eternity, and no person would want to come to this place." The angel explained.

"Where is Hell located? I thought that it was on earth."

"Yes, Myra, Hell is in the center of the earth."

"In the left leg of Hell are located many pits. The tunnel will branch off into other parts of Hell. Our first stop will be in the left leg."

Myra felt the fear and dangers that lurked on every side. Screams filled the air, and evil creatures flew past them. She looked at her arms and noticed that she was in a spirit form that resembled her physical body.

They stepped from the tunnel onto a path. As far as the eye could see there were pits embedded into a wide swatch of land on either side of the path. Each pit measured four feet across and was three feet deep. The bowl shaped pits had red hot coals embedded in the sides. In the center of the pit was a lost soul who after dying was damned to this eternal place. Fire began at the bottom of the pit and swept upward and clothed the soul in flames. Then the fire would reduce to ambers before blazing forth with a rushing sound to engulf the soul once again.

"Angel, can't you help them? Can't they get out of this horrible place?"

As they passed one of the pits, a soul in the form of a skeleton cried out to Jesus asking for him to have mercy on her.

"Listen, she is crying out to Jesus." Myra said, her heart breaking at the plight of the wretched woman.

"Please talk to Jesus for me. Get me out of here, " the woman pleaded with them as they passed. They knew by the voice that it was a woman, even though all they could see was a skeleton with a dirty gray mist inside. Decayed flesh hung by shreds from her bones, and as the fire raged, the flesh burned and fell off her bones and into the pit. Where she once had had eyes, there were empty sockets. She had no hair.

Myra watched as the fire started at her feet in small flames and engulfed her body. She seemed to be constantly burning, even when the flames reduced to embers.

"Hell was never created for people, but for fallen angels." Said the angel. "That is why you must tell people about this place. The Lord never intended His people to end up here."

Myra looked at the woman again and saw with horror that worms were crawling out of the bones of her skeleton. The fire did not harm them. Myra wondered if the woman felt the worms.

"Yes," said the angel in answer to her thoughts, "She feels the worms."

"This is terrible, I don't know if I can stand to see anymore. It is

THE SPIRIT'S APPRENTICE

awful beyond belief." Tears filled her eyes as she looked at the scene. As far as they could see, souls were burning in the pits of fire.

"My child that is why you are here. Heaven is real as you saw a few days ago. Hell is real. Come we must continue, there is more that you must see." The angel replied.

They walked past another woman, who stood on one leg. The other had been amputated, and holes had been drilled in her hipbones.

"What happened to this person?" she asked.

"This person had cancer, and many surgeries. At one time she served the Lord. But later in life she became very bitter. Many people came to pray for her, but finally she turned them away. She grew to hate our Lord. In fact, she told people that she didn't need God to heal her."

"I am sorry I didn't repent while I lived on earth, please give me another chance." The old woman wailed. "Haven't I suffered enough? I promise to do things right and to be good." She began to climb the side of the pit.

At that moment a large demon sprang to the side of her pit. His great wings appeared to be broken at the top and hung down against his sides. His hairy brown form resembled that of a bear with sunken yellow eyes. Baring yellow fangs, he gleefully shoved the woman back into the pit.

Myra wanted to help the woman, and yet she knew that there was nothing that she could do.

"Once judgment has been set, there is nothing that can be done." Said the angel.

"This is awful," said Myra.

"I will show you one work of Satan that will amaze you," continued the angel.

They entered an area where lovely music filled the air. In fact, they seemed to be in some sort of a beautiful ballroom on a well-lighted dance floor. There indeed were five beautiful women dancing to the music. The women stood in a line, and appeared to be in some sort of beauty contest. Each woman was startlingly elegant, such a contrast to the ugliness of Hell. The women wore expensive clothes and dressed like princesses. Their flawless beauty was stunning to behold.

"What are they doing in Hell? They don't look evil."

"Look closer at them and tell me what you see." Said the angel.

"Oh, they have fire racing up and down their bodies. In fact, they seem to be dancing to the movement of the flames. They don't even seem to feel the pain of the flames, unlike the others in the pits."

As they talked an evil presence filled the room. Fear swept over Myra in waves, as the presence of evil became tangible.

A dark person emerged from the shadows, dressed in a long robe and a black cape. Two others flanked him, and were obviously his bodyguards. Myra knew immediately that she faced Satan himself.

The women began to chant and bow, "Hail Satan, hail Satan!"

"My daughters, you have obeyed my commands and now you must go upon the earth to fulfill my will." He said. He laughed wickedly, and said, "But first a little reminder of my power, just in case you decide not to obey me.

"Please, no, don't Satan. Please don't torment us." The women said as they groveled and pleaded with him. Satan laughed as he ignored their pleas.

The women transformed before her eyes from beautiful creatures, to skeletons. Snakes slithered out of their bellies, and many evil spirits filled their forms.

"Please Satan, give us back our forms, and let us have our beautiful bodies back. We promise to obey you." They cried.

Immediately a movie screen appeared, and Myra could see that the images on the screen were taken from scenes upon the earth. Displayed upon the screen were common everyday scenes from life in several cities. Satan began to instruct them on where they were to go and what they were to do.

"Go and find a soul, especially a weak Christian. Work with that soul for about three weeks and report to me. Money is no object. Whatever you need to get the job done will be provided. Use your bodies, lie, cheat, steal and seduce them in order to get your victims to commit the sins of the flesh. Then I will have their souls." Satan laughed.

Immediately the women disappeared, as did Satan and the two men.

"Those are seducing spirits, and they are very real." Said the angel.

"Do you mean that these women actually walk the earth and seduce men?"

"Yes, and they lead many to Hell. Do you remember the sacred words in Proverbs 7 says, 'She seduced him with her pretty speech. With her flattery she enticed him. He followed her at once, like an ox going to the slaughter or like a trapped stag, awaiting the arrow that would pierce its heart. He was like a bird flying into a snare; little knowing it would cost him his life

'Listen to me, my sons, and pay attention to my words. Don't let your hearts stray away toward her. Don't wander down her wayward path. She has been the ruin of numerous men who have been her victims. Her house is the road to the grave. Her bedroom is the den of death.'"

"Angel, we must warn people of this terrible place." Myra cried.

"That is why you have been brought here. By the way, these women are the strange women talked about in scripture.

"We have another stop to make, one that you will find most interesting." Said the angel. They continued walking and came to a bank of cells.

"The cells that you see are stacked 17 miles high. In between the cells are strips of dirt two feet wide. The cells measure four feet square. In them are hundreds of tormented souls. These contain the souls of Satan's servants."

Myra peered into one cell. The woman in the cell kept transforming from a beautiful woman in the 1930s era to a woman of today, to a skeleton with a gray mist. Her flesh hung in shreds, and the smell of decaying flesh filled the air.

"This woman served Satan all her life. In her lifetime, she was renowned for her preaching as an oracle for Satan. He promised her a kingdom. In life she had commanded demons, and they had obeyed her. Until one day, when she died, and those same demons that she had controlled turned on her and dragged her away."

"Oh!" Myra cried.

"Upon entering Hell, she demanded to see Satan. She was brought before him. She asked him where was her promised kingdom. He laughed and produced a black book, and running his bony finger down the list of souls, he read her name. He laughed again, and told her that he had lied, and that she would serve him in his kingdom.

"A mighty wind had thrown her to the ground, demons had ripped her flesh off her bones, as she cried in torment. That is the plight of his servants, and that is their reward for their loyalty.'

"What a contrast to Jesus," Myra answered. As she spoke that name, everything around her cringed as if someone had dumped a bucket of boiling water over them. As she watched, the angel once again grabbed her hand. She felt herself being pulled out of Hell, flying through the sky and finally descending through the roof of her home. She sank into her bed, and fell into a deep dreamless sleep.

"Myra! Myra? Can you hear me?"

Myra slowly opened her eyes, and instinctively shielded her eyes from the light. Pastor Tom and Victoria stood over her, their faces etched with concern.

"Are you OK?" Victoria asked.

"I think so."

"You didn't hear your alarm?" Victoria asked. "We have been trying to awaken you for hours."

"No, what time is it?"

"It is twelve o'clock."

"Oh no, I missed school…again."

"It is OK, although you have missed more than usual this year." Victoria said.

Myra raised herself on one elbow. Her sheets were soaking wet. Her hair was also damp. She looked at her arms, and saw that she had red welts on them. What had happened to her? Apparently, even though nothing had been able to physically touch her, the trauma of having seen such terrible things had taken its toll.

"You looked like you were dead, and we prayed for you."

"Victoria…I visited Hell, and it was awful." Myra began to weep, great sobs shaking her body.

"We thought that maybe the Lord had taken you for a visit to the underworld, so we left you to rest."

"Thanks, Victoria." Myra felt such gratitude toward her, and knew that if she had lived at her old home, her stepfather might haven given her a beating for having overslept.

"You have a fever," Victoria said, "Your forehead burns like it is on fire." How ironic Myra thought, I just returned from a place where the fire never stops.

"I never want to see that place again! How could anyone even joke about someone burning in Hell?"

"Rest, dear, and we will talk later." Victoria and Pastor quietly tiptoed out of the room. Myra fell asleep immediately and continued to doze all afternoon. When she awakened, the fever had broken, although she still felt nauseated. Her bones ached, and her mouth felt parched. The horrible stench of Hell remained in her nostrils. I guess that is why I am still nauseated, she thought. Later she went to the kitchen, Victoria fixed her some hot lemonade.

"Do you want to talk about it?" she asked.

Myra shook her head, as big tears rolled down her cheeks. "I can't right now. Yet I know that I am supposed to tell people about that terrible place. I just need a little time to think about what I saw."

"I understand." Victoria squeezed her hand.

Myra normally would have been excited about going with the ministry team to do the Street Side Sunday School. However, today, she just wanted to rest.

"Do I have to go today?" she asked.

"The team needs you, and I do believe that it will be a blessing for you." Victoria replied. Myra didn't argue, because she knew that the team needed her. Secretly, she wasn't in the mood to hand out Christmas stockings to a bunch of kids that she didn't even know.

"You'll see, God's grace will be there, and you will have a wonderful time." Victoria continued. Myra knew that the Shepherds took their commitment to ministry to the extreme. In fact, she knew that even if the town had flooded, they would probably deliver the stockings by boat. She did admire their commitment to their word, but today she didn't want to do anything.

"Have you met the team?" she asked.
"No, not all of them." Myra answered.
"I am surprised that you don't want to go, especially with David being part of the team." Victoria knew that Myra listened intently to what she had to say.
"David? Oh you mean the newest volunteer?"
Victoria could tell that Myra was unimpressed with the latest recruit.
"No, he has been overseas with his parents. They are missionaries from Romania, and have returned to the United States. They have even had wonderful tent crusades in Russia. He is already a dynamic preacher, and has seen many fabulous miracles." Victoria added, "All the girls think that he is so cute."
"Oh," Myra said. Suddenly she didn't feel as tired as she did moments ago.
"He probably won't like me."
"Hmm, he does know about you." The words hung in the air.
"I need to wash my hair, so I had better get going." Myra said as she jumped out of her chair and headed for the shower.
"Myra, have fun this afternoon." Victoria smiled.
Myra arrived at the church, just as the yellow ministry trucks pulled up to the curb. One of the volunteers lowered the side of the truck, and the team scrambled aboard to "prep" the truck before leaving for the outreach. Myra helped pack the boxes and bags of stockings in the cabinets, and under the storage areas. Kneeling with sweat running down her face, she became engrossed in the task at hand. She didn't notice the young man who approached her.
"Myra?" She looked up to see who had called her name. Immediately she blushed, when she saw him. He smiled revealing a set of perfect white teeth and a dimple in his cheek. Myra's heart skipped a beat. Great, here I am, sweating, my hair is a mess, and I am about to meet the most handsome boy that I have ever seen. Talk about someone who is "tall, dark, and handsome."
"Myra?" he repeated, "Hi, I am David."
"Hi." Myra didn't know what to say next, which amazed her. Especially since she couldn't remember a time when she hadn't had

an opinion and been quick to share it with whoever would listen.
"Would you like me to help you get up?" He asked.
"Oh...sure." He helped her to her feet. Good heavens, she thought, his hands even tingle when they touched mine. Myra knew that David must have a strong gift of healing, which Pastor called the "anointing." Pastor had explained that when God mightily used a person that God's power resided in them. It could actually be felt when a person touched their hands. When the Lord used them in their gift, then the power fully manifested and amazing miracles happened.
"Pastor sent me to get you so that we could pray before going on the outreach."
"Oh," Doesn't it just figure that there would be a reason why David had come to get her. Still, he sure was cute, and she knew that she already had a huge crush on him. She hadn't believed in love at first sight, but now she wondered. I am too young, I guess. He looks like he is a few years older than me.
"So how old are you?" He asked. He must have read my mind, she thought.
"Sixteen but I will be seventeen in a few months. How old are you?" she said. What she said was true, but the fact was the few months made up the better part of a year. Silently, she apologized to the Lord for exaggerating the truth.
"Seventeen."
"I thought that you were older than that." Maybe he wasn't too old for her after all.
"Thanks, but no, I am only seventeen."
"Are you going back to Romania?" she said. Then she blushed. Obviously, she had heard about him with a comment like that.
"Oh?" He smiled, "So you do know who I am." Now Myra felt really embarrassed. All her training had told her to be mysterious and to be slightly aloof when dealing with boys. Here she had just blurted out that she knew a lot more about him than she wanted to admit.
"Well...."
"No, I am staying in the US to finish high school, and then I am going to Bible College after I graduate. Anyway, let's hurry, the

trucks need to leave at 3 pm in order to arrive at 4 pm."

The two joined the rest of the team in prayer. The rest of the team consisted of AJ, Leah, Glen and Emma. The truck would be crowded. After prayer, Glen climbed into the truck, and the rest followed on the back seats.

"Myra, sit in the front with me." Glen said motioning to the passenger front seat. Myra climbed into the seat, secretly wishing that she could sit in the back with David.

The drive to Nuneaton normally took over an hour. The time passed quickly as the team joked and enjoyed each other's company. They arrived at the Housing Project known as Lincoln Village. They pulled into the complex with its white brick apartments trimmed in brown. Myra had heard the stories about this complex. Drugs and crime figures were some of the highest in Nuneaton, yet it appeared to be like any other housing project. They drove around the development with its three hundred units. As they drove, they honked the horn; hundreds of children ran along side of the truck. They jumped up and down and sang as they ran. Around the back of the complex was a covered basketball court. Just as they pulled onto the concrete, one of the teens, named Eugene, walked to the window of the truck. He pulled out a gun and aimed it at Glen's face. Myra sat is total disbelief. The gun was real, of that she was sure. Since Halloween, she had seen more guns at close range then she had in her whole life.

"You can't come up here, we're having a game." Said Eugene.

" Hey, man we come every week, look at the kids. It is the Christmas stocking week." Glen replied while staring down the muzzle of the gun.

"Do you see this? I am telling you to go somewhere else we are having a game."

"Glen that is a real gun." Myra interjected. The young man with the gun remained silent, as he held the gun inches from Glen's nose.

"I know." Glen replied.

"Glen that is a real gun." Myra repeated as she stared at the gun.

"I know." Glen replied again.

"Glen that is a real, real gun." Myra said for the third time.

"I know." Glen replied. Time seemed to move in slow motion as no one moved or said anything for several seconds. The group in the back of the truck was silent.

"Well, you are just going to have to shoot us, because we are going to do Street Side Sunday School." Glen said as he stepped on the gas, nearly knocking the teen over. The young man cursed them as he waved the gun in the air. Great, we could have been shot, and what if he had missed, he might have hit me, she thought.

"What if he had shot us?" Myra asked.

"So, but he didn't. Hey let's do Street Side Sunday School." Glen honked the horn as they pulled into position on the court. The kids swarmed the truck, helping put down tarps, and get ready for Street Side Sunday School. Meanwhile Eugene and some of his friends tried to rock the truck. Myra and some of the others were in the truck when they tried to roll the truck.

"Come on you Christians, we don't want you here, we don't need you. Get off the court or you will be sorry!" Eugene said. Myra marveled that the team didn't retaliate, but just kept playing with the kids, and setting up the truck for the program.

"Leave them alone, we want Street Side Sunday School." Chanted the kids as they sat on the tarps waiting for the outreach to start.

"Should we call the police?" Myra asked.

"No, we don't do that here. We have built trust with these people." John Paul said

"But..."

"No, use your faith. If God has called us here, and he has, then he will protect us." John Paul continued.

"Myra, why don't you and I pray that God changes Eugene's heart?" Said David. Myra and David went beside the truck and prayed together before the outreach started. Myra knew that this ministry made a difference in this community. She also knew that kids, who carry guns, kill. She had heard the stories of how kids kill kids, and then end up getting killed as a result. For the first time in her life, she felt that what she was doing mattered for all eternity.

CHAPTER EIGHT

It is written:
"They shall speak of the glory of
thy kingdom and talk of thy power."

"What time is it?" John Paul yelled. The crowd listened intently. The girls sat on tarps on one side, and the boys on tarps on the other side. The tarps were no longer visible under a sea of children. They sat crossed legged, bunched together in rows. White, black, Hispanic, and Oriental all sat side-by-side, sporting braids, bows, hats, T-shirts, jeans, and colorful sneakers. Hundreds of children responded excitedly as though they were one person.

"Time for Street Side Sunday School!" the crowd yelled back. Even the rules were fun. No wonder the kids loved to come. Myra had to admit that she loved doing the outreach. Even though she got soaking wet assisting with the water balloon games.

After the games and fun, David preached a hard-hitting message to the kids. At the end he asked for a show of hands for those who wanted a changed life. Thirty kids accepted the Lord as their Savior.

"Myra, would you help me to pray for the kids?" He asked. Immediately Myra jumped onto the stage and began to pray for the children. The children fell like dominos, as the power of God flowed through David's hands when he prayed for them. The kids lay without moving on the tarps.

"Are they OK?" Myra asked.

"Sure, the Holy Spirit is working on them. Sometimes he does surgery on them; sometimes he tells them things that they need to know. One girl actually saw heaven."

Gradually, the kids would struggle to their feet after having lain on the floor of the stage. Some had to be helped off the stage because they weren't able to walk. One child dragged another by the foot, until Myra intervened and helped them. The children laughed and seemed happy, even if they had difficulty walking.

"What is wrong with them?" she asked.

"They are drunk." David laughed.

"Drunk?" Myra asked. She was appalled that kids would come to a church function and go home drunk.

"The scriptures talk about this."

"Really?"

"Yes, it is written, "For these are not drunken, as ye suppose, seeing it is but the third hour of the day, but this is that which was spoken by the prophet Joel:

"And it shall come to pass in the last days, saith the Lord, I will pour out of my Spirit upon all flesh: and your sons and your daughters shall prophesy, and your young men shall see visions, and your old men shall dream dreams:

"And on my servants and on my handmaidens I will pour out in those days of my Spirit; and they shall prophesy:

"And I will show wonders in heaven above, and signs in the earth beneath; blood, and fire, and vapor and smoke:

"The sun shall be turned into darkness, and the moon into blood, before that great and notable day of the Lord come:

"And it shall come to pass, that whosoever shall call on the name of the Lord shall be saved."

"Oh, I thought that happened years ago." Myra replied.

"It did, but remember that our Lord is the same today as he was then." Myra felt that he must think that she was really stupid for making such a comment.

"You must think that I am really stupid not knowing what was happening to the kids." Myra replied shyly.

"Not at all, as a matter of fact, I think that you are really cute."

"You do?" Myra said while blushing a deep crimson. Their eyes met, and both looked away.

"I think that you are cute too," Myra added. This time David blushed.

"Do you have a boyfriend?" he asked.

"No, do you have a girlfriend?" she replied.

"No," he answered.

"Oh." Myra didn't know what to say next. They remained silent for a few moments before David changed the subject.

"I guess we had better get back to the kids, but we'll talk later." David said.

"OK." She said. Myra thought that he seemed a little embarrassed. In fact, she knew that they both felt awkward. She was happy, because she knew that he liked her.

They proceeded to hand out the Christmas stockings. How wonderful to see the kids excited faces as they received a stocking.

"Now I have something to put under my Christmas tree," one boy told Myra. "My Mom doesn't have a job, and we don't have any money for Christmas presents."

Myra's heart melted as she heard the kid's stories. How sad, that they are having a rougher time than I am, she thought.

"Can I have another stocking?" one girl asked.

"You are only supposed to have one, because we have several more outreaches to do and we want to make sure that every kid gets a stocking."

"But, if I had another one, when I take out the stuff, I can use them for slippers. I don't have any slippers, and our apartment is really cold. Sometimes the rats try to bite our toes." That brought a lump to Myra's throat.

"Let me ask John Paul if it is Ok for you to have an empty stocking. That way the kids won't think that we are being unfair."

Myra asked John Paul and together they found a stocking that had lost its contents. They gave it to the little girl. She held them to her chest excitedly. John Paul and Myra just looked at each other. How sad, that she didn't even own a pair of slippers. Suddenly Myra felt rich, even though her mother had abandoned her. She lived with the Shepherds, and she knew that the Lord loved her and so did they. Hey, my heart doesn't ache anymore. In fact, I feel this unspeakable joy. I don't dread Christmas anymore! I believe that I can face Christmas day with joy. Besides, David is in town and who knows what the future holds for either of us.

After handing out the stockings, they rolled up the tarps, and loaded the truck. They began the long drive home. This time she sat in the back seat with David. She missed her family, but she also knew that if things hadn't worked the way they had that she would have missed this day. It seems like the Lord could take any situation no matter how difficult turn it for good.

"Could I have your phone number?" David asked.

"Sure, it is (918) 474-3632." Myra wanted to shout for joy. He asked for my phone number. Why everyone knows that it is the dream of every girl to have that special guy ask for her phone number. How I want to pinch myself to see if this was real. I guess that I had better not get too happy. It seems like when I get too happy something happens to mess it up. Nope I am going to enjoy the moment and believe that good things are going to continue to happen for me.

They returned to the church and unloaded the truck. That night, Myra rejoiced as she fell asleep. Who knows what tomorrow holds? But I know who holds tomorrow.

Early the next morning, she awakened and grabbing a glass of milk and her Bible she sat cross-legged in the family recliner. Oh how she loved to feast on the scriptures. She felt strength infuse her body. Suddenly the presence of the Holy Spirit filled the room, and tears began to course down her cheeks. Instinctively she knew that "Comforter" or Holy Spirit as he is called was preparing her for her day. Somehow she sensed that she would need extra prayer today. "What is it Holy Spirit?" she whispered. Her Bible fell open to the words, "Howbeit when he, the Spirit of truth, is come, he will guide you into all truth: for he shall not speak of himself; but whatsoever he shall hear, that shall he speak: and he will show you things to come."

Suddenly, she knew that she needed to expect the unexpected. Quickly, she dressed and readied for school. Today was the last day before Christmas vacation, and all of her tests, reports, and projects had been completed. She couldn't wait for the final bell to ring, and then she would have two-weeks of vacation.

Her first two classes passed uneventfully, except one teacher had served the class Christmas cookies. Just as the third class of the day started, Myra felt uneasiness in the pit of her stomach. The sensation grew steadily stronger. Not long after the sensation began she noticed that one of the office staff had interrupted the class and asked to talk to the teacher in the hall. When her teacher returned she called Myra to the front of the class.

"Myra, you need to go to the office. Your stepfather has had an accident. You have been excused. Your mother and the Shepherds are waiting for you."

"Oh! Is he alive?"

"I believe so."

Myra gathered her things and headed for the office. What am I going to say to my mother? As she opened the office door, Victoria greeted her with a hug. Trust Victoria to be here, she thought. I think that she must be the warmest and most caring lady in the whole world. Her mother stood behind Victoria, and hugged her too. Myra started crying. She cried tears of joy mixed that were tinged with sadness. How wonderful to see her mother again. She had missed her.

"What about George?" Myra asked.

"There has been an accident, and George is not expected to live." Her mother said.

"What happened?"

"He was drunk, and had a head-on collision with a truck. We need to hurry, he is not expected to live." Myra wondered if George's death would mean that now she would have to live with her mother. She didn't want to leave the Shepherds. Victoria apparently sensed Myra's dilemma.

"Don't worry, you can still live with us if you choose." Victoria whispered.

"Thanks, that is what I want." Myra whispered back.

They remained in prayer as they drive from Atherstone to Angleton. Soon they saw the hospital that sat upon the land like a whitened sepulcher. They arrived in ICU, so many machines, wires, and the sounds of staff scurrying about their duties. The smell of medicine and death filled her nostrils. George lay on an air mattress, only partially dressed, exposing the wires that protruded from different portions of his body. A respirator swished as it pumped air through a tube that disappeared into his mouth. She hardly recognized him. His swollen, blackened face was partially hidden by bandages. A cardiac monitor beeped as a neon green line danced across the screen. She couldn't tell if the cardiac pattern indicated an improvement or a drifting toward death. IV's and catheters snaked in and around his body, but to Myra he looked more like a corpse than her stepfather. Her mother cried softly. Is he alive?

As he lay there, Myra remembered how he had tormented her. Here her tormentor lay, totally helpless and at her and other's mercy. She also remembered her visit to Heaven and the Book of Life. George isn't in the book! If he dies he won't make Heaven, but will go to Hell, the realm of the damned. She edged forward and stood near his head. Should she ask her mother if she should say anything to him? It might make him mad and then he might die for sure. If he dies because I talked to him, Mom will never forgive me. Still, if I wait he might die, and then one day I will have to face my Lord and explain why I didn't have the courage to tell George about Him. Sometimes a girl has got to do what a girl has got to do. She decided that it would be easier and better to apologize later, then to regret later.

"George?" she said, "This is Myra."

"George can you hear me? If you can would you move your finger?" There was no response. She remembered from her Health Class that the last sense to go before death is a person's hearing.

"George, I want you to be sure that if something happens that you get to go to Heaven. Did you know that there is only one way to get to Heaven and that is through Jesus Christ? I saw Heaven and Hell, and I want you to know that both places are real." Myra took a deep breath and continued.

"The Bible tell us that whosoever calls on Jesus' name shall be saved." The cardiac monitor began to beep loudly. Great, George is probably furious with me, and knows that he is a captive audience. Her mother stepped toward her, as if to stop her, but a sudden boldness swept over her. Nothing could stop her now; she plowed on with her words.

"I saw heaven recently, and I saw the Book of Life, and your name wasn't in it. But the angel told me to tell you to ask the Lord to be your Savior and you would make Heaven your eternal home." The Shepherds and her mother watched her with their mouths open in shock. I am on a roll now, might as well finish what I have to say, she thought.

"George if you want to be saved, the Bible says that if we will believe that God raised Jesus from the dead, and confess it with our mouth we can be saved. You can't talk but you can move your little finger as a sign that you are asking Jesus to be your Lord."

Nobody moved or said anything, the monitor beeped steadily in the background. Myra knew that all heaven listened and watched the man's hand. Seconds went by and nothing happened, then slowly George moved the little finger on his right hand. Myra and the Shepherds cheered, and squeezed George's hand. Myra's mother stayed aloof. She resisted the urge to look at her mother. Later as they walked down the hall, she could feel her mother's anger. No one said anything as tension filled the atmosphere. They rode in silence down the elevator. When the door of the elevator opened, her mother vented her frustration.

"I can't believe that you said what you did to George. Why you could have given him a heart attack, and killed him. Didn't you see what happened to the monitor?"

"Mom, I prayed about it. I guess I am just concerned about what happens to George if he dies." Myra rejoiced that she no longer lived with her mother, but at the same time her heart filled with compassion. She knew that her mother suffered from a broken heart.

"Mom, I just didn't want him to go to Hell. I saw it, and I wouldn't want anyone to go there, even George." She said. "It is because I care for his soul, I have forgiven him for what he did to me." She handed her mother some Kleenex as she cried. How wonderful to have the comfort of the Holy Spirit, she wished that her mother knew him like she did.

"It is because I care that I said that."

"I know, it is, but he didn't like anyone to talk to him about religion. He felt that it was a personal choice. You shouldn't force your views on a captive audience."

"But Mom...."

"You really should consider other people's feelings about such things. I raised you never to talk about either religion or politics in mixed company. It isn't fitting for a young lady." Myra rolled her eyes discretely.

"Mom, if he was in a burning building wouldn't you try to help him escape?"

"Yes, but he is not, he is in a hospital."

"I know, but just imagine for the sake of the discussion that he was. You wouldn't want him to be burned to death."

"No, but...."

"Hell is like a burning building only it lasts for eternity. I saw it."

"I know that you meant well, but you really need to leave this religion stuff at the Shepherds. You are becoming a religious fanatic, and that just isn't becoming for a young lady. One day soon, you will want to find a young man and that kind of talk will deter your chances of finding a decent man to marry."

Right on cue, the Shepherds joined them and her mother changed the subject. Myra sighed with relief. Her mother stayed with George, and they prepared to return to Atherstone.

"I will keep in touch and let you know what happens." Her mother said as they parted.

"You look like you had a close encounter of the non-God kind with your mother." Victoria joked.

"Yeah, I just don't seem to be able to relate to her."

"Place it in the Lord's hands and pray for her. We think that you

are a fine Christian girl and any man would be honored to have you as his wife."
"Really?"
"David sure likes you." Victoria joked.
"Really?" Myra giggled
"Uh-huh."
"Victoria, why can't my mom be like you?"
"Because God made her unique and special too. Pray for her, prayer changes things."
"I suppose." Myra said. She went upstairs to her room and threw herself upon the bed. Why can't life be simpler? It seems like no matter what I do I get in trouble. Baby rubbed up against her purring, even my cat knows that I am sad.

Absentmindedly, she petted him, and held him close as she rubbed her face against his soft fur. I sure hope that cats go to heaven, and that he lives with me. The phone beside her bed rang. Myra answered it.
"Hello?"
"Myra?"
"Yes..." It sounded like David. Myra listened attentively while trying to act casual. She was very glad that he couldn't see through the phone.
"Hi, its David. What are you doing tonight?"
"Not much, I just got back from the hospital. George, my stepfather had a terrible wreck."
"Oh, I was hoping that you might like to go out, and maybe see a movie? But I guess, maybe another time? I realize that it was such short notice anyway."
"Sure, I mean, I would love to go. I am not going back to the hospital tonight, but...."
"How about if I pick you up around 6 pm? I know that I should have asked you yesterday."
"Oh my, that doesn't give me much time. Let me check with Victoria to see if she has any plans for me." Myra ran down the stairs and found Victoria sewing in the kitchen.

"David asked if I wanted to go out tonight. Is it OK if I go? He says that he will have me home early."

"Go right ahead, but don't stay out past midnight, and have fun." Victoria smiled. She knew that the Shepherds didn't believe in dating. They felt that a young man or woman should pray and let the Lord bring the right person into their life. They felt that dating was actually practice for divorce. The reason being that most young people had many relationships before they found the one that they would marry.

"I didn't think that you would let me go." Myra added.

"I am not in favor of dating, but Tom and I both believe that the Lord has his hand in this. You both have integrity, and know what is right. He has a mighty calling on his life, and you do too. I know that you will have to be careful, and avoid the things that get girls in trouble." Victoria watched Myra's face and added, "You know, obvious things like not being alone with him in a darkened car at the end of a dark road. If you are going to be seeing him on a regular basis, then I recommend that you find another couple and double date. The flesh is weak, and hormones are strong." She laughed.

"Thanks, Victoria," she said.

Right on time, David's truck pulled into the driveway. Myra climbed in, noticing that he had opened the door for her. She had already forgotten the incident at the hospital. She wouldn't be going out with David if she had still lived at home, or if she had moved to Alvin. David was even more handsome than she had remembered.

During the evening, they laughed and shared stories about their lives. Myra had never been with a guy who had treated her with such respect. He opened doors for her, and pulled out the chair so that she could sit. He never tried to kiss her, hold hands, or do anything that most of the others had tried to do. He actually believed in waiting until marriage before getting physically involved with a girl. He told her that he had kept himself pure for his wife.

"I wouldn't want to mess with someone else's future wife." He said. "True love waits." Here was a man that actually believed like she did.

Myra enjoyed his company, and had to admit that she enjoyed spending time with someone who wasn't trying to get her to do things that were wrong. Her mother had never let her date. She had come to expect that all men acted like George.

The movie, they were going to see, was a new animated feature about a horse and had a "G" rating. At school, the kids joked about movies that were "G" rated. Yet, she found herself enjoying a movie that didn't have cursing and lots of bloodshed.

"Hey, David, maybe we will set a new trend."

"How so?"

"You know, it will be the popular to go to a 'G' movie."

"It is the thing to do, if you are six," He laughed. Myra looked around the theater and noticed that children surrounded them. One of them had nearly dumped their coke in her lap.

"I didn't mean by children."

The evening ended too soon, and David watched as she let herself into the house. He didn't try to kiss her, but gave her a "church hug." Great, he hugs me like I am an eighty-year-old stranger at church.

Victoria had been waiting for her and gave her a hug. It sure seemed her day for hugs. Her parents never hugged her nor did they ever tell her that they loved her. Not a day went by at the Shepherds that someone didn't tell her how much they loved her. What a contrast, when I have a family I am going to fill my house with love. My children will know that I love them.

"Sit down Myra, I have something to tell you." Myra felt a lump form in her stomach. Just when things were going well, something had to try to spoil it all.

"What is it?"

"George died this evening."

"Oh," was all that she could muster. "At least he accepted Jesus before he died."

"Your mother stopped by, and told me that she would provide the paperwork for us to adopt you."

"I am sixteen, aren't I too old to adopt?"

"No, because you are still a minor until you are eighteen."

"You mean she doesn't want me to be her daughter anymore?" Myra cried.

"No, she thinks that it would be better for you if you were our daughter. There are certain advantages. She isn't forcing this, she wanted me to talk to you."

"Why didn't she tell me herself? She doesn't want me. I always knew that she never loved me. She probably still blames me for her divorce."

"No, I don't think that is it. In her own strange way she does love you. Even if she has a hard time showing it. She is probably having a hard time coping with everything that has happened." Victoria said.

"What about me? Doesn't anyone think that I have had a hard time too? I am the one who came home and found that my family had moved. This is not fair, I mean it is Christmas and my mom just gave me away. I am sorry, but I need to be alone." Myra said, as she ran out of the room and up the stairs.

CHAPTER NINE

It is written:
"The Spirit saith...to him that overcometh
will I give to eat of the hidden manna, and will
give him a white stone, and in the stone a new name
written, which no man knoweth saving he that
receiveth it."

Thoughts chased each other across the field of Myra's mind. She knew that she needed to apologize to Victoria. She found her still sewing in the kitchen. Trust Victoria to remain consistent no matter what happened.

"I want to apologize for my outburst earlier." Myra said.

"You don't need to apologize." Victoria replied.

"It is just that I have forgiven my mom, but it hurts to know that she would give away her right to be my mother. I feel like a pet that just got dropped off at the pound."

"I really understand, and family is the appropriate place to express your feelings. I would probably have said the same thing."

"Really?"

"Of course, but the good news is that you have a family that loves you very much. You also have your natural mother, and one day the Lord will restore that relationship. Then you will have two moms." Victoria laughed.

"Thanks, I just needed someone to listen. I am going for a walk and to talk to the Lord." Myra added.

She headed down the road outside her house, and detoured into a vacant lot that led to a grove of trees near an old trolley line. She knew a secluded spot with a large pond that she frequented when she wanted to be alone. The December sun warmed her back as she walked around the edge of the pond. She looked for fish, frogs, salamanders, water puppies, or turtles that lived in the reeds of the shallow portion of the pond. Today she hadn't found any. So, she stooped and grabbed a smooth stone and skimmed it across the pond. The ripples spread across the smooth surface of the water. She had thrown it far enough across the pond, so that it wouldn't disturb the wildlife close to her. She hoped that she might still see a turtle that remained sunbathing on a rock at the side of water.

Reaching down she looked for another stone. Her eye caught the glint of a stone that lay half buried by some cattails at the edge of the pond. Upon close inspection, she found that the stone was unlike anything that she had ever seen. It reminded her of a cross between a diamond, radiating a rainbow in all directions, and a fire opal. She pulled the white stone from its hiding place with ease. Obviously someone must have recently left it by the pond. I wonder if I should report it? It must be worth thousands of dollars. She thought as she turned the stone over. Etched on its backside were the words that were written in a language that she didn't understand, or recognize as any language found on earth. Suddenly the sky became very dark, and lightning forked through the sky. A powerful wind began to blow as the trees bent down to the ground. Some looked as though they would break. Myra's hair blew into her eyes obscuring her vision as she turned to run toward home, but an angel blocked her path.

"Hail Myra, favored of women." The angel said. "You have passed the test, and now you hold your reward."

"What test?"

"Instead of staying bitter, you chose to forgive and to seek the counsel of the Lord. It is written, 'seek ye first the kingdom of God, and his righteousness; and all these things shall be added unto you'." The angel's golden hair blew in the wind.

Myra found it hard to concentrate with the extreme weather. Thunder crashed and the lightning forked around them. Dark clouds boiled angrily overhead in a spectacular display that reminded her of a hurricane. Myra didn't want to interrupt the angel, but she wanted to seek shelter before it rained. After all, she didn't want to be rude to the angel who seemed to be enjoying the spectacular weather. Finally, she decided to say something about it.

"Angel! Am I in danger?" she asked.

"No, the wind, thunder and lightning are a sign and a wonder to you of that which you hold."

"What is this stone, angel?"

"You hold a precious stone, and a gift from the Lord to you."

"You mean that I can keep it?"

"It is yours, and only yours. In your hands it will be used to remind you of the special gifting that the Lord has given you. You are not to loan it, or give it away."

"What type of stone is it?"

"It is not like any other stone on this earth. In the book of Revelation, the scripture says, "To him that overcomes will I give to eat of the hidden manna, and will give him a white stone, and in the stone a new name written, which no man knows saving he that receives it. This is the earthly equivalent to the heavenly stone."

"On the back of the stone there are words which I don't understand. Are they written in a heavenly language?" Myra asked.

"That is correct." The angel replied.

"What do they mean?"

" It is written, that if people shall hold their peace the very stones will cry out. Jesus, descended of the tribe of Judah, is the Chief Cornerstone.

"Yes, and don't the sacred words talk about being living stones?"

"It is written, 'Ye also, as lively stones, are built up a spiritual house, an holy priesthood, to offer up spiritual sacrifices, acceptable to God by Jesus Christ.'

"Why me? I am just a girl."

"You are a young woman, and I want to remind you that is it is also written, 'the kingdom of heaven is like unto treasure hid in a field the which when a man hath found, he hides, and for joy thereof goes and sells all that he hath, and buys that field.' In your case, it is the Father's good pleasure to give you this stone. Be a good steward of what has been entrusted to you. You have been given a treasure similar to that which is in heaven."

"What am I to do?" Myra asked.

"You will be given assignments from heaven." The angel answered. "Pray, and wear this stone about your neck, as a reminder that the Lord has transformed you into a new creature. Many will marvel at the power entrusted to you, because they won't understand the power of a true believer. Always give the glory to Jesus, for without him you can do nothing.

"Although the stone is a reminder of the great power entrusted to you from the Lord, the stone itself is powerless. If it is stolen, it will be returned to you, provided that you have used it correctly."

"That is kind of scary."

"When people see the great things that are done, be sure not to take the credit, but to tell people that this is the Lord working through you. Be sure to take no glory for yourself. The stone is a contact point for your faith that will enable you to reach into another era called a "dispensation." The Lord has seen your faithfulness and is granting you the privilege of reaching into the millennium and pulling the ability to operate like you have a resurrected body. Even though you live in the present dispensation of the church age and are a born-again believer, you will function in another dispensation for temporary periods of time. A dispensation is a period of time, such as the church age, which is the time that you live in now.

You will function as though you have a glorified body. However, only our Lord has a fully resurrected body. All those who have passed on to heaven await the full transformation of their earthly bodies.

"How can I reach into another time?" Myra said.

"Actually reaching into another dispensation has happened before. One example of someone who did this is David. Do you remember in Psalms 51, when he wrote about having a "contrite heart and a broken spirit"? Nowhere in the sacred words at that point had this been discussed. Also the tabernacle of David with the priests worshipped around the ark twenty-four hours a day, seven days a week for 36 years. That was unheard of and actually was something the "church age" would experience, when the Lord's presence is felt while worshipping in church and in their homes. Previously only the priests went into the Holy of Holies once a year. It has been told that they even tied a rope around the priest's body in case he died in the presence of God. That way they could pull the priest out without risking death themselves. Nobody could just go before the Ark of the Covenant in the Holy of Holies whenever they desired. The Ark was where the presence of the Lord dwelled. Now the presence of the Lord is in us and in our churches. Anyone can come into his presence, but not so in David's day. In fact, our body is the temple of the Holy Spirit.

Now back to the stone, when you wear it, you will be reminded that the Lord has enabled you to do things that you normally could not do. Things such as to arrive places supernaturally. It will be as though you had walked through walls, to appear and disappear, to some extent to travel through time. You will still look the same. Yet, there will be times when you will be able to slip through a crowd unnoticed, just like Jesus did when they were planning to stone him. You are to keep the stone a secret. Wear it on your person hidden until told to show it. You will find in your house a sling that can be adapted to hold the stone. Wear it around your neck when on an assignment. Just remember whom you serve, and make sure that He gets the glory. Without Him you can do nothing. The power isn't in the stone, but in Him who gives you power through the Holy Spirit. The sacred words also tell us that he is doing a new thing, and this is that spoken by the prophet Joel."

Suddenly, the sky cleared. The angel disappeared before her eyes. The sun returned and Myra carefully placed the stone in her pocket and walked home. She decided not to tell what had happened. As she opened the back door, she marveled that Victoria was still sewing in the kitchen. So much had happened and yet things had continued as usual.

"Victoria, do you know if we have an old sling?" Myra asked.

"Hmm, let me think. Yes, I do believe we have one that was a prop that we used for a skit about Goliath." They had used a portion of one of the spare bedrooms as storage for props for the outreach ministry. Together they searched through the neatly stacked boxes and containers. Their efforts were rewarded. Victoria held up a sling that looked like a cross between a conventional sling and a large necklace. It had a place for the stone. How appropriate that David had used smooth stones to arm a slingshot that brought down the mighty giant Goliath. Here she was placing heaven's stone in a slingshot to bring down her modern day Goliaths.

"You can have this. In fact, we need to get a regular sling shot if we ever do this skit again." Victoria added. "By the way, you can have our name if you want to be adopted."

"Thanks for the sling," Myra said. She hurried upstairs and then took the stone out of her pocket. The stone fit the sling perfectly. She placed it around her neck and tied the strings. Doesn't it just figure? It fits as though it had been made for the stone to be worn as a necklace. Waves of anointing rolled over her coupled with such thanks and gratitude. She spent the next few hours in the Lord's presence. Here she had been given a new name too, just like the sacred words had said.

As she prayed, she opened the Bible. The words became so alive. This must be the hidden manna. She knew that Manna meant food, and now she knew that the scriptures were spiritual food. As she read, revelation filled her heart and mind. She grabbed her colored pencils, and began to make notes in the margins of her Bible.

How could anyone not want to serve such a wonderful Lord? A knock at her bedroom door interrupted her thoughts.

"Myra?" Victoria asked. "Your mom just called and said that George's funeral is going to be on Friday at 1pm. Tomorrow night, he will be ready to be viewed at the funeral home." How ironic, George lay across the street from the church at Earth Dweller's Funeral Home complex.

"Will my mother be there?" Myra asked.

"Probably," Victoria replied.

"Good, I think that I am ready to see her again." Myra added.

The next day, she found herself staring into a casket at the remains of her former tormentor. How small and insignificant he looks, he seems almost harmless. How could she have let this person control her with his threatening? Now she had outlived him, and he would never be able to torment her again. Silently she asked the Lord to forgive her for all the times that she had secretly wished that George were dead. She hoped that in some way her thoughts hadn't caused his death.

Her mother stood beside her, and Myra had to admit that seeing her again was very difficult. She sensed that it was awkward for both of them. She rode to the cemetery in the funeral director's car with her mother. They didn't talk much. She guessed that there wasn't much to be said.

"I have thought about things," her mother said. Myra remained silent. "I suppose I ought to ask you to forgive me for abandoning you. I hate to admit, but I had hoped that maybe without you George would return. I knew that you were nearly grown and that you would be OK with the Shepherds. Besides you seemed to enjoy them more than you did me."

Myra's lips remained sealed. She couldn't give her mother the reassuring words that she longed to hear. She had been right, her mother had punished her for her devotion to the Shepherds. Yet it had backfired so horribly for both of them. The truth remained that Myra was relieved that George had died. As awful as that seemed. The man had caused her family nothing but misery from the moment he first arrived in their lives. Myra knew that her presence caused an ongoing awkwardness in George and her mom's relationship.

"Do you want to talk about it?" Her mother asked.

"No, not really." Myra replied.

"Oh, I guess this is not a good time." Her mother replied.

"No, not the best." Myra agreed and smiled weakly at her mother. She didn't want to hurt her mother, but she just wished to be left alone. Still, she knew that she needed to be sensitive to others. Sometimes you have to put your needs aside and consider others. Myra knew that this was one of them. She also knew that she was having a difficult time doing this. Great, it seems like I am the mom, and my mother is the daughter.

"Mom, at least George accepted Jesus. I know that he will be in heaven, but what about you?"

"Myra I know that you mean well, but let's drop the subject. I am having enough to deal with enough without my daughter preaching to me. Besides, you know that there may be a lawsuit because George didn't have insurance and he killed a young mother and her baby when he had the accident." Her mother's voice had raised an octave and she knew that she needed to change the subject. She also knew that she had been insensitive. Still, one didn't know the time that they would step out of this world and into eternity. By then, it may be too late to decide where you planned to spend it.

"Mom, I am sorry I didn't know that anyone else had been killed."

"Yes, this whole thing has been so terrible." Her mother replied.

They arrived at the graveside, and Pastor Shepherd gathered the small crowd under the canopy. Six pallbearers had carried the casket out of the hearse and placed it under cover before the rain began. He performed the graveside ceremony as a light drizzle fell around them. Afterwards, the mourners dashed to their cars, as the rain grew heavier. The whole ceremony had been somber, and Myra had such relief that it was over. The Shepherds invited her mother back to the house, and Victoria served roast duck for dinner. Myra suppressed a laugh, since the duck reminded her of George. *Oh Lord, I can't believe that I thought such a horrible thing.* She was glad that no one could read her mind.

The Shepherds house glowed with Christmas decorations and lights making such a dramatic contrast to the sadness of the occasion. A Christmas tree aglow with lights, bows, and ornaments filled the foyer from floor to ceiling. Garlands with bows, lights and Poinsettias cascaded down the stair banisters, and the smell of apple cider filled the air. Normally the Christmas season is such a joyful occasion. This year's tragedy had cast a dark shadow over her mind. Still, Myra was determined that nothing would ruin her Christmas. Dinner ended and her mother left. Myra rejoiced that tomorrow was

Saturday and she could sleep later. Usually the ministry conducted Street Side Sunday School on Saturdays in Atherstone, but all the stockings had been delivered and the ministry's fall semester had ended. With Christmas just a few days away, she would help Victoria with the baking and preparations. The Shepherds usually entertained a lot over the holidays; so many considered the Shepherd's house to be a home away from home. Missionaries from all over the world came to visit, and to be refreshed. The Shepherds door was open for all. The phone rang and Myra answered it.

"Myra?"

"Hi David."

"I am sorry that your stepfather died. Do you want me to come over for a bit?"

"Sure!" Myra replied. What timing, he must have known that she needed a friend. Myra marveled that David seemed to be in tune with her even though they hadn't talked. As though some sort of "mind reading" occurred between them. She knew that the "mind reading" was none other than the Holy Spirit revealing things to them. People who pray tend to know things that are beyond their ability to know through the natural senses. Should she tell him about the stone? Immediately, she felt the Holy Spirit impressing her not to say anything. She felt the stone under her blouse. She prayed silently, "Holy Spirit this is our secret."

Later that day, after her mother had left, Myra relaxed in the Shepherds study. She feasted on the scriptures and enjoyed her "quiet time" with the Lord. As she was waiting upon the Lord, David's face materialized before her. The image reminded her of a hologram. He spoke with urgency.

"Myra, I tried to call you. I need your prayers urgently. The Protégé Cleaner is on fire! My cousin owns the diner next to it, and the buildings are attached. Pray that the diner doesn't burn."

Myra felt the stone that lay beneath her blouse. "Holy Spirit what do I do?" Immediately she felt an urgency to go to the Diner. She scribbled a note explaining where she was going, and left it in the kitchen for the Shepherds.

Just before leaving the house, she stepped into the bathroom and placing her hands on the stone whispered, "Holy Spirit, transform me and use me for the Master's glory." Immediately she began to shake, electricity began to race up and down her arms and legs. Even her face felt the anointing descend, literally transforming into a stronger more powerful person. Peeking out the bathroom door, she looked to see if anyone would see her. All clear, she hurried out of the house and ran down the road.

"Ask me to translate you, like I did Philip."

"Holy Spirit, please translate me." She said, and immediately felt herself being carried by the Spirit through the air, and being lowered gently onto the pavement in front of the diner. All around her were fire trucks, and firemen feverously working to contain the blazing fire. How am I going to get inside the diner? No sooner had the question arisen in her mind, than she remembered the angel had told her that she could walk through walls. She remembered that Jesus had appeared to his disciples through locked doors. She started to walk toward the diner expecting someone to stop her, but no one seemed to even see her. Am I invisible too?

Myra closed her eyes and walked toward the wall, she extended her hands and felt them go through something. She opened her eyes to find that she was on the inside of the smoke filled diner. Had the Lord supernaturally translated her? Or had she actually walked through a door, she couldn't say. One thing she knew, one moment ago she had been outside and now she was inside the dinner.

A fire kindled in a corner of the diner, but it looked like it could be contained fairly easily. The smoke wasn't very heavy, and she knew that some how she could still breathe in it without being affected. This is too marvelous! Her eyes surveyed the room, and she wondered what she was supposed to do next. The presence of evil filled the room. The temperature plummeted in the room as the smoke swirled and formed a face formed overhead. An evil, horrifying face glared at her. She had seen him before when she had visited Hell. Myra knew immediately that she faced the devil himself.

"What are you doing here little girl? You are all dressed up with no where to go?" He leered.

"It is written, submit yourself to God, and resist the devil and he will flee from you. Go devil!"

"I know who you are…you're the young lady who gave kisses to George," He laughed. "And now he's dead and you will be soon too. Let me remind you of some more of your past."

"If you do, I will just remind you of your future. You know where you are going."

"No!"

"Oh yes!"

"You can't make me leave this place, and I am going to burn it to the ground. Thanks to those idol worshippers next door who conveniently made a place for me." He laughed again. "Fools, I am not prejudiced, I hate everyone! I am an equal opportunity destroyer."

"Wrong devil, I command you in the name of Jesus to go. The blood of Jesus is against you."

"Don't say that! I am going to strike you dead now. You will die in this place."

"I said go in the name of Jesus!" Myra took a step toward him.

" I will be back and next time I will win."

"No you won't ever win. You are a defeated foe, read the book!" Myra added. The devil vanished in a puff of smoke.

Her attention turned to a corner of the diner. A small partially opened package had been placed there. She walked over to see what it was, and discovered that there were several sticks of dynamite placed strategically. The fire burned just ten feet away. She knew that she had to act quickly. She grabbed them and opening a window, hurled them outside the building.

Myra tried to walk through the wall, but it wouldn't give. She looked at herself in the mirror in the bathroom. She looked like she normally did. I guess that I will have to go out the door, just like anyone else. She opened the door and found herself in the midst of the firefighters and news reporters. David ran to her side. She told the firefighters about the dynamite.

"Myra! Where you in the diner all this time? Why you could have been killed. Are you OK?" He said.

•

"I am fine, a little shaken that is all."
"How long have you been in the diner?" A reporter asked.
"I don't know, but it sure seemed long."
" Look at these buildings. It is a miracle that none are destroyed, apart from the back part of the cleaners. The firefighters say that they don't know what happened to stop the fire. One even told me that they had lost whole shopping centers with this kind of fire. They said that the trucks were about of water too." David continued. "They say that there isn't even much smoke damage."

How I want to tell him what had happened, but I know that the Spirit wants it to be a secret, Myra thought. That way the Lord gets the glory. He uses people as his willing volunteers, or containers for his power. I guess I am like a garden hose. The hose is just the instrument through which the water flows. The hose can't do anything without the water flowing through it. The sacred words tell us that no flesh will glory in His sight. She decided to tell him as much of the truth as she could, without revealing the Lord's secret.

"When I heard about the fire, I prayed that the Lord would stop it and save the diner. Looks like he sure did!"

"My cousin will be so happy! He will be here tomorrow. He is coming from Austin. I want you to meet him." David said.

"I would like to meet him."

" Hope that you won't like him better than me…just kidding." David said. Myra smiled shyly.

"Would you like to go to dinner?" He added.

"Great! By the way, I thought that you were going to come to the house." Myra said,

"I was, but then I got the call about the diner. Then I tried to call you, but you didn't answer your phone."

"It needed charging, because of all the calls that were made because of the funeral. I forgot to switch over to the regular phone. Anyway, I believe that the Lord had his way today." David looked at her confused, and she knew that she just wouldn't be able to explain what she meant. So she changed the subject.

"Hey, let's get that dinner," Myra said.

" I know a nice spot where we can sit, talk, and look at the water."

David replied. "Use my phone and tell everyone that you and I are going to Baytown for dinner."

"OK!" Myra replied as she called first her family and then his and informed them of their plans. Meanwhile David drove them over the Causeway and headed up Highway 105 toward Baytown.

"Is this someplace special?" Myra asked.

"Special place for a special lady," David replied.

Myra didn't know what to say, so much had happened in last few weeks. They arrived at the restaurant just as the sun began to sink toward the horizon. The waitress ushered them to a table overlooking the water.

"Order whatever you want, tonight is special." David said. They both ordered the marinated steaks that made the restaurant famous. Myra couldn't help noticing that David was the most handsome man in the place. She had never gone to such an elegant restaurant, especially with such an arrangement of the knives, forks, and spoons. She didn't know which one to use first. David sensed her awkwardness and said, "Follow me and I will show you which ones to use." Once again he had read her thoughts.

"You are so special, and I do believe that the Lord has brought you into my life." He said.

One of the waitresses announced that they would be celebrating the beautiful sunset. She told them that they did this daily. Tonight the water glowed, a symphony of color, reflecting the sky's brilliant orange, yellow and purple colors that also reflected the lights of the bridge. One of waiters blew a large Conch shell, and all the customers cheered. David said, "Let us honor the one who made the sunset."

"Do you think that I am, well, do you…um, you know?" he asked lamely.

"What? Do I think that you are special too?"

"Yes, and…."

"Do I believe that the Lord has brought you into my life?"

"Well…."

"Yes I do." She said, feeling a little bit like she had just recited a wedding vow.

"I don't believe in dating, because couples can get into trouble that way and sin." He said, "But I don't want to lose you either."

Myra blushed and played with the food on her plate, she didn't want to look into his eyes. She thought that she might say something really stupid and spoil the whole evening if she did.

The sun had set, and now darkness descended as the lights of the marina and the bridge illuminated the night. Truly tonight proved to be such a spectacular sight, and one that she would remember for the rest of her life.

"What I am trying to say is that I believe that you are supposed to be my wife, but you need to finish school."

"And…." Myra asked.

"And I want to officially date you, but I want the church to know so that it can be done right." Myra wondered what that meant.

"How do we…you know?"

"Date, court, whatever you call it?" He replied.

"Yeah." She answered.

"For one thing, we don't need to be alone like we are tonight until we are officially engaged. I think that we need to go out with other couples, and get to know each other. We need to be friends first. We should wait on the engagement until you are closer to graduating. Besides I am not able to support a wife until I finish more of my schooling." He continued.

Myra listened quietly, and considered what he was saying. Her heart leaped, but she didn't want to appear too eager. Still, she knew that he was the man of her dreams. She couldn't imagine anyone more suited to her.

"What do you think?" He asked. "Would you consider me?"

"Yes! Of course, I mean I feel the same way."

"I know that people talk about falling in love, and I must say that what I feel for you is more than that."

"Me too!" Myra agreed. "I think that I fell in love with you the minute I saw you."

"The same happened to me. In fact, they told me about you and I thought, 'Oh no, not another ugly preacher's daughter.' Honest, I have had so many ministers introduce their daughters to me. Most of them are not good candidates to be the wife of any minister."

"Really?"

"Yes, it is hard to find a young woman such as yourself that is totally sold out to the Lord." He answered. "When I saw you I knew that you were different. So many have nothing to say."

"I feel the same way about the guys that I meet. Their conversation is so boring."

"I am glad that I met you." He blushed.

"Me too." She replied. "But are you sure? You haven't had much time to get to know me."

"Yes, that is true. However, when the Lord tells you that this is the one then you know."

"Did he really say that?"

"Yes."

"Oh, I mean am I glad that he did." She answered.

"I suppose that this would be the moment when a couple should kiss, but we really can't here. Can we?" He asked.

"No, not really, and perhaps we do need to be careful." She replied. "I am determined not to do anything that would be morally wrong. I am saving myself for my husband."

They continued eating and enjoying the romantic evening. Here they were enjoying such wonderful company, a beautiful place, and the most wonderful food. Should she tell him about her special empowerment? Immediately, she felt the Lord impressing her not to say anything at this time. Evidently some things needed to be shared only with the Lord.

The long drive home was filled with excited chatter as the two shared their dreams for the future. David stopped the car at the curb outside Myra's home and turned to look at her. He held her in his arms and gently kissed her on the cheek. In spite of her earlier speech about not kissing, Myra felt disappointed that he hadn't kissed her on the mouth. Even though she slid her face over, hoping that he might miss her cheek and kiss her lips. David pulled back and shook his head.

"Myra, Myra you are so wonderful, but I won't kiss you on the lips until we are standing at the altar…that is, just having been married. It isn't that you aren't desirable, but you still have a year of

school. Still, I can't wait until we can tell the world about us."
"Why can't we?" she said.
"Because I want you to pray and be sure that this is what the Lord wants for us."
"But...."
"No, but about it, the flesh, as the Bible says, is weak. Just because we are attracted to each other doesn't mean that this is what the Lord wants. You have to know the Lord's will in this too."
"I guess that you are right." She had already begun her mental checklist of people to tell. In fact, she would have liked to shout it from the rooftop, she felt a little disappointed.
"I tell you what, pray about it and if by Christmas Eve you feel that this is the Lord's will for us then we will announce it. Besides that will be the best Christmas present that you could ever give me. Then we can be officially declared a serious relationship. We might want to wait until next Christmas to be officially engaged. Besides I need time to save to buy you a really nice ring." David added.
"There is something that you need to know about me." Myra began. She found it difficult to tell him about George. She fought the fear that he might be appalled that such a thing had happened and decide that she wasn't fit to marry.
"You mean about George?" He said. Myra's mouth fell open.
"How did you know? Does everyone know?" Myra asked.
"No one told me but the Holy Spirit." David said, "And no, everyone doesn't know. Nor do they need to know. The Holy Spirit doesn't embarrass people, but he does reveal things that we need to know. When Jesus heals and forgives, a person is cleansed like it never ever happened. To me nothing ever happened to you, it is as we say "under the blood.""
"Under the blood?" Myra looked puzzled.
"That is right, Jesus' blood works like vanishing ink on any sin. It causes the sin to be wiped away as though it never happened. In the eyes of God it never did happen to you."
"I have heard that, but people don't forget."
"No, people don't forget, but that is their problem."
"You mean you don't hold that against me?"

"Of course not, you couldn't have prevented it from happening. However, even if you could have, you asked for forgiveness. When God forgives your past is totally wiped away as though it never happened. You have a new beginning and a fresh start."

"You mean that don't you? Up until now, I have to admit that I hated myself for what happened. I felt dirty and used. I felt like I had been ruined forever, and that no man who knew my past would ever accept me as a virtuous woman."

"God sees you as a virtuous young woman, and so do I." David replied.

"Will I see you on Christmas?" Myra said changing the subject. "I mean you probably want to be with your folks."

"I wanted to surprise you. Our folks will be celebrating Christmas Eve dinner with the Shepherds." Myra hugged David.

"How wonderful, I can't wait. I am sure glad that Christmas Eve is only three more days. But do you think that your folks will like me?" Myra asked.

"Of course they will."

"Sure?"

"I'll tell you on Christmas Eve."

"Tell me now, please?"

"I can't it is another surprise." David walked her to the door and made sure that she was safely inside before turning and walking back to his car.

Victoria had been waiting for Myra. "Did you have a nice evening?" she said.

"I had a heavenly time." They both laughed. Victoria knows something and she isn't saying. They talked briefly before they said good night. Upstairs, Myra stared at the ceiling for hours, too excited to sleep. She decided to find Baby. Barefoot she padded through the house until she found him curled up next to the Shepherds cat. She picked him up and carried the reluctant animal upstairs. Typical cat, no matter how she tried to get him to lie beside her, he attempted to escape. So much for my wonderful fur-buddy, I guess life changes for all of us. She felt him leap off the bed as she drifted into a dreamless sleep.

CHAPTER TEN

It is written:
"Therefore if any man be in Christ,
he is a new creature: old things are
passed away; behold, all things are
become new."

Only two more days until Christmas...hurray! Myra leaped out of bed, startling Baby, who lay beside her bathroom door. She couldn't believe how marvelous her life had become. In fact, she fought the uneasy feeling that something would happen to spoil it all. The uneasiness persisted as she read her Bible and prayed. *Maybe I am just being a pessimist because so much bad has happened in my life. On the other hand, maybe the Lord is trying to warn me about something.* She continued to pray in her heavenly language. The perfect prayer was beyond human understanding. Although, she knew that the Lord could reveal the interpretation to her.

After dressing and eating a quick breakfast, she headed for the church. Her duties this morning included updating the extensive mailing list. Something she didn't mind doing, since it involved computers. Pastor Shepherd came into her office and asked to speak to her.

"Myra?"

"Yes?"

"Today, I need you to go down to Clayton Village and visit one of our families. They haven't been coming to church, and their son has been missing Street Side Sunday School. You can take the bus or perhaps David could go with you on the visitation."

"I think that David had some plans with his parents. So I'll catch the bus and visit them." She proceeded to get the information and headed down the street to the bus stop. Just as well that Atherstone abounds with buses. Now that I have a license, maybe I can start saving for a car, she thought.

The bus dropped her off a couple of blocks from the Clayton Village Housing Apartments. She headed to Apt 44A. The apartments were in the process of being condemned. Some had broken windows, and many had been boarded up to prevent looting. As the leases expired, the apartments were being vacated in preparation to demolish them. Huge oak trees provided ample shade in the playground. The grounds were dangerous as drug dealers did their trade in open view. Often disputes would erupt and so would gunfire. Myra had learned to walk carefully through the complex, and to watch her surroundings for signs of trouble. One day just a month before, she had been handing out flyers when she saw several children playing on the playground. One older child chased several younger ones. She noticed that the afternoon sunlight streaming through the trees made such a pretty scene, as the children appeared to be playing. Until that is, she noticed that the older child, a girl, was chasing the others with a large butcher knife. Needless to say, Myra didn't hand them a flyer. She just kept walking and watching. She didn't know whether to report it, and she didn't want to approach them because she didn't know what the older child might have tried to do. Her first few visits to Clayton Village were filled with fear. Now she had learned how to conduct herself. She also knew that even the drug dealers wanted her to come, because they too wanted their kids to grow up and live a different life than what they lived. Even the dealers would tell her that Street Side Sunday School gave their kids hope of a better life.

Just as she approached Apt 44A, she heard the sounds of kids running and shouting to call an ambulance. What in the world had happened? Kids were running toward her.

"Jerry has been run over by a train, and we saw it!" One of the kids cried. Just at that moment Jerry's mother opened the door and rushed out into the street. Two large kids carried Jerry. It wasn't long before an ambulance arrived.

"What happened to my baby?" His mother cried.

"Marcus pushed him onto the tracks just as a train was coming."

"It was an accident." One of the older kids protested.

"No it wasn't. He was pushed, and I saw it." Said four young kids.

"Let me see my baby." His mother shrieked.

"I took one of my shoelaces and made a tourniquet." His brother said.

Jerry moaned as he lay in the two young men's arms, one leg ended in a bloody stump. The ambulance attendants gently lifted his small blood soaked form, and carried him to the stretcher. They all sighed with relief when they saw that he was alive. Although the train had severed his foot, the rest of him seemed to have escaped injury. A shoelace that had been used as a tourniquet dangled from the stump.

"I am not surprised that Marcus pushed Jerry onto the path of the oncoming train." Said one boy.

"Someone ought to whip his rear for this."

"Yeah, why don't you do it?" Said another.

"Not me, I am not messing with him. Everyone knows that he is real bad. I am staying in the house if I know that he is around. Besides, he's got his spies everywhere, and they come looking for you after dark. I don't want to be no homicide."

"Did you see that car they towed into the parking lot? It was all shot up?" Asked one of the kids.

"Yeah, Marcus said if we told that it happened in a gang fight, he'd make us look like that car. He brags too much about killing folks." Said Alex, Jerry's youngest brother.

Myra remembered when he had threatened to kill a church staff member, and that Pastor Shepherd had made arrangements for him to go to camp in Alvin. Yet after returning from camp, the very next week he had been arrested for attempted murder.

"Do you think that this time he will get sent-up for a long time?" His brother said.

"He may be tried as an adult for what he did to Jerry." Myra added. Once more the grim reality of life in the ghetto hit her full force. How ironic that just as soon as a bit of happiness came into her life, it vanished in a moment due to a tragedy. Two days from Christmas, and instead of enjoying the holiday cheer, she watched as the ambulance with sirens and lights flashing disappeared down the street heading to the hospital.

"Do you want me to give you a ride to the church? It is on the way to the hospital, and you can tell Pastor Shepherd." Asked Chris, one of Jerry's cousins.

"Sure." Myra said.

"Let me get some of his things, first." Chris said as he went inside Jerry's house. The sparsely decorated house contained a tiny Christmas tree that was draped in tinsel. There were no packages under the tree.

"Do they have any Christmas presents?" Myra asked.

"I don't know, Jerry's dad lost his job and his Mom works as a cleaning lady for the school. They probably don't have any."

"Oh, maybe our church can help."

"I don't have any presents either, except for the Christmas stockings that you gave us."

"Really?" Myra asked. "I'll see what I can do."

"It has been a tough year." Chris said. They arrived at the church, and found Pastor Shepherd studying in his office.

"Pastor Shepherd, Jerry's foot got run-over by a train and they have taken him to the hospital."

Pastor Shepherd loaded them into the church van, stopping at the Shepherds house to get Victoria before continuing to the hospital. They eagerly awaited news about Jerry. At the triage desk, a nurse told them that he had already been taken into surgery.

The gray waiting room buzzed with conversation. Across from them, Jerry's mother sat rocking absentmindedly in a chair. Her lips continually moved as she prayed for her child. No one could comfort her or distract her as she continued to pray. Time crept slowly as they waited to hear news of the surgery. Several times, Myra glanced at

the clock only to find that the minute hand had barely moved.
"What is taking so long?" Annie, Jerry's mother, asked one of the nurses.
"It is Saturday night, and the ER is full." Replied the nurse.
"But he has been in surgery for hours." Said Myra.
"Sometimes it takes a long time, especially if they are trying to save part of a foot."
"There wasn't anything to save. I suppose though that they have to reconstruct his foot."
"That will come later, he will most likely have to have more than one surgery." The nurse answered.

David joined her at the hospital; he grabbed her hand. How amazing, she thought, that we don't even need to say anything and yet we understand each other. Together they prayed for Jerry and his mother.

A nurse announced that they needed blood donors for Jerry, so Myra and David arranged to donate blood.

Finally, the doors opened and a tired doctor called for Jerry's family. They gathered around him as he prepared to tell them about Jerry's prognosis.

"He is doing fine, and will make it. He is a tough little guy. In a few weeks he will be fitted for prosthesis and will eventually be able to run with the other kids. That is once he gets used to it."

Later they were allowed to see him in the Recovery room. He smiled weakly at them and drifted into sleep. Tubes and wires coursed over his body, and a monitor recorded his heartbeat. He looked tiny and so vulnerable lying amongst so many tubes and machines. She had to admit that hospitals were intimidating.

"I want to believe that the Lord will regrow his foot." Myra told David. David looked at her, and she could tell that he didn't want to quench her faith. Yet he didn't know what to say.

"Don't you believe that God can do a creative miracle on his foot?" she said.

"Yes, " David stammered.

"That is OK, I have enough faith to believe for both of us." Myra continued. Already the Lord had given her a plan.

The next two days were filled with preparations for Christmas. Delivering toys to the needy families of the community and getting the house ready for Christmas visitors. Myra delivered toys to Jerry's family and cousins. They were so excited since they didn't have money for presents. The two days had passed like a whirlwind.

Now Myra found herself wishing that she had more time to prepare to meet David's parents. Tonight was Christmas Eve and in a few minutes they would arrive.

"Myra would you help me in the kitchen?" Victoria asked. Myra hurried into the kitchen. The crowded counters contained a myriad of casseroles and serving dishes. Steam rose from several of the serving dishes. Pies, cakes and cookies lined the breakfast table. All around her people worked on the evening's preparations. The aroma of roasting turkey filled the air, mixing with the inevitable cinnamon smell of apple cider.

"I have such butterflies in my stomach." She told Victoria, "I am so nervous about seeing my mother and meeting David's parents. Plus, I don't know how my mom is going to act around David's parents. I sure hope that she won't embarrass me." Victoria had invited her mother to come for Christmas. "Maybe since it is Christmas, mom will be on her best behavior."

"You will handle it all like the champion that you are." Victoria beamed.

"Victoria, would you pray with me?" "My mom can be so unpredictable. She has a penchant for telling stories about me. The stories usually humiliate me, and they make me look so stupid."

"Of course I will pray with you." Said Victoria. Immediately they joined hands and Myra began to pray.

"Please Lord, don't let her humiliate me in front of David's parents. Let them understand that she isn't as spiritual as they are. Let me find favor with his parents."

The doorbell rang, and Victoria went to answer it. David's parents entered the room. His father towered over Victoria. His striking white hair and charisma surprised Myra. He greeted her warmly with a hug. Next, she met David's mother, Joan, an elegant lady, who oozed warmth and friendliness. She reminded Myra of Victoria in so many ways. Myra felt their acceptance.

The doorbell rang again and Myra's mother stood at the door.

"I hope that I am not too early." She apologized.

"Nonsense, you are right on time." Victoria replied. Myra felt such compassion for her mother. She hugged her, and her Mom wiped away a tear.

"I decided that I want to know this Jesus that you talk about so much." Her mother said. "All these years I have been to church and I never knew him. I always knew about him."

"Great, Mom!" Myra didn't know what else to say. Her prayers had been answered.

Pastor Shepherd called them to the table for dinner. The long table was resplendent in beauty with swatches of evergreens and holly. Red Poinsettias and candles trimmed the table. Myra sat at David's left side. Her mother sat on her other side. After they prayed and gave thanks, they passed the food.

"I want to make an announcement." David said as he tapped a glass with his fork.

"Here, here," said Victoria.

"It is my intention to officially date Myra with the intentions of having her be my wife." No one said a word as they waited for him to continue.

"I ask that you pray for us and give us your support and guidance."

"Here, here," said Victoria. Thank heavens for Victoria; she knew what to say and when. Myra's mother's mouth hung open in shock. David's parents smiled.

"I have heard such good things about this young lady." David's father, Robert, said, "I look forward to getting to know her." After they all agreed, they began to pass the food. Myra felt more than a little embarrassed.

"Now it is official," David whispered.

"Yes I noticed." Myra replied.

"How do you feel?"

"A little like a bug under a magnifying glass, but apart from that just great." Never in her wildest imagination, would she ever have dreamed that he would have made such an announcement. So much for thinking that they could read each other's thoughts.

As if in answer to her thoughts, David squeezed her hand. Myra wanted to kick him in the shins under the table. However, she merely smiled having decided to play the part of the doting bride-to-be. She knew that what happened next was inevitable.

"I guess that I am always the last one to know, seeing how no one ever tells me anything." Said Myra's mother.

"Mom, I am as surprised as you are." Myra whispered to her mother.

"Do I have anything to say about this?" Her mother continued.

"By all means, make a speech." Said David. Myra immediately wished that the floor would open up and swallow her, allowing her to vanish from the table. A speech about her was what she had wanted at all costs to avoid.

"Honey," she said to David, "Could I talk to you in the kitchen for a moment?"

"Sure, right after your mother has her say."

"Whatever," Myra said. She felt that the relationship might be over before it had even officially begun. She was desperately trying to avoid making a scene.

"I just want to say that I think that David seems to be such a nice young man." Her mother said.

Myra waited for more to be said, and was relieved that her mother quit speaking and started eating. In a few moments her mother nudged her and whispered, "I can be tactful too, you know."

"Thanks Mom, I am so embarrassed."

"Don't be, I think that your young man is quite quaint and proper."

"See I do hear from God, now we have everyone's blessings," David whispered. "Still want to talk to me in the kitchen? We might need a chaperone." He laughed as Myra rolled her eyes.

Evidently there was more to David than met the eye. At least life with him would not be boring.

The rest of the evening seemed like a dream. After dinner, they opened presents. Myra gave David an ornate sterling silver cross. David presented her with a friendship ring. The gold ring contained a tiny diamond. Although smaller than an engagement ring, it never the less symbolized the seriousness of their relationship. She knew that she would treasure it forever.

"Oh, it is so beautiful." She said. David had surprised her again. "This is the best Christmas that I have ever had."

After dinner, they went to the church for the midnight candlelight service, and enjoyed singing Christmas carols with the church choir. After the carols, the church celebrated the Lord's birth, with a Christmas play. The curtain rose showing a stable with Mary, Joseph and the baby Jesus. A cow and donkey chewed on the hay in a manger behind the holy family. A wise man rode a real camel down the aisle and onto the stage. Shepherds herded two lambs onto the stage to present to the baby Jesus. The tangible presence of God descended upon the audience as the drummer boy presented Jesus with his drums. All over the sanctuary the muffled sobs of people crying could be heard. Myra had never seen such a drama done inside a church. She knew that the drama team of the church had been rehearsing for weeks. At the end of the play, Pastor Shepherd called for people to come to the altar who wanted to accept the Lord as their Savior. Myra's mother went forward with the others.

"Would any of you like to say something?" Pastor Shepherd asked those at the altar. Her mother raised her hand, and he gave her the microphone. Her sad countenance had changed to one of joy. Myra no longer felt embarrassed about her mom. She was proud of her.

"I just gave Jesus a Christmas present." Her mother said. "I gave him my heart." The church cheered.

"That is the best present anyone can give him." Pastor Shepherd replied.

"When I first saw you, Pastor, I thought that you were a cult. But now I see how you have helped my daughter. I know that what you have is real, and I want what you have."

Pastor Shepherd laid hands on her, and she dropped onto the

floor. She remained there for twenty minutes. "Don't worry she is fine," he said to the church. "The Lord is healing her heart." Myra had never told anyone in the church that her mother had suffered for years from a cardiac ailment. Myra stepped to her mother's side.

"My Mom never told Pastor about her heart condition. Several years ago, she had a severe heart attack and has been on medication ever since." Myra added. The audience cheered while her mother cried tears of joy.

"I am so happy, for the first time in years." Her mother said. Eventually everyone returned to their seat and the service dismissed.

"What an evening, " he said. "I do like your Mom." David said as he took her home.

"Really?" Myra asked. "I mean she is a little...."

"Different?" He finished the sentence for her.

"Yeah."

"I am looking forward to what the Lord is going to do in her life." They arrived at the door, and Myra anticipated a good night kiss. Instead, he leaned over and kissed her on the cheek.

"That is it?" she asked.

"Yep," he said. "True love waits."

"But tonight was special." Myra said.

"Believe me, I would love to grab you into my arms and do more than kiss you."

" I guess, that I just needed to know that. How funny, I am the girl and here I am having my boyfriend tell me to wait. Usually it is the other way around." She laughed. "I mean how many times have I visualized you sweeping me into your arms and kissing me on my front door step. Still, in another year or two, I'll be able to kiss you any time that I want."

"You'll probably be the one who says quit kissing me I am not getting my work done." David laughed as he walked her to the door.

"Hey at least I can hug you." They hugged and pulled apart reluctantly.

"Good night, and remember I love you." She said as she opened the front door.

THE SPIRIT'S APPRENTICE

"Myra I am so glad that I met you, and I love you too," he replied, "Good night." She watched as he walked down the sidewalk to his car. What a handsome man, he was everything that she had ever dreamed of having in a husband. She knew that he loved her. Standing beside his car he said, "I can't wait until we are married."

"Me too," she replied.

A fire crackled in the fireplace as she joined her mother and the Shepherds. Victoria poured her some hot chocolate.

"We never thought that you two would quit saying good night to each other." She laughed.

"Yeah, you forget that you left the front door open." Pastor Shepherd remarked.

"Oh, no did you hear what we were saying?" Myra asked.

"Uh-huh." They chorused.

"So young, and so in love," Victoria said, "Why I remember when Pastor used to date me." Pastor Shepherd blushed.

"As the days of heaven on earth, or so the sacred words say," Pastor replied. "It is getting late, and I am tired. I believe that I will be the first to officially wish everyone a Merry Christmas."

"Merry Christmas," Myra's mother replied.

"I have had a full day, and I am ready to go to bed." Said Victoria.

"I second that motion," said Myra's mother.

"I am cooking breakfast at 4 am if anyone wants it." Pastor said. "Just joking, that is only 2 hours from now.

That night Myra fell asleep thinking about sugarplums, weddings, and Christmas Carols.

CHAPTER ELEVEN

It is written:
"Be not forgetful to entertain strangers:
for thereby some have entertained angels unawares."

Rain beat upon the windows as Myra gazed outside. Heaving a sigh she decided to go into the kitchen and find Victoria. All the preparations and excitement of Christmas was gone. Now life returned to the same old routine, only the cold, drizzly wintry days didn't help her mood. Where is David she wondered? So much for the love of her life, he had disappeared Christmas evening and hadn't even called her. Isn't that just like a man, once they know that they have you they decide to ignore you? The sound of the telephone made her jump.

She opened her cell phone and noticed that her caller ID listed David's number. "Hello." She said as casually as she could.

"What's up?" David asked. Seems like David had a habit of proving her wrong.

"Just watching the rain, and reading, why?"

"Want to go Roller Skating?"

"Sure," she said. Was she crazy? She hated to roller skate, being literally terrified of falling. However, she wanted to be with David.

"Victoria asked me to check on one of the church kids."

"She did?"

"The girl is staying with friends because of a death in the family. She asked me to find something that the two of you could do. She felt

THE SPIRIT'S APPRENTICE

that you would be good for the girl. Sort of a big sister thing, are you game for it?"

"Sure why not, truthfully I was a little bored."

"I'll pick you up about six o'clock, we can eat at the rink." Great, that gave her time to do her hair and nails, if she rushed. She still couldn't shake a feeling of uneasiness; in fact her inner peace had vanished. She knew the 8 yr. old girl, whose reputation preceded her. The kids called her "Ghetto Bunny" because of her protruding front teeth, and the fact that her nose twitched when she got angry.

David had already gotten Emily, when he arrived to get Myra.

"Next stop, Fun Time Skating Rink," said David.

"Do you like to skate?" Myra asked Emily.

"Uh-huh I love it." Emily replied. What Emily hadn't told them was that although she had come to the rink she didn't know how to skate.

Fun Time Skating Rink was packed as they waited in line to enter the building.

"These prices are a lot, I only have enough for us to eat. Am I glad that I have gas in the car." David said as he paid for their admission and skates.

"I don't have any money on me either," Myra said. They both knew that Emily didn't have any money with her.

"Do you like to skate?" Emily asked, as they were putting on their skates.

"Nope, I just like being with David. In fact, I usually hang onto the rail. I can skate real well if I am holding onto someone like David."

"I can teach you to skate." Emily said. Myra sensed that the girl was lying.

"Really, how long have you been skating?" Myra asked.

"Oh I come here all the time." Emily continued. Myra felt the stone under her blouse; she knew instinctively that something about tonight was terribly wrong. Yet she didn't want to ruin anyone's fun.

As they entered the rink, Myra held onto to the rail. Couples skated past, as the music played her favorite songs. A kaleidoscope of color cascaded onto the floor from the rotating lights. Emily launched onto the floor, and fell; David and Myra tried to help her onto to her feet.

"I don't need any help," she protested. She skated awkwardly away, and a few minutes later they noticed that she had joined some girls her own age on the sidelines.

"Looks like Emily has found some friends." Said Myra. "I do hope that she is going to be all right.

"It is going to be a long night," David whispered to Myra. Little did they know that those words were prophetic.

David took Myra's hands as they skated onto the floor. Together they flowed around the rink. Skating with David was effortless, such a contrast from her own efforts. She loved it when he placed his arm around her waist and gently spun her. I can do this with him, but I would never do this on my own. The evening passed fairly quickly, until the inevitable happened.

Suddenly the music stopped, and they heard Emily crying. People were rushing to the center of the floor. There in the middle her small form lay crumpled on the floor. She rocked herself in pain. One look convinced Myra that her arm was broken. It hung at an unnatural angle.

"David, do you have insurance?"

"No, do you?"

"No, I guess that I could call Pastor Shepherd."

"Yeah, but is this a church outing?"

"Didn't Victoria ask you to take Emily?"

"Yeah, she mentioned it as an idea for something that we could do that was sort of chaperoned."

"An eight year old chaperone? Really David has it come to that?"

"No, I mean it is just best that we don't spend too much time alone together. You know what I mean."

"So what do we do now?" Myra asked

"I think that we had better take her to the hospital, that is unless someone has already called an ambulance." David said pointing to the office.

They comforted Emily. The skating rink attendants suggested that they should take her to the hospital. One of the officials asked

David if he could talk to them privately.

"Are you responsible for Emily? Were you aware of how recklessly she had been skating? In fact, several times, we asked her not to go into the middle of the floor, but to stay on the sidelines," he said. Myra knew that they were covering themselves against any liability.

Meanwhile, a crowd of skaters surrounded Emily as she lay on the rink floor groaning and crying. Nobody seemed to know what to do.

"Can't you see that she is hurt," David said, "Someone please help her get to the sidelines."

"Stay with her Myra, I am going to get the car and bring it to the door." While David went to get the car, Myra and another girl helped Emily walk to the door.

They waited for several minutes for David to drive up to the door. He seemed preoccupied, and his face had lost its color.

"What is wrong David?"

"Nothing, I will tell you later."

At the Emergency room, they prayed over Emily's arm, while they waited their turn for her to be seen by the doctor.

"They sure are slow." Emily said. A few minutes later an orderly helped Emily into a wheel chair.

"They are going to do an X-Ray, I'll bring her back in about an hour." David and Myra waited in one of the examination rooms. Maybe the church's insurance will cover this. She fingered the insurance form, but knew that it probably wouldn't cover Emily. I wonder how much the bill will be.

"How are we going to pay for this?" Myra asked.

"Don't worry, the most amazing thing happened a few minutes ago." David said.

"Is that why your face is so pale?" Myra asked.

"I guess. When I went to get the car, a tall man with blonde hair approached me in the parking lot. I thought great, just what I need someone asking for money. Although the man looked well dressed. The man said 'Are you David?'"

"But you said that you didn't know him."

"I didn't."

"What happened next?"

"He said that the Lord told him that he was supposed to give me this." David said as he opened his hand and produced three $100 bills.

"What did you say to him?" Myra asked. "I must admit that you are a man of surprises."

"I said thank you, and reached for my wallet, I had only looked down for a moment, but when I looked up he had vanished. I looked all over the parking lot and he was nowhere to be found. I wanted to say more, and to ask him how he knew who I was, but he had vanished. I do believe that he was an angel. The scriptures say, "'be not forgetful to entertain strangers: for thereby some have entertained angels unawares.'"

"An angel!" said Myra.

An attendant wheeled Emily into the room. The doctor followed and told her that her arm most likely had been broken but must have spontaneously healed itself.

"Doctor, have you ever heard of a broken arm spontaneously healing itself?"

"No, but we don't know what else to call it. You see the first X-Ray showed a break, but the second X-Ray didn't. We had to repeat the X-Ray because there was movement around the bone. We thought that the girl wasn't holding still, but the movement was just in the area of the break."

"Doctor, do you believe in miracles?"

"Yes I do!"

"We do too." David told the doctor about the man and the $300.00.

"That is funny, because your bill will probably be just about that amount." The doctor said.

Emily was discharged. They rejoiced when the bill came to $270.00. Myra knew that the Lord had intervened.

"Isn't that like the Lord? He gave enough for us to tithe on it." David said.

"What is a tithe? Emily asked.

"No, the tithe is what you are supposed to give God. The Bible instructs us to give God the first ten percent of all that we make."

"That sure does seem like a lot." Emily said. "I could sure use that $30.00."

"Yeah, it is a real mystery, but it works and the Lord blesses you financially when you tithe. In fact, if you don't tithe it seems that you lose the money plus your money doesn't last."

"I don't know about that," Emily said.

"Really, then why don't you pay your bill?" David said.

"No, I would rather that God paid it." Emily said.

"Me too!" Myra said.

"In fact, give this to Pastor Shepherd when you get home. Tell him to put it into the church funds, that it is my tithe." David handed her the thirty dollars.

The next morning, Myra awakened early. She hadn't heard from Jerry in several days, and she wondered how he was recovering from surgery on his amputated foot. The sun streamed through her bedroom window sending shadows across the floor as she lay across the bed reading her Bible. Such a beautiful day for mid-winter, a great day to go bike riding or for a walk, so she decided to visit Jerry. It might be too soon, suppose that his stump still hasn't recovered? Maybe I should wait a week or two longer. However, her heart told her that now was the time. Maybe I can borrow Victoria's car and take him to the Mall.

Would she have the courage to ask him to go to a shoe store? Her friends would think that she was crazy. However, she believed that the Lord wanted to do a mighty miracle for Jerry. She decided to call him.

"Jerry?" she said. "This is Myra and I was calling to see how you were doing."

"I miss everyone, and my leg is doing great."

"Hey, how would you like to go to the Mall? I mean, are you up to it?"

"You mean it? I haven't been out of this house in days. Let me ask my mom." He dropped the phone. The phone clattered against wood, making a loud thump that resounded in Myra's ear. Myra winced. He sure sounded excited about getting out of the house. Myra waited on the phone, she could hear the muffled exchange of conversation that Jerry was having with his mother.

"It's OK. I can go, but I can only go for an hour. Mom says if I get tired that you are to bring me right home. Is that OK?"

"Sure," Myra answered. "Let me check with Victoria and see if I can get the car. If so, can you be ready in about an hour?"

"Uh huh."

"Great, I will ask Victoria and then call you back." Myra wished that she had asked Victoria before she mentioned it to Jerry, because if she couldn't borrow the car then she knew that he would be disappointed. Still, she could visit him anyway; it was a great day for a walk. Myra sighed, and decided that she had better gather the courage to ask Victoria if I she could borrow the car for an hour or two. She found her as usual, sewing in the sunroom of the kitchen.

"Victoria, can I borrow the car to visit Jerry?" she said.

"I suppose, let me check with Pastor." Victoria replied. " Saturday is his busy day to prepare for his sermons so I doubt that he will want to use the car this morning." Victoria went to ask him in his study. She returned a few minutes later and told Myra that she could use the car.

"Seems to me that you need to start saving for your own car." Victoria said.

"Really, I mean you would let me have one if I raised the money for it?"

"Of course, and I know that you have the faith to do it."

Myra called Jerry and arranged to collect him in an hour. Images of people laughing at her floated through her mind, because of what she was about to do. "Lord, help me have the courage to do this," she whispered as she drove toward Jerry's apartment. How would she explain that she wanted to take a crippled boy to the Mall? Everyone would say that she was "a dumb blonde." Only the Lord knew her true purpose.

Jerry hobbled out to the car on crutches. Myra gulped, what in the world had she been thinking about to ask him to go to the Mall? Still, she resolved to do what was in her heart.

"Jerry, do you believe that the Lord wants to heal your leg?" she said as they drove.

"Yes, I sure do. You ought to see my stump it is almost all healed."

"I mean, more than just healing your stump."

"Huh?"

"Yeah, like maybe growing a new foot?" Myra asked. Jerry remained silent.

"Jerry? Are you OK?"

"Yes."

"Did I upset you saying that?"

"No." Jerry said as he began to cry. Great, now I have made him cry.

"I 'm sorry if I upset you."

"I'm not crying because I'm upset. I'm crying because the Lord told me that I could have a new foot."

"He did? That is wonderful. Do you know that he told me to take you to a shoe store and have you buy a pair of shoes? I am going to pay for them."

"I don't know if that means that I will be able to wear the second shoe when I get fitted with my prosthesis in about three weeks."

"No, Jerry, I mean for you to try on the shoe today."

"Oh." Jerry said. "But...."

"Can you believe that the Lord will grow that foot when the shoe hits it?"

"It might hurt, because the stump is still tender." Jerry replied. Myra hadn't thought about that. She sure didn't want to make Jerry's mother mad by hurting her son. She shifted uneasily in her seat. Why did things have to be so complicated? Why did the faith walk seem to have to fly in the face of obvious facts to the contrary? I guess that is because it wouldn't be faith otherwise.

"Hey, let's do it anyway. I won't tell if you don't tell." Jerry said. Myra was surprised; he had taken the words out of her mouth. Except now she wouldn't get in trouble for having said them.

They arrived at the Mall and walked into J.C. Penny's. Jerry hobbled on his crutches. Myra looked at the shoes and ignored the salesman who was following her. They wandered around for about ten minutes before she looked in the salesman's direction. Immediately he hurried to her side.

"Can I help you with some shoes?" he asked.

"Jerry needs a pair of sneakers." She said pointing to Jerry.

"What size does he wear?" The salesman asked. Jerry shrugged obviously unsure what size he needed. The salesman had him stand with his good foot on the store's floor measure. Jerry had found a pair of Nike sneakers that he liked. The salesman returned with a box in his hand. He took out one shoe and tried it on his good foot.

"This seems to fit, and it looks really nice." He said.

"I want to try the other shoe too." Jerry said. Seconds passed slowly as the salesman stared at first Jerry and then at Myra. His eyes pleaded for understanding.

"Are you sure?" The salesman replied. Myra shifted in her seat, wishing that she were anywhere but in the store. By now some of the customers were watching them. I sure hope that none of them go to our church, she thought.

"Uh huh." Jerry replied.

"How do you...um...well, plan to try it on?" The salesman asked.

"You mean because I haven't got a foot? Jerry asked.

"Yeah, I didn't want to say that, but...."

"Oh, it's going to grow the minute you put the shoe against my stump." By now there was a crowd standing around the three of them.

"Yeah, right." The Salesman said.

"You'll see." Jerry protested.

"Jerry..." Myra asked. Trying to talk to him privately was futile. Not only were there people watching, Jerry seemed very sure that something miraculous was about to happen. Great, this was my idea and now he is going to look stupid if nothing happens, Myra thought miserably.

"Put the shoe on, or I will." Jerry said. No one moved for several moments.

THE SPIRIT'S APPRENTICE

"Are you going to put it on or not?" He asked. The crowd hushed as they waited to see what would happen next.

The salesman reached down and picked up the shoe. His hand shook as he moved it toward Jerry's bandaged stump. The moment the stump touched the shoe; Jerry's foot grew into the shoe. Evidently the bandage grew too. His foot filled the shoe and was normal in size.

"Jesus Christ!" The salesman said.

"Yeah, he is the one who did it! See I told you." Jerry proudly proclaimed. "Jesus healed my foot!" By now he had leaped to his feet and walked around the room, while the crowd around them gasped. He didn't even have a trace of a limp.

"Jerry, does your foot hurt?" Myra asked. Myra's knees felt weak, so much for being a mighty woman of faith, she thought.

"Of course not." Jerry replied. A few minutes later, they called Victoria and told her what had happened. She shrieked with delight on the other end of the phone. Within a few more minutes the manager of the store arrived to see the miracle. He took pictures of Myra, Jerry, the salesman, and the new shoes. Then he gave Jerry an extra pair of shoes, and Myra a gift certificate.

"My God is an awesome God!" Jerry told everyone who would listen. Later, she returned Jerry to his home. His mother fainted at the door when Jerry walked into the room wearing his new shoes and carrying his crutches. Myra left as Jerry's sister was fanning his mother, as she lay sprawled on the couch. Although she was now conscious, she kept repeating, "Thank you Jesus, thank you Jesus." Myra would have liked to have stayed longer and savored the moment, but she had promised to return the car by a certain time. What a day this has been she thought. She couldn't wait to tell David all about it.

CHAPTER TWELVE

It is written:
"And he sent them to preach the kingdom of God, and to heal the sick."

Triumphantly, Myra returned to the Shepherds. Such power, such miracles, how could anyone not be high because of the Most High, God? She bounced into the kitchen and sat in a chair. The mood was decidedly somber, to say the least. An evil foreboding tugged at her heart. Why did it always happen that one minute her joy knew no boundaries, and the next minute disaster knocked at her door and heart?

"What is wrong?" she asked.

"It is Donny Faye" Victoria answered. "She is in the SICU at John Kemple Hospital and she isn't expected to live."

"Oh no!" Myra cried. Donny Faye and her husband were favorites amongst the parishioners. Having had a mission years ago that fed the homeless, they were loved by all the street people.

"She has been so sick." Victoria continued, "I just knew in my heart when they were doing all those Angioplasties that things were turning sour."

"She is such a fighter though." Myra added.

"Yes, she is, and I am about to go visit her in the hospital. Do you want to come? She would love to hear about Jerry's miracle. Even though I am told that she is in a coma. The hearing is the last sense to leave before death, so people in a coma are usually able to hear what is being said around them. Be careful, we don't want to say anything that would upset her or hurt her faith."

"I understand."

"The family isn't handling it well at all. In fact, her husband hasn't been able to see her without crying because it is too painful."

"How awful!"

"We need to pray for her."

"Yes, but be sensitive to the family. This will be a good lesson for you in ministry. Follow my lead, and then we can discuss things after the visit."

The two drove silently to the hospital. Myra clutched her Bible as she reviewed healing verses.

"How long has she been sick?" She knew that Donny Faye seldom came to church, because of her heart condition. At 76 yrs of age, she spent most of her time on the Internet, especially in the Chat rooms sharing her faith with those of other religions.

"She had a Quadruple Bypass two years ago." Victoria answered.

"Really? I didn't realize that it had been that long ago."

"She has been in the hospital for eight weeks because she got an infection in her Angioplasty site." Victoria added.

They arrived at the hospital and found a space in the parking garage. As they walked the short distance to the hospital, they passed several patients in wheelchairs with IV poles in tow. Evidently, their relatives had taken them outside the hospital to enjoy the fresh air or to smoke cigarettes.

The SICU waiting room buzzed with people waiting to see their friends and relatives. Victoria called on the red phone and asked permission to visit Donny Faye.

As usual, they were asked to wait for several minutes. Victoria rolled her eyes and smiled.

"Guess that they are bathing her. Seems like they bathe her a lot." She laughed. After several minutes, a nurse called and gave them permission to visit. As they walked into the busy Intensive Care, sounds and smells bombarded Myra's nose and ears. They washed their hands and entered Donny's room after donning the disposable yellow isolation gowns and gloves.

Nothing prepared Myra for what she was about to see. Her heart fell when she saw Donny. How could anyone have faith in this place, she wondered. Donny lay surrounded by tubes, wires and machines. So much equipment was attached to her that it was difficult to make a path alongside the bed. A respirator rasped next to Myra as she stood beside Donny's swollen body.

Donny 's swollen body lay lifelessly on the bed. At first, she hardly recognized her due to the blemished skin. She hadn't been prepared for the sight of blood oozing out of her nose, eyes and ears. Her blackened toes and bluish feet stuck out of egg-crate booties. The Dialysis machine filled one side of the bed, with its tubes, bottles as it monitored the procedures. Overhead monitors beeped and occasionally set off alarms, everywhere that Myra looked there were tubes connected to tubes, IV's with their monitors. How did anyone pray a prayer of faith with all this complicated equipment?

"Donny can you hear me?" Victoria asked.

No response came from Donny apart from the regular rasping of the respirator.

"Do you think that she hears you?" Myra asked.

An oriental nurse bustled in and around them. "I am sure that she hears you, because the last sense to leave a dying person is hearing. Even if they are in a coma, people can still hear what is said around them."

"In that case, I am going to tell her about healing." Myra replied. Victoria nodded in agreement, but remained silent.

The nurse began to cry, and Myra didn't know what to say, "She is so special, there is something different about her. I want so much for her to live." The nurse replied.

"Did you know her…before she got sick?"

"No, all I know is that she is already a miracle. She had a condition that causes her blood not to clot. In all my years, I have never known anyone her age to survive it."

"Does she still have it?" Myra cast an anxious glance at the bed while wondering if Donny could hear them speaking. She wanted to ask the nurse to step out of the room, but didn't want to interrupt her. Yet the nurse spoke words that she knew Donny needed to hear, words that brought hope and not despair. She couldn't imagine what it must be like to lie in a bed day after day with all the wires and tubes attached to her body.

"That is the amazing part, she doesn't have it anymore. What happens is that with this disease, a massive blood clot forms in the body and all the clotting factors go to it. Which is normal, if for example you cut yourself, then the body forms a clot to aid in the mending process. The person literally bleeds to death." The nurse continued.

"Is that why she had all that blood pouring out of her eyes, nose, ears and mouth? " Myra shuddered. "Her family told us about that."

"Yes, that is what happens. We give them transfusion to replace the blood, and some get as many as 40 or more pints of blood." The nurse continued. "Donny's age was against her. Like I said, I have never known anyone her age survive this condition, and I have been a nurse for many years."

"But she did survive."

"Yes, most don't last more than a week."

"Are her clotting factors?" Myra's voice trailed away as she asked the question.

"Yes, they are normal now, and the bleeding has stopped." The nurse continued. "I pray for her every day."

"You do? The Lord gave Donny a praying nurse." Myra said clapping her hands.

"I kept getting her as a patient." The nurse added, "and that doesn't happen very often."

"Isn't the Lord wonderful!" Myra exclaimed.

"Yes he is!" replied the nurse. Victoria handed the nurse a pamphlet on healing and they both left the SICU.

Myra and Victoria were rejoicing as they headed for the elevator. Little did Myra know that her joy would face a serious challenge in the form of Donny's daughter.

Victoria excused herself and left Myra talking to the daughter.

"Francis, I just came from your mom and she has received a healing."

"Yes, she is better for now, but we are still making funeral arrangements just in case. Today, we bought a cemetery lot, and made preliminary arrangements for the funeral."

"But your mom is going to make it."

"The doctors told us that she only had a twenty percent change of surviving. The family decided that it would be a good idea to make the arrangements now, so that we won't have to deal with it when she dies. Besides at 76 yrs of age, she is going to need it one day anyhow."

"But she is doing so much better, and they are talking about taking her off the respirator and moving her to a room." Myra couldn't believe the cold hard glare in the daughter's eyes. Her daughter had stayed faithfully at her side for weeks, why wouldn't she be excited that she was doing better.

"I plan to be here until the end."

"But...." Myra protested.

"Let's just say that we have differences in theology and so let's not go there, O.K." Francis spoke kindly and yet with such finality. Myra knew that it would be futile to continue the discussion.

"I am going to see mom, are you staying or leaving?" Francis asked as Victoria rejoined them.

"Leaving, Victoria needs to get back to the church." Myra answered. They watched as the SICU doors swung open, admitting Francis. The doors swung closed blocking their view of Francis or the unit. As they headed toward the elevators, Myra's heart became heavy. A premonition of doom hovered over her like a ghostly garment.

"My, my, my what happened? Did the daughter say something to you? Why, your shoulders are drooping and you look like you just lost your best friend." Victoria said.

"I hope not."

"Tell me about it." Victoria asked.

"Francis told me that the family had just made arrangements for Donny's funeral. She says they went together and bought the plot, and even picked out the casket. She isn't even dead."

"Oh," Victoria said, and remained silent.

"I want her to live, and I don't understand how her family is already making funeral arrangements. That is so cold! Don't they love her like we do?"

"I am sure that they do, but they don't believe like we do." Victoria continued, "Doubt and unbelief in family members is a real issue when dealing with healing. It kills people faster than the disease."

"What do we do?"

"Pray!" Victoria answered. "It isn't like the family members don't know the Bible, but they believe differently than we do."

"I wish the whole world believed our God like we do."

"That is our mission, and why we must continue to love and help people." Victoria replied. Myra marveled at the wisdom and loving way that Victoria handled every situation.

Little did Myra know that the next few days would challenge her faith, and bring her to a crossroads in her faith.

The next evening, Myra and Victoria visited Donny. This time she had been moved to the Geriatric unit, and had a spacious room. Donny slept with an oxygen mask strapped over her face. Many of the tubes and machines had been removed after being moved from the SICU. She looked frail and thin compared to her pre-hospital days. They didn't want to disturb her, but she opened her eyes and greeted them.

"I'm going to make it, but I am in so much pain. I just wish that I could go home." Donny said. She hadn't been able to speak in over a month and her voice sounded normal in spite of the tracheotomy wound.

What does she mean go home? Myra wondered, did she mean back to her house in Atherstone, or to her heavenly home.

Myra and Victoria talked with her for several minutes, before leaving her to sleep. The next morning, Donny's husband called to tell them that Donny had been found unconscious and without a pulse. Two days later, Donny went home to be with the Lord. Myra's faith was challenged as she cried in Victoria's arms.

"But she was healed, and then she died. I don't understand. She was doing so much better and she had normal clotting factors. I was just sure that meant she would live. Why did she die? People didn't die when Jesus prayed for them, they lived." Myra cried.

"Everyone Jesus prayed for lived, but Jesus didn't pray for everyone." Victoria said.

" I know, but I feel that is just an excuse to explain why a person didn't get healed. Yes, and I know she is healed now, but I am sorry I just don't consider someone dying as healing. That is just a poor excuse if you ask me." Myra's eyes were so swollen and her nose stuffy from crying.

"Did you ask the Lord if it was time for Donny to go home?"

"No," Myra replied.

"I must admit, that I didn't think that the Lord was going to heal her." Victoria said.

"You are kidding, you of all people didn't think that she was going to be healed?"

"No, I didn't think that she would be healed."

"Why?" Myra asked, startled at this confession.

"Unbelief is powerful, and I had actually warned her about continuing to have the Angioplasties performed. I knew that it would be difficult for her to survive. Every time that she had one done, she nearly died. The hospital was scheduling her for one to be done every two weeks. Her family's continual statements of unbelief didn't help either. Unbelief is contagious. That is why the Bible tell us to surround yourself with people of like precious faith."

"Don't let any doubters be around me if I ever have to go to the hospital." Myra said.

"I know that this has been hard on you, and that it is so much fun when people live. Don't let this affect your faith. Remember healing was accomplished on that cross two thousand years ago. It isn't up to the Lord to do anything now, it is up to us to receive what he already did."

"Have you ever been healed?" Victoria asked.

"Of course, remember my broken nose."

"Do you think that God changed?"

"No, the scriptures say that he never changes."

"So are you still going to believe for healing in the future?" Victoria asked.

"Yes, it sure beats the alternative!"

"Sometimes people don't want to be healed."

"What? I mean I know, it just amazes me that they don't."

"If you are sick enough for long enough, and you know that you are going to heaven. Think about it, a new body, streets of gold, no pain, no bills, wouldn't you be tempted to yield to death?"

"I suppose."

"Maybe Donny really wanted to go home, and knew in her heart that it was her time. Sometimes we can outlive our appointed time on earth. Remember, we are citizens of heaven and temporary residents of earth. Medical science can maintain a life past its normal time."

"So, how do you know when to believe for someone to be healed?"

"As long as there is life there is hope. Do you remember the story of King David and Bathsheba having a son?

"Do mean Solomon?" Myra asked.

"No, Bathsheba became pregnant before they were married. David arranged for her husband to be killed, and then married her."

"Oh yes, I remember the story of her bathing on the roof."

"That's right, and this was the son that was born as a result of that incident. Anyway, the baby became ill. David fasted and prayed, and he heard the servants discussing the child in hushed tones. He knew that the child had died, so he quit fasting and mourning. The people asked why he had quit grieving when the child had died."

"What did he say?"

"He said that as long as the child lived there was hope, but once the child died that was the end."

"So I guess, we need to pray and believe for healing. The results are up to the person and their belief that the Lord meant what he said in the Bible."

"Even though healing is available for all. It is up to the person to believe that they can have it, and then to receive it. David and Bathsheba had committed sin, and so the baby died. It is important to live a holy life if you want miracles in your life. So many people think that us preachers just want to talk about sin and ruin everyone's fun. What they don't know is that the opposite is true."

"That is true. But Donny loved the Lord and surely she didn't sin." Myra said.

"I am not saying that she did, but I do know that if you are sinning you need to stop if you want healing. We aren't to judge people, and if the Lord tarries, we will all die."

"I don't want to think about death." Myra said.

"No one does." Victoria agreed. "One day we will understand these things, and when I get to heaven I plan to ask lots of questions."

"Me too," agreed Myra.

"By the way, did I mention that David was coming to see you tonight?"

Myra marveled that once again David knew instinctively when she needed him. She looked at her reflection in the hall mirror.

"Oh great, my hair is a mess, and my eyes are swollen half-shut, not to mention that my nail polish is messed up." Myra said, "I had better go wash my hair and put a cold pack on my eyes."

"That's my girl," Victoria laughed. "It is amazing what love will do for a hurting heart."

"I just hope that love is blind, where David is concerned." They both laughed.

Myra's heart ached and she needed David's loving arms. She would miss Donny more than she cared to admit. She knew that this had made her question her faith. Up until now, her success rate in praying for the sick had proved phenomenal. She remembered the newspaper article about the accident, and Scott being raised from the dead. How powerful and wonderful she had felt.

Here I thought that I was God's woman of faith and power, so what had gone wrong?

Why did Donny get healed of the clotting disease and then die? She wasn't even in the SICU; she was on a normal hospital floor. She remembered Victoria saying that sometimes a person gets healed of a sickness, but then the person dies not too long after that. Donny had died peacefully, so maybe it was her time to go home. She didn't know, and now she would have to deal with death on a new level.

I wonder if I will continue to pray for the sick with as much boldness as I have had before? Her heart said yes, but new seeds of doubt raced through her mind. If she didn't stop the negative thoughts, she knew that the seed would grow and hinder the Lord's plans for her.

The Lord's presence seemed far away. Maybe God is through with me, or maybe I wasn't even called to the ministry, she thought miserably. She couldn't seem to shake the heaviness that hung over her like a moist, oppressive blanket.

"Hurry David, I need you. Why is he taking so long to get here?" Myra said to herself, as she stroked Baby under the chin. Sullenly she sank into the recliner in her room, "Might as well read a few chapters from the Bible while I wait," she explained to Baby. Baby rubbed against her legs and purred. She thumbed through her Bible, but found herself yawning.

"Myra, David called and said that he was running late. He said he might be as long as an hour." Victoria's voice traveled up the stairs, although she couldn't see her.

"Thanks Victoria." Myra pondered what she would do for the next sixty minutes. "I suppose that I will take a nap," she replied as she stretched herself across the bed. In just a few moments, she had drifted into an uneasy sleep.

In the dream, Myra stood by her dresser in her bedroom. She sensed a powerful presence and heard a loud voice behind her that sounded like a trumpet blast. "Myra, I have called you for such a time as this, write down the things that you are about to see. This is your time of visitation, things are quickly coming upon the earth and you are to take my words and power to the people. Will you go for me?"

Myra turned to see who was a speaking to her, she gasped as she saw a brilliant light. In the middle stood someone she instinctively knew to be the Lord. He wore a long robe with a golden sash draped across his chest. His hair gleamed like fresh fallen snow, as he gazed at her with blue eyes that blazed with love and fire. She looked down to avoid his gaze and noticed that his feet were as bright as bronze that had been refined in a furnace. He spoke with a voice that thundered like a waterfall, or an ocean wave. His face glowed like the morning sun.

She fell at his feet, and noticed the nail scars, and she knew that she was on holy ground.

"Yes, Lord."

"Are you sure? Much danger surrounds this assignment, and you will have to stay close to me to succeed."

"Lord, I..." She didn't want to admit that she was afraid. In a moment she saw something that she did not understand. Masses of children wearing uniforms marched in columns. They carried automatic weapons. In a second, she saw first one plane and then another crash into the World Trade Center. She saw a militant leader receiving the Nobel Peace Prize, and then issuing orders for suicide bombings against Christians and Jews.

Men cheered and celebrated as they held the bloody entrails of a human in the streets of Jerusalem. What did this mean, and what could someone as small and insignificant as a young girl from Atherstone do against such violent hatred? She shuddered at the images that the Lord revealed to her.

"My daughter, don't be afraid. I am the one who died, but look I am alive forever and ever. He jangled large golden keys and said, 'I hold the keys of death and the grave.'

Myra remembered how the word of God gives precious promises, and a guarantee that as a believer she could overcome any problem.

She knew that her Lord loved her, but that he is a jealous God. He keeps his promises and expects us to keep ours. The Bible tells that he has not forgotten the Jewish people. How he will avenge his faithful servants in all the earth. The Bible foretells that one day there would be a final battle and a Day of Judgment would come. Once again he seemed to speak into her mind.

" Write down what you have seen, not just the things that are happening now, but also those things that are to come.

"I know of your love, faith, your service, and your patient endurance in the face of hard times. I know all the things that you do, and I have opened a door for you that no one can shut. You have little strength, yet you obeyed my word and did not deny me.

"Because you have obeyed the things that I have asked you to do, I will protect you from the great time of trial that is coming upon the whole world. Hold on to that which you have and let no one take your crown. Remember that all who are victorious sit with me on my throne."

What kind of crown do I have, she wondered. What does that mean? The Spirit spoke into her mind; "I have great plans for you, thoughts of good and not evil. But you must be patient, for there are perils ahead. Hold fast to what I have given you, and promised you and you will be victorious and cause multitudes to be saved. I am going to show you a glimpse of the evil that is to come upon the earth. You will to be strong, and you will only survive if you follow me closely. I will lead and guide you through these perilous times."

Myra felt the stone that lay under her blouse. "Yes, daughter it is my gift to you, and to remind you of your unique gifting." He seemed to speak into her mind, and she received revelation of assignments. The Spirit answered her unspoken questions. "Yes you will be able to continue to arrive and escape places that would seem impossible. When my Spirit is upon you nothing shall be impossible for you to do through me, prepare to be "translated."

"What is that?" Myra replied in her mind. It seemed that no speech was needed. She also noticed that she didn't seem to need to breathe. How amazing heaven proved to be.

"You will find yourself moved by the spirit to another location for a special assignment." The Spirit spoke into her mind again. "At such times, you feel as though you are indestructible and that no weapon could prevail against you. However, only when you are in my shadow are you totally safe. Otherwise you must use my word if attacked. Of course you are safe in heaven, no being would dare challenge you there."

"What weapons?" Myra wondered.

"The two-edged sword in your mouth." Speak my written words, for they have power to change your world.

"Oh." Myra said, as truth flooded her mind. She had heard it said that the spiritual world was more real than the one that she could see and touch. Now she understood that her very life would depend upon the knowledge of this truth.

A door opened through the ceiling; it seemed to be standing open in heaven. She heard a voice, the same one that had been speaking to her. The voice sounds like a trumpet blast, she thought. I wonder if trumpets are living creatures in heaven with voices. Then she remembered that she had never read anything about that in the sacred words. The voice called to her, "Come up here, and I will show you things that must happen."

"How will I do that?" Myra replied, but as she spoke she felt herself floating upwards toward the ceiling. I wonder if my whole body is going or just my spirit. She looked back and saw the room getting further away as she floated effortlessly upward. Soon she saw heaven, and then a bright light that grew brighter as she approached. She had arrived at the throne in heaven. She could just discern the shape of someone sitting upon the heavenly throne. What a fabulous sight, Myra strained to discern the form of the one who sat upon the throne. How brilliant he was like gemstones—jasper and other stones. She could not see his face, and she knew from the sacred words, that would not be permitted to see his face and live.

A rainbow circled his throne with the glow of an emerald. Twenty-four golden thrones surrounded him with twenty-four persons seated upon the thrones. An angel stood beside her and spoke to her mind, telling her that these were the Elders. Twelve from the ancient patriarchs of the Old Testament, and twelve were apostles from the New Testament. Elders wore gowns of unearthly, spotless white, and a golden crown sat upon their heads. Deafening sounds of thunder and flashes of lightning issued from the throne. Myra gasped as the thunder crashed and lightning forked around her. Flames danced as they rose from the seven lamp stands in front of the throne. She trembled and had great difficulty standing, an angel held her arm in support. The angel spoke into her mind, telling her that these were the seven spirits of God. They represented the seven facets of his work in the lives of his creation. These angels certainly weren't the wimpy looking creatures that she had seen pictured on the Christmas cards.

"Fear God and keep his commandments," The angel spoke into her mind. Myra felt God's love extending toward her. She knew that he wouldn't hurt her, but he had the capability of doing so if he had so desired. Myra wondered if the sea of glass in front of the throne was ice or crystal. She even wondered if anyone skated upon it. However, those thoughts passed as another peal of thunder brought her back to the awesome majesty of the throne. She sure wouldn't like to be the first one to zoom onto the glassy sea in a pair of skates in such a sacred place. She shuddered at the thought of the reaction that such behavior would invoke. Then she remembered that the angel could read her thoughts, and wondered if she was already in trouble for considering such a thing. However, the angel didn't say anything. *I suppose that he knows that I am a child.* To which the angel reminded her of the scripture that said, "Even a child is known by his doings whether they be good or bad."

She diverted her attention to the four living beings. Myra found it hard to look at them without wanting to run, they were frightening to say the least.

Eyes covered each of the four living being's bodies both front and back. They sat in front and around the throne. Myra knew that literally every eye focused upon her. The first creature resembled a lion, the second looked like an ox, the third had a human face, and the fourth had the form of an eagle with its wings spread as if in flight. She noticed that each of them had six wings. *How ironic, even the wings are covered with eyes inside and out.*

"Holy, holy, holy is the Lord God Almighty—the one who always was, who is, and who is to come." They cried in unison, and as they praised the one sitting on the throne, the twenty-four seated around the throne fell down and worshipped the one on the throne.

"You are worthy, O Lord our God, to receive glory and honor and power. For you created everything, and it is for your pleasure that they exist and were created." They said as they laid their crowns at his feet.

Suddenly, Myra saw a scroll in the right hand of the one who was seated on the throne. She noticed that there was writing on the inside and outside of the scroll. The scroll bore seven seals. An angel shouted with a strong voice. "Who is worthy to break the seals on this scroll and unroll it?"

But no one answered, and it seemed that no one in heaven or on earth was able to open the scroll and read it. Myra felt such sadness that she began to weep, because no one was worthy to open the scroll and read it.

One of the elders, comforted her and said, "Stop weeping, my child! Look, the Lion of the tribe of Judah, the heir to David's throne has conquered. He is worthy to open the scroll and break its seven seals." What does all this mean? She wondered.

Myra dried her eyes and looked. A beautiful yet wounded lamb stood majestically between the throne and the four living beings. The wounded lamb bore wounds on its body that would normally have been fatal. Yet it stood very much alive between the throne and the four living beings and among the twenty-four seated on the thrones. The Lamb had seven horns and seven eyes. The angel spoke to her mind, and she knew that the Lamb was symbolic of her wonderful Lord and that the seven eyes represented the seven spirits of God that are sent out into all the earth. The Lamb approached the throne and took the scroll from the one on the throne. Immediately he transformed into her wonderful Lord. As he had reached for the scroll, the four living beings and the twenty-four elders fell down before him. Each elder had a harp, and they held golden bowls filled with incense.

"What is in the bowls?" she asked in her mind.

"The bowls contain the prayers of God's people." The angel replied into her mind.

All of heaven burst into a new song:

"You are worthy to take the scroll and break its seals and open it. For you were killed, and your blood has bought back the people for God from every tribe and language and people and nation. And you have caused them to become God's priests and kingdom. They shall reign on the earth."

Myra looked again and she heard the singing of thousands and millions of angels around the throne, the living beings, and the elders. They continued singing in a mighty chorus:

"The Lamb is worthy—the Lamb who was killed. He is worthy to receive power and riches and wisdom, strength, honor, glory, and blessing."

Then it seemed as if she heard every creature in heaven and in earth and even under the earth and in the sea singing:
"Blessing and honor and glory and power belong to the one sitting on the throne and to the Lamb forever and ever."
"Amen," the four living creatures said, as the twenty-four elders fell upon their faces and worshipped God and the Lamb. They laid their crowns before the throne.
Myra marveled as she watched her Lord.
"Oh, angel, the Bible is true...every word of it."
"Look closely and see what happens," said the angel.
As Myra watched a globe appeared before them. It hovered before her as it slowly revolved. The United States drew her attention. An invisible force seemed to be propelling her toward the globe. She felt herself sliding into the globe. Continents whizzed past her, then states, then cities, and finally neighborhoods. She recognized the coastland of Atherstone Island. Soon her feet landed softly on grass. How amazing, she had landed just a couple of streets away from New Life Christian Youth Center. Towering above her was the old orphanage, known as "The Cradle." The moon silhouetted the imposing brick structure. Often she had passed by the old orphanage, she had wondered if anyone lived there, as she never saw lights or any activity around in the building. Now however, the building teemed with activity, every window was lit, and it was obvious that some kind of meeting was in progress. I wonder what the Lord wants me to do? Surely this can't be the purpose of my heavenly visitation. She crept quietly through the bushes until she was standing in the shadows of the massive front stairs. She heard voices, but could barely discern what was being discussed. She eased herself along the brick wall that seemed to be a basement that was partially buried in the ground, perhaps if she could get closer, she could hear what was being discussed. As she peered through the windows she saw several people in turbans.
Myra gasped, in the center of the group was a very tall bearded man dressed in a robe and a turban. He looked just like the leader of the organization responsible for blowing up major buildings in America. All the newscasters say that he is supposed to be in

Afghanistan and not Atherstone. No wonder the worldwide manhunt for this man had been unsuccessful, who would have thought of looking in Atherstone? What should she do? Surely the police would laugh at her for suggesting that he was in the small city of Atherstone. Then she remembered that this man's organization had declared war on America, especially on the Jews and Christians. She remembered someone explaining that the attacks were a result of their religious beliefs. They considered that the holy war, known as Jihad, which involved destroying America, Christians, and Jews was pleasing to their god Allah. Myra began to tremble, surely the hooded group that had been chasing them a couple of months ago were not as big a danger as these people.

"Lord," she whispered, "What do you want me to do? I am just a girl, and what am I against such people?" Then she remembered that Atherstone was near the area that produced much of the nation's oil. To make matters worse, she remembered hearing the Shepherds say that the Medical center, located in Atherstone, had a lab that was developing antidotes for chemical and biological warfare. Also there was a Mosque less than two miles away. As if that wasn't bad enough, she had heard that the coast guard base located just four miles away was being used to train military for the War on Terrorism.

Just as she was watching, she noticed one of the men looking in her direction. Terrified, Myra decided to inch her way toward the driveway gates. She had descended into the complex, so she had no way of knowing if the gates were locked. Above her, a door opened and she heard voices speaking in what sounded like Arabic. She bolted toward the driveway crashing through the bushes. The leaves crunched loudly under her feet as she hastily exited the property. Surely they had either seen her or heard her by now. If only she hadn't panicked. Gratefully, she noticed that the side entrance gate was open as she bolted down the driveway. She ran the two blocks to New Life Christian Center. She listened for the sound of footsteps, but heard none. Never was she so glad to see the Youth building. She fumbled in her purse and found the key. After she got in the door, and locked it she began to cry. She sank onto the couch by the door and sobbed. "Oh Lord, what do you want me to do?" It took her several minutes to regain her composure. She decided to call the Shepherds.

"Where have you been?" asked Victoria.

"I don't know, I must have been translated." She replied.

"David came to see you."

"Oh…I laid down for a nap, and then suddenly I saw heaven. I must have dreamed because I ended up outside the old orphanage." Myra replied. "Victoria, this is so scary I saw several men in turbans, and they resembled the terrorists."

"I thought that you were upstairs taking a nap." Replied Victoria. "My, you are a girl who has many strange adventures."

On the way home, the Shepherds listened to her story of all that had happened. They listened grimly without saying anything.

"You do believe me don't you?" she asked.

"Yes, of course." Pastor Shepherd replied. "This is very serious, and I sincerely hope that you are mistaken. However, given the nature of the vision that you have had, I am sure that the people you saw were the terrorists. Much prayer needs to be given to this situation. Say nothing of this to anyone, apart from David, until we have heard from the Lord on this matter."

"Yes but can't I tell Louise?" she asked.

"I suppose," he said.

"Remember that we do prayer walking on Wednesdays and we pray over the city." Myra said. "We will be careful, but I know that you can trust Louise. She is such a powerful intercessor."

"Yes, but the fewer people who know about this the safer we will be." He added.

"Let us refer to the man as "Esau," and his organization as merely, "the Terrorists." That way no one needs to know that we know his true identity." Pastor Shepherd said. "Remember these are dangerous people who hate Christians."

CHAPTER THIRTEEN

It is written:
"Surely you desire truth in the inner parts:
you teach me wisdom in the inmost place."

Louise listened distractedly as Myra talked.
"Louise? Are you listening to me?" she said. She had just finished telling her about hearing the Arabic voices, and seeing the turbaned men at the old orphanage.
"Yeah I heard you. Don't you remember what happened when we did prayer walking around the new Mosque, while it was under construction?"
"Oh yes." Myra answered. Immediately she remembered how the two of them had gone to the place. The foundation had been laid, and skeletal beams had been placed. No one had worked on the building in several years. Rumor had it that the Mosque was about to be finished. So this particular day, Louise and Myra had decided to "Prayer walk" the property. Prayer walking consisted of the two of them praying, and placing wooden Popsicle sticks containing scriptures in the ground or around the strategic site.
As they walked they were reclaiming the City's land, particularly land that was being used for purposes that were viewed as being harmful for its residents. With all the terrorist activity in America, most citizens viewed mosques with suspicion. Even though most people knew that the majority of those that would attend, would be law-abiding citizens who didn't support the Jihad agenda of the fanatics.

They had gone to the site, and were in the process of walking around the foundation, and placing the Popsicle sticks inside the structure, even in the cracks of the foundation. They were almost finished when a turbaned, bearded man approached them.

"What are you dong?" he asked.

"We were just looking at the land. Is it for sale?" Myra asked.

"No, do you know what this is?" the man asked. He seemed highly agitated that they were walking on the land.

"Is it for sale?" Myra asked again. Louise remained quiet.

"Don't you know what this is?" The man asked, his face inches away from Myra's. She decided that she had better play the "dumb blonde role." She chose to pretend that she was stupid. She didn't like the man's attitude or the tone of his voice. Meanwhile, Louise was praying under her breath.

"You mean that this property is not for sale?" Myra asked.

"No, it is a mosque." He said.

"I thought that maybe you were going to sell the land, since nothing has been done with it."

"No, it is a mosque, do you know what a mosque is?" he asked.

"Yes, so I guess that means that you aren't selling the land? We have been looking for land. I suppose that we will have to tell our people that it isn't available." Myra said, realizing that she was wearing the ministry t-shirt that bore the legend, "We dare you to experience the power of God" on a patch resembling a brick wall. Although the patch was on her back, she was sure that he had seen it. Louise and Myra excused themselves and left the property.

"That was too scary. Did you see the way the man looked at you?" Louise asked.

"Yes, I knew that he didn't buy the dumb blonde approach." Myra answered.

"Yeah, did you see the sign on the building across from the Mosque? It was a circle with a cross in it with a slash through it. That means that they are Anti-Christians. I wanted to say, Myra let's get out of here." Louise said.

"Me too, but I was trying to say something that would explain what we were doing. Thank heavens he didn't see us place all those

Popsicle sticks, especially the ones that talked about the blood of Jesus. I'll bet that mosque will never be the same," Myra added. They both laughed.

"Prayer walking with you is an adventure. I never know what you are going to do next. I thought that I was going to faint. Do you know who that guy looked like?" Louise asked.

"I think so."

"He looked like that terrorist guy, you know."

"You mean Esau?"

"Yeah, and they say that they can't find him." Louise added.

"It sure looked like him."

"Wouldn't that be something if he was in Atherstone? They have searched all over the world and here he is right in our back yard." Louise said.

"I think that he is too short, Esau is really tall." Myra added.

"I heard that he had a brother that kept his plane on an airfield in Sealy." Louise said.

"Really?" Myra asked. "That is only thirty miles away."

"Yes, we had better be careful, that guy was really mad." Louise said. They had left the mosque and were returning to New Life Christian Center.

"Hey, do you want to walk over to the orphanage?" Myra asked.

"Why did I have the feeling that you were going to suggest that?" Louise asked.

"I just wondered if all those people were still there." Myra replied.

"Just what are you going to say to them, especially if the guy from the mosque goes over there? Surely you are not going to ask him if he is selling property?" Louise asked.

"Well...."

"I am waiting to hear how you are going to explain this one. You are going to get us in trouble." Louise said.

"You are right, and I am sorry. Let's just go back to the church." Myra said. Louise looked thoughtful.

"I think that maybe we need to ask what God wants us to do. I didn't want to go, but maybe this is a divine assignment." Louise said.

The two prayed silently for several minutes, before anyone broke the silence.

"You know what?" Louise said.

"What?"

"This could be an assignment, but we are going to have to be careful."

"You mean walk by the orphanage?" Myra asked.

"Do you have any more Popsicle sticks with you?" Louise asked.

"No, but we could make some. After all the church is only two blocks away. Myra added.

They went back to the church and made the Popsicle sticks with the scriptures.

"Maybe we had better pray a little more before we go." Myra said.

"What? You want us to pray? Has it come to that?" Louise joked.

"Yeah, we had better pray!"

They were about to leave when Pastor Tom called them into his office.

"You wouldn't be making those sticks so that you can go and 'Prayer Walk' around a certain orphanage would you?" he asked.

"How did you know?" Myra asked.

"The Holy Spirit told me."

"Oh." Myra and Louise said in unison.

"Maybe we had better go somewhere else," Louise suggested.

"I think that is wiser." Myra added.

"This might be perfect. Do you remember me telling you about the research building near the hospital? You remember, the one that has the terrible odor, and the razor wire on the top of the chain link fence?" Louise said.

"Yes," Myra answered. "Why don't we go pray around it?" Louise said.

"Good idea." Myra said. The two drove toward the east end of Atherstone. The hospital complex sat on the edge of the city perched like a huge octopus with its tentacles spreading in many directions.

The complex gobbled neighboring properties in a never-ending quest to meet the growing, health demands of the community.

They parked and walked across to a small brown building, wedged between two other hospital buildings. Myra wrinkled her nose as the pungent odor of hay and urine reached her nostrils. The place gave her eerie feeling, and she felt that they were being watched.

"What is this place?" Myra asked.

"I don't know. But I do know that something is horribly wrong with it." Louise said. "My daughter and I walk past it, and sometimes the smell is so bad that it makes us want to gag."

Louise looked around and whispered in Myra's ear. "Yeah, rumor has it that they were doing research and using the prisoners." Louise added.

"How do you know that?" Myra asked as she glanced up at the structure of the prison hospital that towered over the other hospitals. The massive structure resembled an impenetrable fortress. Joseph, one of the prison ministers, had told them about a prisoner who had begged the Amityville Department of Corrections not to send him to this hospital. He said that he was afraid, and felt that he would die if they sent him there.

"I wonder if this has anything to do with the Research Institute?" Louise asked. "I had a dream that someone was experimenting on the prisoners." Louise said. "Like I said, this place gives me the creeps when I walk by it, and why would anyone need razor wire to keep out caged animals? Surely no one would want to steal them."

"What kind of research are they doing?"

"No one seems to know, but I want to find out." Louise said. "I have been wondering ever since I heard from the Mission that some of the homeless men have been disappearing." Louise added. "I can't help but think that this place has something to do with it. If a homeless man disappeared, it would take a while before anyone knew that he was missing."

"Great, as if we don't have enough problems. I mean considering that the man I saw could be the infamous Esau. Now I am wondering about people disappearing. Our city is small. How could all this be happening in our little city? Surely it couldn't be connected?"

Myra gazed up at the razor wire, and tried to see through the decorative openings in the brick wall in front of the building. She could vaguely discern cages, but that was all. They continued walking and praying but neither of them spoke.

"You wait and see, something evil dwells here." Louise said.

Later that evening, Myra excused herself while the family watched television. In her room, she knelt beside the bed. Absentmindedly, she fingered the stone that hung around her neck.

"Holy Spirit, you said that this stone would be a contact point for you to take me places that I cannot ordinarily go." She paused and added, "Would you take me into the hospital's Research Institute? I want to know the truth about it."

She scarcely breathed, sitting as still as possible. Silence overwhelmed her as she waited; the second hand crept around her watch slowly. Once again, she glanced at her watch, only to notice that less than two minutes had elapsed. What if there were murders being done, and someone discovered that she knew so much, should she ask to know more? She already knew enough to threaten her safety and those that she loved.

"Holy Spirit, maybe I don't need to know more." The minutes continued to crawl past as she waited. Slowly a light began to fill the room. Her body shook uncontrollably, until she lowered her body to the floor. She fell on her face as an awesome fear swept over her. A holy presence had begun to fill the room; slowly a swirling mist began to form in front of her. An invisible wind blew her curtains upward. At first, she rubbed her eyes thinking, is this real? A wonderful fragrance reached her nostrils, like the scent of roses. Surely this couldn't be her imagination.

"Holy Spirit?" she whispered.

"Daughter, you have asked a difficult thing, nevertheless come and see," spoke an audible voice. The voice terrified her as she shrank away from it. She dismissed the thought that someone could be hiding in the room. No amount of money could have convinced her to move from her spot.

Within a few minutes, her body began to lift into the air, propelled by what she believed to be the Spirit. The bedroom windows flew open as she approached the windowsill. Once again she was being supernaturally transported. Can people see me she wondered? Yet no one seemed to notice. What if the Shepherds come looking for me, she thought. Immediately, She heard the Spirit, "Do not fret, for they will not even know that you are gone."

Soon she felt her body descending though the roof of the prison hospital and into a room. Standing behind the team of doctors, she strained to see the object of their attention. A man who was covered with horrible ulcers on both his upper arms and face lay on the bed, occasioning coughing a rasping cough as he gasped for air. His chest rose and fell erratically. She listened to the doctor's conversation. A stench filled the room, probably as a result of the oozing ulcers on the man's arms and face.

"We are going to be giving you daily cleansing baths for these ulcers." One of the doctors said. "Tell me, were you exposed to a white powder within the last three weeks?"

"No, just when I went for tests last week."

"You mean at the Research Institute?" They asked.

"They gave me a strange powder to place on my tongue." The man said.

She heard them discussing amongst themselves. "Who scheduled an inmate to be sent there?" Another added, "Maybe we need to recheck this chart. Why would they have ordered the Research Institute to be conducting tests on this man?"

"I don't know," replied a small man in a lab coat. "Perhaps because they suspected that he had contracted an unusual ailment."

"Yes, but everyone knows that no unorthodox treatment is to be done on the offenders," said another. The team member scowled and shook his head, "Most unusual and definitely not with hospital protocol for prisoners." The team finished concurring and turned to the patient. Myra strained to listen and see the man's face. Apparently no one had noticed her in the room.

"It is possible that you have contracted Anthrax." The doctor said. The group around him nodded in ascent.

"Anthrax, oh my God, how could I have gotten that? I am in prison." The offender said.

"We don't know, but you will be in strict isolation while you are being treated. The source of this must be found. It must be kept a secret to prevent mass panic," said another.

"Anthrax...." Myra gasped, but no one seemed to hear or see her. So this is what they were doing, they were using the prisoners to contract diseases suspected to be used by the terrorists in biological or chemical warfare.

"Were you around any cows or sheep?" One of the doctors asked.

"No, I have been in prison. I have never even seen the prison farm," replied the offender. He appeared to be very frightened.

"We need to find out where he was exposed to this disease, and then notify the authorities before there is an outbreak," another added.

Perspiration suddenly drenched the offender's face as he lurked forward, his eyes staring as if he had seen an apparition. The man coughed and blood poured out his mouth and onto the bedclothes.

The team hurriedly left the inmate's room; no attempt was made to resuscitate him.

Holy Spirit, the man is dying and no one stayed to help him, what do I do? Louise was right something was horribly wrong. The man lay with his eyes staring toward the ceiling, how Myra hoped that he knew the Lord before he had taken his last breath.

A nurse wearing a gown, mask, and gloves scurried into the room and covered the corpse with a sheet. Didn't they know that Anthrax was so deadly that it could easily spread and that the whole city could be affected?

What if the Research Institute was a cover for an inside terrorist operation? Myra knew that she already possessed dangerous information. These people would stop at nothing to hide the truth from being discovered. If what she suspected proved to be true, the city could be at risk, and she would be a marked woman.

CHAPTER FOURTEEN

It is written:
"Therefore judge nothing before the time, until the Lord come, who both will bring to light the hidden things of darkness, and will make manifest the counsels of the hearts: and then shall every man have praise of God."

    Myra and Louise stared at Hank in disbelief. Surely they were mistaken, a homeless man who appeared to be wearing mascara and lipstick, and if that wasn't enough he had on gold slippers. Yet he was a man. They knew that he had been healed of many ailments such as Multiple Sclerosis and Cancer. They listened as he excitedly told them of his treatments at the hospital.
    "Tomorrow I start a new treatment," he said.
    "What kind of treatment?" Myra asked.
    "They said it is so new that they ought to take it out and spank it." He laughed.
    Louise looked confused, "What do you mean?"
    "Oh you know, like spanking a brand new baby." Hank joked.
    "Just where do you go for this?" Myra asked.
    "It isn't in the regular part of the hospital." Hank pulled out pieces of paper covered with numbers and handwriting. He wrinkled his nose and continued to search through his papers. "Got it here somewhere," he added before proudly flourishing a scrap of paper. "Here it is," he said as he pressed his eye as close as possible to the paper. Obviously he had problems with his vision, and was extremely near-sighted. "Have to go to the Research Institute tomorrow first thing in the morning."

"The Research Institute," Myra and Louise chorused.

"Yeah, that's the one, they have some kind of special treatment that they are testing." Myra and Louise stared at one another. Neither one spoke for several minutes.

"Is there a problem with that?" He asked. He had a habit of raising one eyebrow, giving him a comical appearance.

"Hank, can we talk to you for a few minutes?"

"Sure," he said.

"I mean alone and out of earshot of people." Louise added.

"I haven't eaten today, so how about if we go somewhere and eat. We'll buy you lunch." Myra added.

"Sounds good to me," Hank said smiling. Myra thought, how are we going to tell him our suspicions? She already knew that Hank was under Psychiatric treatment. He suffered from Paranoia, and her suspicions would only make this problem worse.

Hank gobbled his sandwich quickly while gesturing with his hands, and talking excitedly between swallows. He seemed so happy that the Research Institute was using him to test a new drug. He talked about his long illness, and the problems of being homeless.

"Hank, why don't you let us go with you?"

"Why?" He said once again wrinkling his nose and raising an eyebrow. He looked at Louise, and winked saying, "I think that Myra likes me." Louise rolled her eyes.

"So why do you want to go with me to the Research Institute?" He asked again.

"That way you wouldn't have to ride the bus back to the Mission." Myra replied.

"You mean you weren't going to stay with me?" he asked.

"Well...I, we...weren't really sure. As a matter of fact we had kind of wanted to see the inside of the place."

"Thanks but Sherry, my MHMR counselor, is going to take me there." Hank said. Myra searched for the right words to say. She didn't want people asking questions about why they wanted to see the inside of the place. Yet they were concerned for his safety, but they didn't want to alarm him, especially if their suspicions were unfounded. Finally she found the right words.

"Actually, we are doing some work on the gym, and had hoped that you would be able to work tomorrow. We will pay you and provide your meals while you work." Hank eagerly agreed to see them the next day. She knew that he wouldn't be able to resist the thought of money and food." We didn't know if you would be able to work the day after treatment."

"No problem, I'll see you the day after tomorrow." Hank said. As he walked away, Louise and Myra shook their heads. "This is not good," Louise added. "Maybe we should follow him tomorrow?"

"We don't know where he stays. Besides you can't follow a street person without them knowing it." Louise said.

Two days later, Hank failed to come to the church. Myra paced the floor while remembering that he wasn't always reliable about his commitments. Later that afternoon, Myra and Louise walked to the Mission.

The sight of Sherry's blue Honda parked by the curb, and a long line of homeless people waiting outside the MHMR office told them that Sherry was counseling in her office. After waiting for several minutes, their patience was rewarded as her office door opened. She greeted them warmly.

"Have you seen Hank?" Louise asked.

"Not today, I took him to an appointment yesterday." Sherry replied.

"Didn't you stay with him?" Myra asked.

"No, I just dropped him off, because I had a full case load that day."

"When did he return to the Mission?" Louise asked.

"I don't know that he did, he doesn't stay here." Sherry replied. "Why has something happened?"

"We told him that we had some work for him to do today." Louise said, "He knew that we were paying him, and feeding him."

"That's not like him to not show up for food," Sherry laughed. Her eyes sparkled as she tossed her raven hair, "Hey, he is a survivor and I am sure that he is all right." Myra tried to smile, even though she knew that Sherry would be very upset if she knew the reason for her concern. Sherry eyed them and said, "Talk to me. What's going on?" Sherry's sensitivity to the Holy Spirit was well known, "Come to think of it, I didn't like that place. So let's pray," she said as she grabbed their hands and made a circle. "I am sure that I will hear from him, but let's pray for his safety." The three bowed their heads and prayed. As they prayed a wind blew through the trees as if to confirm the urgency for prayer. "Let me know if you hear from him." Sherry said.

"Likewise, would you let us know if you hear from him?" Myra replied.

They were driving along Harbor Drive when Myra turned toward the hospital.

"Where are you going?" Louise asked.

"Call it woman's intuition or just a hunch, or the Holy Ghost." Myra smiled.

"Uh-oh, sounds like trouble," Louise laughed.

They rounded the bend and Myra pulled the car along a side street. " Let's walk over to the Research Institute." As they walked down the sidewalk, they noticed a blue van parked in the driveway. A labyrinth of pipes and tubes, resembling ductwork, connected the van to the building. "What in the world is all this?" Louise asked. They heard the sound of voices, and decided to hide behind some bushes near a rose garden that was adjacent to the building. Fire ants bit Myra's foot. She brushed them off while trying not to make a sound.

"Look they are carrying something," Louise said. Two men emerged from the building with something heavy in a black plastic bag and loaded it unceremoniously into the truck. The two men strolled casually back to the building.

"What do you think is in the bag?" Louise asked. "It looked really heavy. Surely it wasn't just trash."

"I don't know. The twilight makes it so hard to see, and soon it will be dark," replied Myra.

"I sure would like to know."

"Me too," replied Myra

"Do you think that we ought to follow the truck?" Louise asked.

"You read my thoughts, exactly," Myra said. The men went back into the building. They waited for several minutes to see if they would drive away, but there was no more activity.

"Maybe we had better go home," Louise said.

"Patience my friend, let's wait. If my hunch is correct they will not want to leave that bag in the van in this heat for very long." Sure enough, within fifteen minutes, they returned with another smaller bag. The two men climbed into the cab, and started the engine.

"We need to get to the car, so that we can follow them before we lose them. However, I don't want them to see us, pray for all red lights on Harbor Drive, provided that is the direction that they are going." Just as they were about to cross to their car, they saw Hank.

"Hank! What happened? Why didn't you come yesterday?" Myra asked.

"I overslept and missed my appointment with the Institute. That is why I was here. I was hoping to get it rescheduled. However, it seems that isn't going to happen anytime soon. They are quitting the new program!"

"Great!" Louise said.

"What do you mean?" Hank said eyeing them suspiciously.

"That's O.K. You don't want to know. Hey we were just leaving, have a great evening." Myra yelled as they ran for the car.

Once they were in the car, they drove frantically trying to catch up with the blue van. They could just see it several blocks away. "Hurry we are about to lose it," Louise said.

They had gone just a couple of blocks when a big UPS truck pulled in front of them from a side street blocking their view. Myra craned her neck straining to see.

"I can't believe that I lost the van!" she moaned.

"Let's just ask God to show us where it went," Louise said. The two prayed as Myra drove. Myra made a sharp right turn. They drove for several minutes in silence, stopping the car at every intersection, as they scanned the street in both directions before proceeding. "I think I know where they are going!"

Myra drove the car onto the bridge leading to an adjoining island. One could sense the ghosts that hovered over the bridge, most likely a result of the island's history of slave trade. They drove down the main road on the island, before they spotted the blue van. The van was parked in the distance on what was known as "the flats," which was the leeward side of the island. They drove slowly down the road and parked. The island had few scrub bushes and places to hide. The oppressive atmosphere settled on them as a misty fog blew across the road.

"I wonder why they call it "Flamingo Isle?" "Raven Isle would be more like it since this place is creepy. I wonder if anyone has seen us." Myra said. They knew that the probability was high that they had been seen. The van sat at an angle, perched on deep ruts most likely from dirt bikes, and vehicles that had been stuck in the mud from the recent flooding. The island was also known for its bike trails.

"What is on the side of that hill?" Myra asked.

"I think that there are rocks, and water but not much of a beach. No one goes out there, and it has been years since I have been on the island." Louise said.

"Great place for a murder," Myra said. "Besides I heard that the crabs will eat a body in just a few hours."

"Thank you for that wonderful piece of information!" Louise laughed. "Do you think that they are disposing of people over there?"

"I don't know. What do we do now?" Myra asked.

"Maybe we should come back later, like tomorrow during daylight and see if anything is left."

"Good idea, I think that we need to get out of here before anyone wonders what two girls are doing in the dark in this deserted place." Louise said.

"Louise, look gun shells…lots of them."

"Either some one liked to do target practice or something really bad happened here."

"What could they be hunting on this island?"

"Maybe they are shooting some birds?" Louise said. "I heard that they have wild pigs on this island."

"Let's get out of here now." Myra said. "I don't have a good feeling about this."

Her stomach had a distinct scratchy, queasy feeling. She had learned to listen to her gut feelings. Often it was the Lord trying to warn her that something was horribly wrong.

They hurried back to the car, and left the island. "Let's come early tomorrow morning and see if we can see anything." They agreed to meet the next morning.

That night sleep eluded Myra, as she tossed and turned before drifting into a light sleep. She dreamed about the van and the island. In the dream the two girls were running over the flats looking for something but unable to find it. She heard the voice of the Lord say, "Look over here." When she looked to her left she saw a pile of rocks just off a makeshift jetty. A piece of black plastic seemed to be caught on a portion of the rock that jutted out of the water. Soon after the dream she awakened. She tried to remember the dream, and then she remembered the part about the voice of the Lord saying, "Look over here." She bolted out of bed and quickly showered and dressed. Louise would definitely want to know about her dream.

They drove to the site, where they had seen the van; Myra shared the dream with Louise. As expected, the blue van was gone. They walked toward the hill carefully stepping around the ruts on the soft ground. Trash abounded on the flats, each having a history that pricked their curiosity. "Wouldn't you like to know what really happened out here?" Myra said. Just as they spoke a biker rode past them. "Where did he come from?"

"This whole thing is making me nervous." Louise said.

"Let's pray, and bind any enemy from harming us. " Myra said. "The Bible says: 'No weapon that is formed against thee shall prosper; and every tongue that shall rise against thee in judgment thou shall condemn. This is the heritage of the servants of the Lord, and their righteousness is of me, says the Lord.'"

"Here is another one, just in case that we run into snakes. 'And these signs shall follow them that believe; in my name shall they cast out devils; they shall speak with new tongues;

They shall take up serpents; and if they drink any deadly thing, it shall not hurt them; they shall lay hands on the sick, and they shall recover.'"

With that, the two continued walking up the worn dirt bike trail on the hill.

"Don't move, look right over there is a snake...a Pigmy Rattlesnake," Myra said pointing to a spot on the path a few feet away.

"Where is it? I don't see it." Louise asked.

"Right over there, it blends in with the rocks."

"Look, it is stiff and it isn't moving."

"That is because we prayed." They decided to climb the hill another way. As they reached the top of the hill, a panoramic view of the bay unfolded before them. The surf lapped upon the rocks about forty yards away, and the grass rustled in the light breeze. The salty smell of the ocean filled their nostrils. They walked through the scrub brush as they carefully made their way to the water. Myra couldn't help looking more at the ground than where they were going. Especially after having seen the Pigmy Rattler.

"I wonder where they went, and what they did with those bags." Myra said.

"My thoughts exactly, but you know what?" Louise said.

"What?" Myra replied.

"I believe that God is going to show us. Remember the dream, where you saw a piece of black plastic near the rocks?"

"Yes?"

"Look over there," Louise said pointing to her left, "There is the makeshift jetty, and I see some rocks nearby. Let's check it out."

The two walked over to the jetty and noticed the rocks, but they were just far enough that they couldn't reach them, even though they reached out with stick. "I wonder how deep the water is." Myra asked.

"Looks pretty deep to me," Louise said. "Can you swim?"

"Yes, but I don't have my swim suit with me, and I don't want to get these clothes wet. Do you have a swim suit?" Myra laughed for she knew that Louise carried a large black bag, and that she seemed prepared for every emergency. One time they had needed a screwdriver, and she had reached in her bag and produced exactly what they had needed. Another time it had rained, and once again she had reached into the bag and produced a yellow plastic raincoat.

"Yes, as a matter of fact I came prepared, I am wearing my swimsuit." After pulling a towel out of her black bag, she took off her blouse and slacks. "I am ready if you are?"

"Hey, I am just going to cheer you on from the jetty!" Myra replied. She dipped a hand into the water; it was clear and cool to her touch. She looked to see if she could see any fish.

Louise eased herself into the water, "I'd dive but I don't know how deep it is. I don't want to dive into two feet of water." She laughed. "It's cooler than the ocean, and it is deep here too." She swam to the rocks, once she reached them she ran her hands over the sides of them, and then reached under water to feel any evidence of the plastic bags. "I don't see or feel anything yet."

Myra saw the piece of plastic. "Look to your right," she said, as Louise moved to her right. "There under that one rock on the side." Louise swam over to the rock and grabbed the plastic. She looked around, evidently to see if anyone was watching, "It is stuck pretty hard." After tugging on it, her efforts were rewarded when the bag pulled free.

"Careful whatever is in it might be contagious," Myra cautioned. "Remember the guy who died of Anthrax."

"Now you tell me, now that I am in the water with it! I am glad that I believe the scriptures that say, if I drink any deadly thing, or in my case even if I touch any deadly thing it will not harm me."

"Thank God for the scriptures!" Myra said.

Louise dragged the bag to the shore, and the two of them lifted it to the jetty. "I wonder where the second bag is. Weren't there two bags loaded on the truck?" Myra asked.

"Yes, this is the smaller one." Louise said as she opened the bag and dumped the contents onto the jetty. Out rolled a human head, one that had begun to smell. The nauseating odor caused Myra to wrinkle her nose. "I wish that I had a clothespin to put on my nose. The smell is nauseating." The head looked like that of a balding Hispanic man, his mouth drawn open in a silent scream. Myra and Louise both recoiled in horror.

"That looks like a real, human head." Myra said.
"It is, and it looks like one of the men who come or I should say, came to the Mission." Louise said.
"Whose idea was it to follow the truck?" Louise added.
"Yours."
"No it was your idea." Louise said.
"Fine, just blame me!"
"What do we do now?" Louise said.
"I suggest that we leave." Myra said adding, "We can call the police from the church."
"You aren't going to leave him here are you?" Louise said.
"What? You mean that you want me to put the man's head back in the plastic bag and put it my car? Myra asked. "Besides it stinks. I sure hope that isn't Warren, although it looks like him."
"I don't know, but you can't leave him."
"Right, I can just see what could happen. We are on our way back to Atherstone, and a policeman just happens to pull us over, and he notices the smell and the bag. What do I say when he asks about it? 'By the way I have this head in the back seat that I just happened to find.' I don't think that story will work, do you? They are going to say that we murdered him. This is not my idea of how to start a prison ministry. Besides what if he died of Anthrax? I sure hope that neither of us touched him. Be sure and wash your hands carefully."

As they made their way back to their car, they followed the small but well-worn path up the hill. The sound of an animal's squeal reached their ears, the closer that they got to the top of the hill. "What was that?" Myra asked.

"Sounds like a pig, doesn't it?" Louise asked.

"Look over there," Myra said pointing to a clump of scrub trees. A small piglet had caught its foot in a scrub tree's trunk. It squealed and yanked its foot, staring at them in wild-eyed terror.

"Look, its trapped, and it is kind of cute." Myra said.

"Don't touch it; you never know where the mother is." Louise said, looking around nervously.

"But it is caught, and it would be so easy to free it. Besides, I have never seen a wild pig before." Myra added. The little piglet was blackish gray and somewhat resembled a domestic pig. "It probably weighs about fifteen pounds."

"Don't look now, but its mother doesn't weigh any fifteen pounds. That is the biggest pig that I have ever seen. She looks like she weighs about five hundred pounds." Louise said as she pointed to an object that was walking toward them in the distance.

"Let's get out of here; have you seen the size of her tusks?" The animal's tusks were long and curved viciously upward.

"Why do I feel like I am on an African safari with a Rhinoceros walking towards us?" Louise said.

"No time to talk, let's just run!" Myra said as the two girls broke into a run, as they closed the last few yards to the car. The sow had increased her pace to a lope and then a full charge as she bore down upon them. Myra fumbled with her keys.

"Hurry, she's closing in, she is really big, and she looks really mad!" Louise said.

They could hear the grunts of the enraged sow as she hurled herself toward the car. At last Myra got the doors of the car open, and they climbed in and slammed the doors. The sow still charged toward the car, undaunted by the vehicle as it sprang to life when Myra started it. Fortunately Myra was able to drive away from the charging sow, but she couldn't travel very fast on the soft flats. She dodged the water-filled ruts as she drove the last fifty yards toward the gravel path that led to the road. The sow continued to charge, and was now only a few yards away.

"What do you think that she is going to do if she catches us before we get on the road? Do you think that she will try to attack the car?" Louise asked.

"I don't know but I think that this is the time to exercise our authority as believers!" Myra said. Abruptly the car hit a rut and lurched forward, before settling back on the ground.

"That is enough," Myra said, "God has not given me a spirit of fear, but of power, love and a sound mind." She stopped the car, and rolled down the window just as the sow angrily changed direction and charged toward her door.

"I can count every hair on her back! This is not good," Louise said.

"In Jesus name, I command you to stop!" Myra yelled at the sow. The sow slowed and looked at Myra with a strange expression.

"In Jesus name, I bind you from touching this vehicle or either of us." Myra added.

The sow abruptly turned and trotted back in the direction that she had come. Myra and Louise were shaking, but happy. They shouted and laughed all the way back to the church.

As they pulled the car alongside the curb outside of the church, Myra said, "What a day that we have had. I don't know about you, but I won't forget this day any time soon."

"I told you that going places with you is an adventure. Why can't we go prayer walking like everybody else without wild sows charging us, and getting stuck in the ruts?" Louise paused, and added, "Oh yes, I forgot, what about the head?"

"I think that it is time that we tell our Pastor what two of his parishioners have found." Myra said.

The Pastors listened to the two girls told about the day's events. Pastor Tom was known for his endless teasing. As usual he attempted to add some humor to the horrible situation. "Why, you are two girls just looking to get a-head."

"That is not funny." Myra said, giving him a reproachful look, "I am going to call the police and tell them what and where we found the head."

"Yes of course, that is the right thing to do," Pastor Tom said, trying to recover from his ill-timed attempt at humor.

"Seriously, do you think that they might suspect us of having anything to do with the murder?" Myra asked.

"Do you think that anyone in their right mind would report such a find if they did the crime?" asked Pastor Tom. "Besides people know of your character, and the fact that you are girls. It would take a very physically strong person or persons to do this crime."

Nervously, the girls waited for the policeman to arrive. Myra paced the floor like a caged lion. Two Policemen arrived about thirty minutes later, and took the information from them. As they were leaving, Myra asked, "Would you let us know what happens?" She hoped that her questions wouldn't cause the policeman to wonder if she was guilty.

"I can't promise you anything on that, because it could jeopardize the investigation. However, I will do what I can." The policemen promised.

Just hours later, reporters were knocking on the church door. "This is a small city; you can't do much of anything without reading about it the next day in the paper." Myra said.

"True but you must admit it is a gruesome find." Louise added.

That evening David and Myra listened to the evening news and the report of the head that had been found. They listened as the newscaster showed both bags. They explained that a second bag had been found nearby. The second bag contained the remains of a torso and an arm. The man had been identified as one of the city's homeless men.

"Oh, that was Warren, and we all knew him," Myra said to David.

"I remember him; he was such a harmless man, although he did have an irritating personality. I remember when Warren had visited our church. He complained that our music was too loud and would wake the babies across the street."

"David, I wonder if they tested the man for any diseases, you know like...Anthrax."

"Anthrax is a disease that terrorists use." David said, after she had told him about the Research Institute and the blue van. Together they told the Shepherds the whole story.

"Let's pray about this. After all, Myra would not be able to explain how she had gotten into the prison hospital to see the man die of Anthrax." Pastor Tom said. "We don't want to obstruct justice, but we don't want to endanger Myra and Louise. Also, the terrorists might be wondering what you know about the Research Institute. Not to mention what you were doing following the blue van."

CHAPTER FIFTEEN

It is written:
"I can do all things through Christ which strengtheneth me."

Myra leaned on her mop, and glanced at her watch. Could it really be eight thirty? She felt so fatigued, and yet there was so much to do, even though it was past time for her to go home. She continued to lean on her mop, while she reflected on the events of last few days. They had been traumatic to say the least. Not only had they found a decapitated human head, but also a wild sow had chased them. To make matters worse, just a couple of days ago, she and David had decided to eat dinner at a local diner. No sooner had they been served, than a man had walked in and sat adjacent to them. His head resembled that of the decapitated man. He had turned and smiled at her, revealing a row of yellowish teeth that reminded her of the homeless man. Her reaction had been immediate; she had burst into tears, and left the restaurant sobbing. A bewildered David had offered apologies to the waitress, as he hastily paid the bill and followed her. David had been very understanding, even though she had felt like an idiot.

Talk about being an idiot, here she was cleaning at night in a floodlit gymnasium, clearly visible to the outside world, in a dangerous part of town. Not the safest thing for her to do, considering that she might have been seen discovering the head. She never knew if someone had been watching them the morning that they found it. Especially since she might also have been seen spying at the old orphanage, and then beating a hasty retreat by running through the grounds. What if the two had been connected, and someone had wondered, just how much this strawberry blonde knew about their unsavory business.

This had been her first time to be in the building alone at night, and she had to admit that it gave her a creepy feeling. The building had been the old YMCA, and the former director swore that it was haunted. However, with her experience with the supernatural, she knew that ghosts were disembodied spirits that tried to counterfeit a real person. She also knew that as a believer, she had authority to make the most determined ghost leave.

She had helped Pastor pray over parishioner's homes. She had even prayed over one person's home that reported having a poltergeist. The homeowner reported that things flew around the room. They had prayed over the home, and now there were no more ghostly sightings. They had prayed over a haunted hotel across the street, and it now was a successful Bed and Breakfast Inn.

She stopped and listened for noises outside, and then she heard an unexplained noise within the building. Must be my overactive imagination she thought, maybe if I listen to a teaching tape, it would help me finish my work faster so that I can go home. The church had a special kid's crusade the next day, so she had volunteered to clean the big gymnasium.

Dropping the mop, she walked over to the soundboard and placed a teaching tape in the cassette player. At first, she was hesitant about operating the soundboard. She had been told that there was a specific order in which to turn on the different parts of it. One of the technicians had told her that she could ruin the system if she turned the different parts in the wrong order. She turned it on, and sighed with relief when she heard the speaker begin his message. After turning up the volume, she resumed mopping. She had mopped about a third of the floor, when she heard a loud bang.

"Darn!" Myra said, as she stopped and listened. Instinctively she ran to the soundboard, but the tape was still running. Yet there was a distinct odor in the air of something having burnt. What is it? Then she noticed that not only was the soundboard working, but the odor smelled like gunpowder. One glance at the windows told her that the

metal screen on one had been bent. Then she looked toward the door, a tall thin man wearing a red bandana that covered the lower part of his face, stood at the door. Remembering the noise that she had heard, she whispered, "Holy Spirit please tell me if someone is in the building."
"Hey!" yelled someone outside the windows. The sound echoed in the big gymnasium. Myra bolted for the side gymnasium door. As she ran down the dark and musty hallway, a peace that made no natural sense enveloped her. She had an understanding that she couldn't explain. Somehow she knew that no one was in the building with her. Still, she wondered about the unexplained noise within the building. She felt her way down the back hallway bumping into walls in the pitch dark. No lights were on anywhere in the hallway, which was good since she knew that she couldn't be seen. However, she also knew that someone could be hiding and that she might run right into them. She wouldn't know that the person was there until they grabbed her.

She rubbed her eyes hoping that they would quickly adjust to the dark. Every second counted as she felt her way down the hallway, the hallway led to one of the exit doors. Vaguely she could see the red exit sign and the door. Should she go out the back door? What if someone had been waiting for her, knowing that this was one of only three ways out of the building. No, she didn't have peace about leaving the building. So she felt her way down the hallway to her left. Unfortunately the building's hallways formed a labyrinth, and the back hallway became a locker room with showers, and bathrooms. She stopped and listened for sounds, her heart beat so loud that she was sure that if anyone had been nearby they could have heard it. Silence, blessed silence greeted her ears. She proceeded cautiously down the hall and into the locker room. She continued to an open area, and then came against a wall. Frantically, she groped to find the door, just as her foot kicked against what must have been a tin can. It clattered on the tile. She stopped and listened again, knowing that if someone had been following her they would now know exactly where she was. The building remained silent, and Myra felt safer. However, she didn't know where she was in the building. Inch by inch her hands searched the wall until she came to the opening. She had forgotten about the six-inch retaining wall that marked the entrance to the showers. Myra stubbed her foot on the tile wall, causing her to lose balance and fall in the dark. She landed hard on the floor tile. Her breathing came in gasps as she calmed herself, and examined her legs. She couldn't see, but apart from being bruised, she didn't think that she had broken any bones. Although in the dark, she didn't know if she was bleeding. After regaining her feet, she continued her way around the shower wall. After several minutes, she came to the opening of the pool. How would she get past the huge windows that went from just below the ceiling to the floor? She would be an open target if she walked around the pool.

"Holy Spirit, what do I do?" She whispered. The minutes crept by as she searched for any sign of outside activity near each window around the pool. To make matters worse, something tall stood near the entrance to the pool on the opposite side. Which was the side that led to the offices, the phones, and the door. She hovered in the shadows for several more minutes before deciding to stay close to the wall on the far side of the pool. She hoped that no one on the outside would be able to see her. Slowly she made her way around the pool. Drawing closer to the pool's entrance, what is that? Whatever it was, it didn't seem to be moving. What if it was someone who was waiting for her? Then she remembered the peace that she had, and the knowing that she was alone. Do I run? No, that would be unwise, because someone outside could see the sudden movement. She also remembered that window pane of the door at the entrance to the pool had a gun shot hole in it. Nobody knew how it had gotten there, perhaps there had been a street fight and someone had been shooting. She hoped that it wasn't a bad omen for her this night. Why did I have to live in such a violent little city?

She continued to make her way along the wall. She could see the tall object that stood by the door. When she got close enough to see it in the hall light, she laughed. It was a helium tank that they had gotten to blow up balloons for the crusade. Someone must have moved it to the entrance of the pool. The hallway leading to the pool was brightly lit, and could also be seen from the street, and she knew that she could be seen from the windows. She ducked out of sight and scurried down the hall, and into an office. The office was in plain view of the door where she had seen the man. What do I do now? She sat on the floor for several minutes and listened for activity on the street. Unfortunately, the phone sat on top of the counter, and in plain sight of a window, and just a few yards from the door. She decided to call Victoria, but first she had to reach the phone. Maybe she should call the police or perhaps Victoria could call them for her.

Mustering all her courage, she reached up and grabbed the phone, pulling it down to the floor. Once again she listened for any sound of activity either in the building or outside. With shaking hands, she dialed Victoria's number.

"Victoria?"

"Hello…who is this?" Victoria replied. Myra tried to speak but couldn't.

"Hello…hello?"

"It's me…Myra…I am at the church. I think that someone shot at me, but I am not hurt."

"I'll call the police, you just stay low and we will be right over." Victoria said.

"Thanks," Myra said gratefully. How could she ever repay the Shepherds for all that they had done for her? She waited for about ten minutes, when she heard the sounds of a police radio, yet she wasn't sure that she wanted to stand up to look. She tried to peer over the counter to see a police car. After several minutes, she stood up. A policeman stood at the door. Shaking, she opened the door and let him into the church. Pastor Tom and Victoria arrived minutes later. The police asked her questions, but she couldn't speak. No words would come out of her mouth, but words that resembled her prayer language more than English. The police searched the building, but found little evidence apart from the damaged window, and a damaged fan. The police assumed that the stray bullet had hit the fan.

"Myra you need to tell the policeman that you are the one who found the head." Victoria said. "Tonight's events might be connected. You also might mention what you saw at the old orphanage." Myra couldn't believe that Victoria was telling this in front of the policeman.

The policeman shifted his weight from one foot to another as he reopened his notepad. "Myra, it might be wise for you to stay close to the Shepherds for the next couple of weeks. Either that or perhaps you could go away for a week, that would certainly make our job easier." He said.

Before the policeman left, the Shepherds had agreed for Myra to leave the area for a few days.

Later that night, Myra reflected once again on her increasingly bizarre week. This time, she wondered if the person who had shot at her knew about her finding the head. She had told the police that she didn't want her identity known, for security reasons. Still, Atherstone was a small city, and it seemed that people knew each other's news in a matter of minutes after it had happened.

"Where will they send me?" Then she remembered a Renewal Center located about 30 miles away. She could go there for two or three days, that is if the Shepherds would let her. She wouldn't miss many days of school due to an In-Service on Monday. Although the teachers told her that she couldn't miss any more school after these days. Her teachers loaded her with homework, and a teacher volunteered to visit the center to help her with any questions. That way she wouldn't miss as much school.

The doorbell rang interrupted her thoughts. Billy, a friend of the Pastor's, stood at the door with a book in his hand.

"This is for Myra." He said.

"Thanks," Myra said wondering why anyone would give her a book at a time like this. "Oh," she gasped as she opened it. Recessed in the book was a handgun. He had evidently heard about the shooting.

Great...a gun, just what she every girl wants to carry in their purse, she thought.

"I'll teach you how to use it." Billy said.

"Thanks Billy, but I don't want the gun." She said, he started to say something but she silenced him with a wave of her hand. "I don't want to be known as the girl that shot someone, besides the Lord is my protection."

"O.K. but if you change your mind, I'll be happy to bring it back and show you how to use it." Billy said. "Don't be too brave, I don't want to attend your funeral." He added as he was leaving. Great, just what she needed to hear, and they expected her to be excited about the Kid's Miracle Crusade tomorrow. Yeah right, she thought as she flopped into bed and fell into a dreamless sleep.

The morning sun blazed against the pavement as the children started to arrive. Myra and the Crusade team had been up for hours preparing the auditorium. David and several of the men had spent several hours the night before setting up the props and the set for the crusade. Excited children laughed and talked as they waited for the crusade to start. Forty-five minutes before the crusade someone told the crusade team, that the power of God was so strong, that people were being 'slain in the spirit' in the bathroom. The workers hastily explained to people, that the term being "slain in the Spirit" meant that the Holy Spirit had laid the person on the floor. Many times the Holy Spirit did that in order to talk to a person, impart a gift, do supernatural surgery, or to prove to that person that He was real. A girl had been "slain in the Spirit' in her wheel chair. Several people had tried to rouse her or talk to her, but without success.

Earlier that morning Myra had withdrawn to an office. She planned to stay in prayer for several hours before the crusade began, because so many children needed a miracle, and she knew that she had to focus on cooperating with the Holy Spirit. She had to be like a hose, for the power of God to flow through her.

The crusade began like Street Side Sunday School, with games, songs, and high action. After this, the teaching included object lessons, and drama. At the end, they asked for every head to be bowed. A hundred children responded to the altar call. They came forward to accept Jesus as their Savior. Myra's heart overflowed with the excitement at seeing so many children accept Jesus as their Savior.

After the break, the children were given a choice of leaving or staying for the rest of the healing crusade. If they stayed, they had to be very still and not interrupt the service by getting out of their seats or leaving. This gave the restless a chance to leave without disturbing those who desperately needed to receive a miracle.

The tone of the crusade changed as the children began to worship the Lord. Tears flowed down many of their faces. As Myra worshipped a sensation of electricity covered her body. She felt like she had been plugged into a light socket. In addition, she had a sensation of floating. How awesome to be allowed to be a connection between God and hurting people. She started receiving supernatural knowledge about different children in the audience. "Multiple Sclerosis is being healed," she said. "Heart disease is being healed. Someone in the wheelchair section is receiving a healing."

"If I have called out your healing, then don't wait, come down to the front. You need to give a testimony of your healing, or you could lose it." Children got out of their chairs and filled the aisles on either side of the gymnasium. One or two came pushing their wheelchairs in front of them.

One by one they came and told what had happened to them. Myra prayed for them, and without exception, every one of them fell to the floor, 'slain in the Spirit'.

"Don't be afraid, sometimes the Lord will lay children down to talk to them. Sometimes he does surgery on them. Some boys and girls say that they have seen heaven. Sometimes children are so active, that the Lord has to temporarily stick them to the floor." Myra explained.

Someone brought a girl in a wheelchair to the front. Myra went over to talk to her. As she talked, the camera crew videotaped the crusade. Two teens dressed in black, with tattoos and nose rings, accompanied the girl.

"What is happening?" Myra asked.

"The power of God is all over me," the girl sobbed. She shook from head to toe. "I was born with Spinal Bifida, and I have never walked." She said, clutching a crusade flyer in her hand. The flyer had a picture of a girl jumping out of a wheelchair. "I want to walk like other kids walk. I am twenty years old, and I have never felt my legs, but as you were praying I felt fire and electricity race up and down my legs. Now I have feeling in my legs."

"Can you stand up?" Myra asked, excitement overwhelming her.

"I don't know." The girl said.

"What is your name?" Myra asked.

"Kelsey," the girl said. "I want to walk, but I don't know if my legs will hold me."

"Take my hand," Myra said, "Let's walk together." Slowly the girl started to stand up in the wheelchair. Myra laid her hands on the basketball-sized tumor on her back, and it shriveled to the size of a golf ball before disappearing totally.

Glen, one of the crusade team members, had pushed up the silver footplates where her feet had rested so that she could stand. Myra took Kelsey's hand, and David took Kelsey's other arm. She took her first step and started to fall. They held her upright, then she took another step, and then another. The crowd cheered. The cameraman fell to the floor, evidently 'slain in the Spirit', Myra noticed that he had cradled the camera when he fell and it didn't seem to be damaged. How wonderful, since it had been rented. The two teens with Kelsey had accepted Jesus during the altar call. When asked what they thought all they could say was, "Only God could have healed Kelsey!"

One after another the children testified of their healings: Asthma, heart disease, Multiple Sclerosis, Cancer, Pneumonia, teeth problems, hearing problems. Such a fabulous night, Myra didn't even think of terrorists, decapitated heads, or even any threats on her life.

Monday morning had arrived all too soon, she had hastily packed, and now she left the protective walls of her home. After a glorious weekend, Myra found herself driving to the Renewal Center just thirty miles away. She needed time for the police to investigate the case, and for her to spend time with the Lord. Not every one had agreed with her plans. After church on Sunday evening, her friend Maureen had warned her.

"Myra, have you prayed about this? I just don't feel good about you going. Something is not right." She said.

"That is precisely why I am going, to spend time with the Lord." Myra answered.

"Alright, but know that I will be praying for you." She said. Maureen wasn't known for trying to scare people, and her accuracy in perceiving things was well known. However, Myra's mind resounded with the glory of the weekend, she didn't give the warning a second thought; she just wanted to get away for a few days.

CHAPTER SIXTEEN

It is written:
"For I know the thoughts that I think toward you,
saith the Lord, thoughts of peace,
and not of evil, to give you an expected end."

Myra kicked off her shoes, and sat on the bed of her cabin. Victoria had said how much she enjoyed coming to the Renewal Center. Looking around the sparsely decorated room, she noticed that it had only a bed, desk, lamp, and chairs. No phone, television, or radios were allowed in the rooms. This enabled the guest to spend time focusing on the Lord without the usual distractions of every day life. After a brief nap, she decided to walk around the pond. She had been told that if you looked carefully you could see a bullfrog hiding near the water's edge. It's amber and black eye would see one's every movement. She enjoyed the peaceful and relaxing atmosphere. Here she could forget all that had happened, and focus on hearing from her wonderful Lord. She sighed before walking the short distance to the dining hall, when she remembered that the cook was off-duty this week. Looks like I will have to fend for myself, she thought. She walked into the kitchen and opened the refrigerator door. She found very little food and most of it unappetizing. I suppose that I could drive to the town and find a restaurant. She hadn't wanted to do that, but perhaps she could go to a local store and stock up on some snacks. Victoria had told her about the exquisite food served in the dining hall.

She drove the winding road that led from the cabins to the administration buildings. The contemporary blue-gray buildings sat on manicured grounds, which were nestled in the woods adjacent to a bayou. Swings, chairs, and religious statues adorned the grounds. She continued onto the quarter-mile, tree-lined driveway that connected the Renewal Center to the main road. Absolutely no one found this place by accident; even the sign had been partially hidden. If you wanted to be alone this was the place.

Myra found a diner and hastily ate her hamburger. She wanted to be back to the Renewal Center before dark, but she had miscalculated the time. Darkness greeted her as she emerged from the diner. Too late for a stroll when I get back, she thought as she climbed into the car. She never thought to look at her surroundings. She had enjoyed her dinner, and now she looked forward to her return when she would be able to pray and read her Bible. It wasn't until she had driven several hundred yards along the feeder road that she sensed that something was wrong. I guess I am just feeling spooky since I am driving by a cemetery. In fact, a friend of hers had been buried there. She cast a wistful glance at the grounds. She missed her friend, and then she remembered that she had read of young women disappearing along this part of the freeway. I need to meditate more on the sacred words, because my nerves are on edge, she thought to herself. Still she shifted uncomfortably in the driver's seat. She had lost her peace. Come to think of it, her spirit had a prickly sensation that seemed to be increasing with each passing minute. I am getting superstitious, she thought. Shaking her head, she thought, no, something is wrong, and that is why I have lost my peace. "Lord are you trying to tell me something?" she said to the empty air. At that moment her eyes locked on the rearview mirror. Three cars followed her car down the lonely feeder road that led to the overpass.

As she looked in the rearview mirror, she instinctively knew that the Lord wanted her to notice these cars. "Lord what is it that you want me to see?" She felt impressed to continue to eye the cars that trailed behind her. What am I going to do if they are following me? Maybe this is my imagination? I can't take a chance, she thought. She began to pray in the spirit. Using the gift of tongues, which she knew to be perfect prayer. She had been taught that her heavenly prayer language, or tongues, prayed out the perfect will of God, and the mysteries of heaven concerning her situation.

Nervously she eyed the cars following her, as she entered the ramp for the overpass. The cars continued to follow her. Surely it had to be a coincidence that they followed onto the overpass. She thought that at least one of the cars would continue on the feeder road to the freeway entrance ramp. As she drove over the overpass, she saw that the on-coming traffic lane had been blocked by construction, creating a one-way street. The cars continued behind her. "God has not given me a spirit of fear, but of power, love, and a sound mind." She said to the empty air.

She passed a subdivision, and decided to drive through it, perhaps she could better determine if the cars were following her. Two of the cars turned and followed her at a respectful distance. She decided to turn down one of the subdivision streets, praying that it wasn't a dead-end or a cul-de-sac. The two cars turned also. By now, she knew that she was being followed. I wonder if I should pull into a driveway and knock on someone's door and tell the person that I am being followed? What if the people didn't answer the door, then she could be trapped on foot. No, she would continue driving. She turned down another street, which led back to the main road. The Renewal Center was less than a mile down the road. She looked in her rear view mirror, but didn't see any headlights from either of the other cars. Good, she thought, so she turned off her lights and drove without them. She entered the main road and continued toward the Renewal Center. A brief glance in the rear view mirror showed that no one that she could see followed. Of course in the dark, a vehicle without lights would be difficult to detect. Still, she felt some measure of relief. She drove to the Renewal Center and around to her cabin, and ran the short distance from the parking lot to her cabin.

Hastily, she heaved her suitcase on the bed, and threw her clothes into it. Without considering the consequences, she had decided to pack and return to Atherstone that night. Lugging her suitcase to the car, she started the car without turning on the lights. Cautiously she drove the winding road to the Administration building. She started to cross the parking lot that was situated between the winding road to the cabins, and the long driveway that led to the main road. Just then a large, white, extended cab Dodge Pickup turned on its lights and lurched toward her, trying to block the path of her Honda. The powerful pickup lunged toward her car missing her by inches. She couldn't see her attacker, because of the trucks tinted windows. The fear that had gripped Myra's heart, gave way to anger. I could die right here tonight, she thought." No, I am not going to die at the hands of some stranger," she said out loud as she pushed the gas pedal to the floor and lurched toward the driveway. The Pickup spun around and followed in hot pursuit, Myra took a detour through the woods, hearing the bumps and scrapes on the bottom of her car. I suppose this is going to be one expensive repair. The Honda burst out of woods and onto the driveway.

What a perfect place for a murder? Why didn't I think about this before I came here, she thought. The Pickup sped toward her car, gaining with every passing yard. Soon she would be at the main road, and would have to pull out in traffic. She turned on her lights, and holding her breath turned onto the Main road without checking the traffic. It would almost be better to get into an accident than to risk being over-taken while she waited to get on the main road. The truck followed behind her. She prayed in the spirit as she continued to drive the back roads, hoping to see a police station or a way to get to the freeway, since she was unfamiliar with these roads. The Pickup continued to tailgate her for several miles. Finally she saw a freeway overpass looming ahead. What a wonderful sight. She drove under the overpass, and at that point the Pickup kept going. She turned and drove on the entrance ramp to the freeway. How strange that she had never seen whoever had been chasing her.

About thirty minutes later, she pulled up on the side street beside the Shepherds and ran to the back door. No one appeared to be following her now. However, she had not stopped shaking. Victoria greeted her at the door.

"What happened? You are white as a sheet." Victoria said.

Myra opened her mouth to speak, but no words would come forth. Her tongue wouldn't cooperate with her, except to speak in her heavenly language. Finally, after about twenty minutes Myra was able to tell her what had happened. Once again, the police were called. David arrived within minutes clad in a bathrobe. The police offered advice, but admitted that they didn't have any foolproof solutions for her safety. They had spent about an hour discussing her safety and what could be done to help her. Obviously, someone or even more than one person had decided to try to either kidnap her or to kill her. Although she had been scared, a strange peace filled her.

"God protected me from my step-father. God protected me from being shot, and now he is going to protect me from whoever is trying to harm me." Said Myra. What did people do who didn't know the Lord or believe in his divine protection?

"When you get right down to it, the Lord is all the security in life that we have." Said Pastor Shepherd.

"I hope that you don't regret that you decided to have me stay with you," Myra said.

"Why would you say such a thing?" Victoria asked.

"For one reason, I could be endangering you by staying here with you." Myra said.

"Don't you want to stay here?" Victoria said, and softened her voice when she saw Myra's face become downcast. "It isn't that we don't want you here. We just thought that maybe you wanted to go somewhere else. Or that maybe you wanted to contact your mother to see if she is better situated now, and more able to care for you." Victoria said.

"Is that what you would like?"

"No, of course not, we are with you in this." Victoria said. "We just want what is best for you."

"Then I want to stay with you. I believe that I am supposed to be in Atherstone." Myra said.

"We do too," said Pastor Shepherd.

"Of course she could always marry me." David smiled.

"Not till she finishes school," the Shepherds chimed. Myra wistfully wished that she could elope with him. How nice it would be to drive into the sunset with her new husband into a new life. She dreamed of a life that wasn't complicated by things like decapitated heads, terrorists, and stalkers. However, she had to face reality, and that someone, or several people wanted to end her life. Haven't I had enough people trying to harm me, she wondered? Pastor Shepherd eyed her strangely and seemed to be reading her thoughts.

"Things like this will either be the making or the breaking of you. Like finding the head, you will either grow stronger and bolder or weaken. It will depend on your relationship with the Lord. In life one becomes either bitter or better. The difference is the 'I'. God must have a tremendous calling on your life for the enemy to be so determined to destroy you. Remember what the sacred words say, 'No weapon that is formed against thee shall prosper'.

Myra marveled once again, at how the Lord hearing her thoughts had sent encouragement when she desperately needed it.

Several days passed uneventfully, as Myra learned to relax. At first, even unexpected noises had caused her to jump. "What kind of woman of God am I?" She didn't think it was very funny when Pastor Shepherd had joked, "Myra are you a woman of faith and power, or a woman of paste and flour?"

"Just keep praying out mysteries," Victoria said. She noticed the confused look on Myra's face and added, "You know…pray in your heavenly language, and ask the Lord to "manifest" them in your life." Victoria had said.

"Would you be upset if I asked you a really dumb question?" Myra said.

"Certainly not, I mean there are no dumb questions." Victoria answered.

"Just exactly what does praying out mysteries so that they manifest mean?" Myra asked. " I didn't want to appear stupid, but I have wondered, and everyone else seemed to know so I just decided to act like I knew too."

"Good question, my dear, and I am glad that you asked," Victoria answered. "Mysteries are the plans and purposes for your life that you don't know about, but God does know. He hasn't told you for various reasons or perhaps it is his timing. Also, he doesn't want the enemy to know so that he can try to stop the plan of God. The word 'manifest' means that they have become a reality where you can see them. That means pulling them from the spiritual realm into your physical or natural realm where you and everyone else can physically see them. You receive things in the spiritual realm first, and then it materializes or manifests in the natural realm."

"Oh, I get it," said Myra. Did she ever, she suddenly had a revelation that sent a rush of joy through her soul. "What power we have as believers. I can literally use my faith through speaking in this heavenly language to pull the vast riches and promises of God into my life, now! Victoria, if this is true why don't more people do this?"

"Because most people haven't been taught what you have just learned. They don't know that they can literally write their own ticket for the perfect will of God. If people knew this, just think of what they could achieve!" Myra knew that she had already tapped into secrets with God that most people didn't know. Now she knew that she could be a young woman without limits. Little did she know that the day would come in the not so distant future when she would need to walk in the fullness of this knowledge just to survive.

Myra felt her spirit growing in power as she spent more and more time with the Lord. She read the sacred words, prayed, and worshipped. One day the presence of the Lord filled the chapel of the church. That day David had decided to surprise her, by coming to see her. He walked into the room, then topped and rubbed his eyes straining to see her. At that moment, the power of God threw him across the room and up against a wall. Stunned, he said, "What was that?"

Myra remained in a trance-like state, and was unable to answer him, so he discreetly left. Later, they had laughed about it. He had reported seeing a mist in the room that covered her. That is why he had rubbed his eyes, because he thought that something was wrong with his vision.

This winter, the Grace Ships had been berthed at the Atherstone docks. The ministry had been a long time friend of New Life Christian Center. The crew eagerly anticipated the trip to Israel as they made preparations to sail. God had miraculously provided for the trip's fuel, and for the crew. Staff from "The Grace" frequently visited the church. They had practiced water survival training in the church's pool. Grace Ships had also donated pallets full of toys, food, and Christian literature to the church to be distributed to the Street side Sunday School ministry.

As the days passed, Myra began to help them with their preparations. Although she had been careful not to go anywhere alone, including last minute trips to the local convenience store. However, with each passing day, she became less cautious. Perhaps it had been a coincidence about the shooting, and being chased by the car. After all, she lived in an area where women disappeared and were never found. Rumor had it that a gang of three vehicles kidnapped young women, and that at least twenty-two had disappeared in the last ten years on that stretch of highway. So with each passing day, Myra became more confident that life would return to normal. Even the traumatic finding of the head seemed to fade in her memory. In America, grisly as it seemed, such things happened. She wasn't the first person to make such a horrific find.

During the Sunday night service, a prophecy had come forth telling her, "Change, change, change." She didn't like prophecies like that, because she found that they proved to be true, and change wasn't always pleasant. For example, the week before her mother and stepfather had abandoned her, she had received such a prophecy. However, after Sunday's prophecy, she had shifted nervously in her seat, and had prayed even more earnestly.

Today she had gone to the church as usual. The church had been working on remodeling the old locker rooms. She had helped the volunteers carry out construction debris to the alley for a special trash pick-up, and decided to remain in the alley and tidying a pile of trash. She noticed that a black car drove down the alley, and parked about thirty feet away. Lots of cars went through the alley, so she paid no attention to it.

Absentmindedly, she continued to pile the last of the trash. I need to finish up so that I can see David, she thought. In her haste, she wasn't paying attention to her surroundings. In fact, her back had been turned to the car, and she hadn't noticed the two men that got out of the car and approached her. She turned around just as one of the men grabbed her, and the other placed his hand over her mouth, just as she started to scream. She kicked trying frantically to escape, as her captors shoved a bag over her head and threw her roughly into the back seat of the car.

CHAPTER SEVENTEEN

It is written:
"Better is the end of a thing than the beginning thereof:
and the patient in spirit is better than the proud in spirit."

Myra fought the bag, and tore a hole in it to breathe. She could barely see her captors, but could not understand their conversation. They seemed to be speaking in another language, and looked like Middle-Easterners. Obviously they thought that they had her secured and had turned their attention to other matters.

After a few minutes of driving, the car slowed and came to a halt. She still couldn't discern where they had taken her.

O Lord, surely this is not the end of my life. You didn't bring me this far to die at the hands of some brutal men, she thought. She continued to pray in the Spirit. Only her lips moved, but she made sure that no sound could be heard.

Roughly someone grabbed her and pulled her out of the car, another grabbed her and tied rope around her arms and shoulders. A hand roughly shoved her forward with such force that she lurched and fell. A man's hand grabbed her and yanked her to her feet. "Ouch!" she yelled. The man had nearly dislocated her shoulder.

"What did you say?" a male voice asked.

"Nothing," Myra answered. A hand pulled the bag off her face, and Myra gratefully gulped the air.

"So this is the scum that has caused all the trouble?" said another man with a turban and a beard. "The Master will be most interested in interviewing her!" He laughed. Two other men joined him in laughter as they shoved her up the massive stairs leading to the old orphanage. Normally she would have admired the beauty of the place. The wooden walls and floors gleamed with a highly varnished finish. Once again she had been propelled toward stairs, only these stairs led to the basement.

Myra continued to pray softly in tongues, while trying not to alarm or agitate her captors. The basement's stale, dank odor added to the horror of the setting. She now stood face to face with a man whose face had been broadcast worldwide on the news. Esau towered over her, his swarthy face a portrait of evil. His eyes mocked her, yet he didn't seem human. The pictures did not do him justice.

"So this is infidel that poked her nose in our business? Someone needs to teach this young woman some manners. Pity that she won't live long enough to mend her sinful ways." He said, waving his hand to dismiss her.

They dragged her toward a cage containing a tiger.

Esau turned and walked back to her and said, "No we won't throw you to the tiger yet. We want to be sure that he has another couple of days without food so that he will be very hungry, and will enjoy his meal." He said. One of Esau's aides bent over and whispered in his ear. He laughed and they both turned and looked at Myra.

"Oh that would be the perfect solution to our…little problem." Evil laughter filled the room, as he doubled over in laughter. "Of course, why hadn't I thought of it, Yasseh you are a genius. The Grace ships berth on this island, and Christians run them, how fortunate to have this young woman in our midst. Perhaps we could strap the suitcase bomb to her and place her aboard the Grace. The ship is supposed to be making a trip to Israel. However, she will be making a detour to Houston. Just think a Christian ship with a suicide bomber. Only this bomb is a hydrogen bomb, and what a mess it will make of Houston. To think that we had thought of giving her a choice of dying by being torn apart by a tiger, or of being a guinea pig to test either Anthrax or Mustard Gas. Where is your God now, sweetheart?" Esau said. "Convert to Islam and confess that Allah is your God, and I might relent and add you to my harem." He said stroking her hair and laughing. "You aren't too bad looking for a westerner. Of course, I would enjoy seeing you beg for your life before you die anyway." He said as he walked away.

"Dear Jesus, help me!" Myra whispered. Esau opened the cage door next to the tiger and shoved her into it. Myra fell against the bars on the far side, just as the tiger lunged toward her cage.

Time crawled by slowly as Myra sat in the cage. She wondered if they were going to feed her, and looked longingly at the Tiger's water bowl. Her tongue licked her lips as she longed for water. She wished that she could reach through the bars and shift it closer. However, she knew that the animal, being a cat, would move with lightning speed.

Myra prayed in tongues so quietly that only her lips moved. She felt a strange peace, and knew that the vision she had and the instructions from the Lord would carry her through this situation. She wondered if the Shepherds had missed her, and had contacted the police.

Every so often one of the men would check on her, then chant something in Arabic to the man who was guarding her cage, before returning up the stairs. After several hours, Myra drifted into an uneasy sleep. There were no windows for her to see if it was day or night, and while she working in the alley, she had removed her watch. She wondered what David was doing, he was so sensitive to the leading of the Spirit, and knew her thoughts. She could feel his prayers.

At least they weren't talking about beheading me, which she knew that Jihadists often did to their hostages.

Her thoughts were interrupted. A man dressed in black ran into the room shouting, "The building is surrounded, the police have found us!"

"They must have been searching for the scum girl." Esau said. "Tell them that we are holding the girl hostage, and that if they don't leave the property that we will feed her to the tiger. We will save one of her bones to show them." He laughed. "They can always do a DNA to make sure it was her." Myra winced as she heard the words. At least being beheaded would be quick. The man ran back up the stairs, and Esau turned to Myra, "Where is your God now? You are nothing

THE SPIRIT'S APPRENTICE

but an infidel and worthy of death. I wouldn't lower myself to touch you." He said as he spat into her cage.

Thoughts of fear and anger coursed through her mind, until Myra regained her composure, and placing her hand on the stone she prayed. "Holy Spirit, you said to touch this stone as a contact point for you to translate me to another place. Remember the book of Acts where Paul and Silas were prisoners, and how you opened the prison door. Lord I ask you to do the same for me. The sacred words say that you are no respecter of persons."

She could hear running footsteps as the men on the floor above scrambled from room to room. Suddenly she heard the sound of squealing pigs. A man ran to the basement and said to the man who was guarding her, "Someone has unloaded a truckload of pigs onto the property. If we touch a pig we are doomed. Allah will not accept a soul that has touched a pig, so we won't be able to go to heaven. They claim that the police have dipped their bullets in pig's blood."

Another man ran down the stairs toward her saying, "Esau said to throw the girl to the tiger." Myra's heart skipped a beat, as her cage door opened, and the man grabbed her and pulled her out. The door to the tiger's cage had been opened. Seconds passed like hours, as once again an anointing and a peace descended on Myra. It seemed as though she had been coated in liquid love.

The man had tied her arms behind her back, and pushed her into the cage, and slammed the door. The tiger lunged toward the door, going past Myra. It was as if he didn't see her. How strange, she knew that the animal hadn't been fed. Yet it didn't seem to know that she was in the cage.

The two men stood in front of the cage as the tiger snarled at them. Mystified, they shrugged and continued to watch.

"Every hand on the first floor," an unseen voice yelled. By this time, shots could be heard as the police and the terrorists exchanged gunfire. No one seemed to care what happened to Myra. She slid to the floor in a corner of the cage. The tiger sank to his haunches and then hunkered down. He began to groom himself just like her cat, Baby did. I can't believe what I am seeing. The tiger sat with one leg hoisted into the air and his head turned to wash his hip. He is acting like he doesn't see me. Evidently he can't sense that I am anywhere near. When she had touched the stone, she had reminded the Holy Spirit of his promise. She knew that the stone itself had no power. She continued to watch the big cat for several minutes before she noticed that the cage door had begun to open.

Slowly, the door swung open, the tiger ignored her and got to its feet, he pushed the door with his paw until it opened enough for him to escape. Once out of the cage, he bounded up the stairs. Shouts followed telling her that the men on the first floor had seen the tiger.

She moved her hands and realized that the rope tying her hands behind her back had fallen to the floor. She got to her feet and bolted out of the cage. She hoped that the tiger preferred eating pigs to people.

She didn't know whether to go up the stairs, but decided to head for the wall. She felt the Spirit leading her toward the wall. She closed her eyes and walked into the wall. Opening her eyes a few minutes later, she found herself on the other side of the wall, having no knowledge of how she had gotten there. A policeman stood about twenty feet away and she ran to him. She hoped that he would be able to see her. Just as she neared him, he turned and waved for her to come to him. Praise God she had been seen, and now she knew that she was safe.

She could still hear the sounds of gunfire on the other side of the building. Pigs roamed freely around the compound. There was no sight of the tiger. She presumed that he had been shot. The battle continued for an hour, while Myra watched from the safety of the squad car.

At length, she saw the tall figure of Esau walking single-file his eyes blazing with defiance. Handcuffed with shackles on his feet he walked with some of his men toward the police van. The man, who had once threatened to destroy America, now held captive on American soil.

Already the news had spread, as ten TV trucks, together with newscasters, and cameras were stationed just outside the wall of the compound. News of the capture had caused the western world to rejoice. Microphones were pushed into her face, as the newscasters asked a flurry of questions. Victoria intervened, and told them that

Myra would answer their questions later, but right now they were taking her home.

She never thought that she would be so excited to see her home and the church. Victoria cried and Pastor Tom kept praising the Lord. She told them about the terrorist's plans, and about the suitcase hydrogen bomb, the plans to use the Grace Ship, the Anthrax and the Mustard Gas.

David arrived and held Myra in his arms. They were interrupted by several phone calls. David and Victoria took turns answering the calls. The press, TV, and other organizations all wanted to talk to Myra.

"The Mayor just called and wants to meet with you. He wants to present you with the key to the city." David said. They decided not to answer any more calls for the evening.

"Sweetheart, I want to be with you, love you, and protect you. To think that I could have lost you," he said as he gave her a small blue velvet box, and dropped to one knee and held Myra's hand.

Myra opened the box and gasped. She thought that the ring was the most beautiful ring that she had ever seen. The heart shaped diamond glittered on the golden band. The larger stone sat delicately balanced between two smaller stones. A cross was etched on either side of the band, creating a perfect symbol of their faith and love, and that the Lord would be the head of their home.

"Will you marry me?" he asked.

"Of course," she said, as he placed the ring on her finger.

"I thought that you were going to wait another year," said Victoria.

"I was, but after tonight I just wanted to make it official." David answered

"Congratulations, God has great plans for both of you. Although I am asking that you wait to marry until Myra has graduated. Remember that true love waits. I do know that the Lord is faithful and he will be with you always, to God be the glory," said Pastor Tom.

"I just want to thank my wonderful Lord. If it hadn't been for him, I would have been a tiger's lunch." Myra said.

They all said in unison, "His mercy endures forever!"

SURVIVING FOSTER CARE

A Journey of Self-Discovery

A Workbook for Empowering Individuals who have Experienced Foster Care to Persevere and Succeed

Janetta M. Coleman, MS, LSW, CMP

Enhanced DNA
DEVELOP. NURTURE. ACHIEVE.
Publishing Division

www.EnhancedDNAPublishing.com
DenolaBurton@EnhancedDNA1.com
317-537-1438

Surviving Foster Care
A Journey of Self-Discovery

Copyright © Janetta M. Coleman, MS, LSW, CMP 2021
All rights reserved.
No portion of this publication may be reproduced, stored in any electronic system, or transmitted in any form or by any means without the written permission from the author. Brief quotations may be used in literary reviews.

ISBN-13: 978-1-7369079-1-7
Library of Congress Number: 2021915329

TABLE OF CONTENTS

DEDICATION V
FOREWORD IX
INTRODUCTION XI
LESSON ONE: EQUIPPED TO LEAD 1
LESSON TWO: YOU MUST BE WILLING TO LEARN 9
LESSON THREE: MISTAKES AND FAILURES ARE NECESSARY FEEDBACK 17
LESSON FOUR: LET THE HURT GO! 25
LESSON FIVE: WALK A NEW PATH 35
LESSON SIX: SAY YES 43
LESSON SEVEN: ARE YOU WILLING TO STAND ALONE? 53
LESSON EIGHT: KNOW THAT YOU ARE STRONG! 61
LESSON NINE: ENCOURAGE YOURSELF! 69
LESSON TEN: STAY ALERT 81
CONCLUSION 89
ABOUT THE AUTHOR 93
MONTRELL PARTNERSHIPS LLC AND GENESIS MEDIATION LLC 97

Janetta M. Coleman, MS, LSW, CMP

DEDICATION

This book was inspired by my parents, youngest sister, and a youth who God blessed me with in my career path.

To Mom and Dad, thank you for having the hearts that you do. Without your love and support my life would never have gone in the direction it has. What was, and still is so amazing, is that you both allowed me to be me and not what you wanted me to be. You allowed me to do what delighted my heart without hesitation, even if that meant wearing chain link belts with a bra under my jacket during the Madonna years! All that I am is the best of both of you. Watching you love other people's children will never leave me. God says to host others, welcome them into your home, feed, clothe, and love them. I also want to thank you both for showing me what love and partnership between a husband and wife looks like. Many people fake it for the sake of the children, but you guys are truly in love! I see that and so does everyone else. No matter how crazy things get or how much you drive each other nuts, your love is an example of God's love manifested in marriage for over 50 years. The devil has tried to come between you, but no weapon formed against the two of you shall prosper. God knew I needed the covering of both of you to be who I am. You were put together by design and through it all God has your back! Dad, you gave me the edge that allows me to have no fear of anyone or anything, and Mom, you gave me the nurturing side that is necessary to do my job and be a great mom.

To my youngest sister, it was you who sealed the deal that the professional field of social work was for me. The day you left our home, it hurt to see you go, and I vowed then that I would never stay silent if the decision were wrong for a child. Many people have been on the receiving end of my wrath when I fight for what is right on behalf of foster youth. In the end, it all worked out and it is how it should be and how God designed it. He knew you would never really leave our family, and nothing would keep you from us. Never once, as a biological child, did I feel like mom or dad's love was taken from me or lessened. I delighted in how much they loved you and many other foster youths. The first time I saw you in the hospital I cried because I felt life had been unfair to you and I KNEW you had to be with us in that moment...no question!

To all the youth I have encountered in my career thus far, it has been a blast knowing, laughing, crying, praying, and caring for you. You **all** were the inspiration for this book. God allowed me to be in your presence and it has been my privilege! You have given me more than I have given you. I may not have always said or done the right things along the way, but I pray that I did not harm you or cause any additional trauma. I am not perfect, but I tried. Thank you for letting me in your life.

To those teachers, mentors, and friends along the way in my career, I thank you! You know exactly who you are. The teacher in high school who trusted my decisions and nurtured my leadership, the undergrad professor who gave me that first job, the Vice-President who gave me creative freedom, and the CEO who allowed me to be under his wing and learn. Ladies in Waiting (LIW) ministries, that was born out of friendships, --I cannot begin to express how this ministry has kept me close to God during moments when I felt like I could not feel HIS presence. I wish everyone had friendships such as ours...rare, honest, unique, and lifelong. I thank you all--1992 and still going strong! You all know the title of friend is earned with me. We ride together we die together.

To my daughter, my only biological child, you are the one who took my breath away and never gave it back. Know that you are loved and occupy my heart in a way that is indescribable. Forever, you will have the words within this book from me. You are one of the loves of my life and nothing you do in life, good or bad, will change my love for you. Thank you for being exactly who you are...perfect! Let NO one tell you any different. On earth or from Heaven, I will always be with you and Jordan. Love Mommy.

To my son, Jordan, while you were not born from me, I love and care for you as if you were my own. I don't use the word "step" because there is nothing "step" about loving and caring for a child. You will always have the title of son with me. You have such a beautiful smile, laugh, and sense of humor. You are a sweet boy and I pray that you reach your full potential. Everything you need is inside of you. Stay on course, believe in yourself by trusting yourself, and the decisions you make (that goes for you too, Victoria). Your spirit (God) will speak to you; so, remember to listen to it and stay focused. Love Mommy

To my husband, Craig, thank you for not running away. You came with a purpose to restore what trust, love, and honesty looks like in a marriage. I appreciate the patient father you are to the kids. I love your attention to details, which is a compliment to my big picture approach. Special thanks to you for creating ALL my websites and creating the book cover. You are a man of integrity who does what is best for the greater good which is a rare find! I am lucky and blessed to have a man with such qualities and talents by my side. This moment could not have happened without you being by myside. Thank you for creating a marriage where I can be my full me. I love you more than you know.

FOREWORD

By
Mary Petty
Former Foster Youth

From the first time I met Janetta, aka Ms. Janetta and Mommy Dearest, I knew she was unlike anyone I had ever come across. In my lifetime, I have met a lot, and I mean a lot, of case workers, social workers, and child advocates. All of which I noticed had the same thing in common. It was not until a short time later after I met Ms. Janetta that I understood why things were the way they were, but I will get into that later. I decided early on I would not talk to the social workers. It was for the best because they had shown me, they only trusted and were interested in what the foster parents had to say about me and their beliefs of me. After having so many people in and out of my life, being silent just seemed best.

When I first met Ms. Janetta, that was my attitude. I will never forget the day she came into my life. She told my foster mother there will not be a meeting where I would not be in attendance. I remember her saying, "…this is Mary's life, so we need to talk to her together." As much as this surprised me, I was not ready to release my protective stance and open up. And, like I did with all the others, I said nothing at all. I did not know I would ever meet such a devoted person. After staring at me for about five minutes, she tilted her head, stood up and walked to the door. My mouth dropped y'all. She turned to me and said, "when you are ready to talk to me, call me. I won't make you talk, nor will I waste my gas." That was the beginning of our relationship, and I cherish it deeply every day. I have two children of my own, and they know her as my godmother.

When I read this book, I knew it took a person of knowledge and compassion to write it. I remember thinking, I am so happy it is not preachy. I know I am one of the lucky ones when they assigned her to me. There are still kids in the system that need and want someone to listen, understand their needs, and who will be empathetic. Someone who will not allow us to pity ourselves. This is our book. The book hits every deep, dark, hopeless feeling y'all. For the people who work with kids who are in the system, I know you have a heavy caseload, but believe me, we wish we weren't one! Hang in there! You do not know how much you are definitely needed.

- Mary Petty

INTRODUCTION

I have always wondered why I was drawn to leadership books. I am not sure exactly when the love affair started, but I believe it began in high school. I began to take mental notes on how successful people thought and was extremely interested in how some were more successful than others. What I have found over time through life experiences, reading leadership books, and through my profession as a social worker, is **'success is always determined by the individual and not by their circumstances.'** Success will always be a state of mind. You can never look outside yourself and measure your success nor can you compare your success to anyone else's success, because what is for you is for you. You cannot take over anyone else's dreams or successes. People are often encouraged to choose a role model but looking at a person for their success is false adoration. Most people look at role models and see only the success and strive to be that person. NO! Admire their accomplishment but study their journey. Admire their guts to stand and keep pushing for their dream. Let that inspire you to have the guts to stand and keep pushing for YOUR dream. Do not let anyone tell you to be like this person or that person. You just be you. God designed you the way you are for a reason and that is perfect. Do not confuse who you are with your circumstances. What we experience is not who we are. It may shape you, but it does not define you. Here is what I do know; success is given in small and large amounts. The best analogy I can use is that of a lottery winner. Most people say, "if I could only win the lottery my life would be so much better." Then they win and realize how unprepared they were for the "extras" that came with it. As Luke 12:48 says, *"to whom much is given much will be required"* or as coined by a now deceased rapper Biggie Smalls, *"the more money, the more problems."* We must be ready for what is given to each one of us. Our life experiences equip us for our next level good or bad. Your worst situation is a testimony to someone else on how to make it through in their darkest hour. We all are destined to endure hardships and then save someone who cannot endure it. That said, success develops out of your pain and saves someone else through acknowledgement, understanding, and encouragement. On the same token, you may be needed to show someone how to succeed in an area they never thought they could. For this very reason you must know you are not alone in your troubles. There have been others before you and there will be others after you. Real success in life is not only having what we want, but helping others get what they want.

I have learned as a social worker that everyone can be successful. Working with foster youth was challenging, rewarding, exhausting, fun, chaotic, stressful, heartbreaking, and refreshing all wrapped up into one. Most of my professional life has been guided by young people transitioning into adulthood. I have been amazed at the leadership skills I found in each of them. Rarely, did I find a youth who did not possess the qualities of a leader. While they may not have been functioning out of that gift yet, I could clearly see the potential for the gift. Systemically, foster youth are viewed as less than, rather than equal to other youth who are not in state care.

- Nothing says you are less than, more than not having a family that will take you in.
- Nothing says you are less than, more than not being able to date.
- Nothing says you are less than, more than not being able to get your driver's license before age eighteen.
- Nothing says you are less than, more than not being able to attend a high school game or dance.
- Nothing says you are less than, more than not feeling like you have the same potential as anyone else.

Because you are a foster youth, these normal stages associated with teenage milestones are all too often extremely difficult to experience. While the system is changing to allow foster youth to accomplish such milestones, it is not changing fast enough. An insurmountable measure of hurtful trauma exists in the bodies of many foster youth. Mostly because the life they have been given APPEARS to be less than. Of course, most of the things I am saying are not new thoughts, but what I am attempting to do is to forever lay it to rest that foster youth are less than. You ARE GREATER than!

I have seen many disappointments that foster youth experience--not having a parent pick them up for visits when they promised, being separated from siblings, watching their parent be consumed by drugs or an abusive relationship, having everyone blame them because they told a "family secret," being shuffled around from one school to another, being pushed away by other extended family members, being labeled as defiant, difficult, non-social, and confrontational. Is this the characteristic of ALL foster youth experiences? Absolutely not! But I ask you, if a person experienced even a small portion of the situations described you might be defiant, difficult, non-social, and confrontational too. Hell, I am fairly sure I would be! Most people cannot imagine not spending the holidays without their family let alone a lifetime without them. I am talking to foster youth, and youth in general, who feel as though their life might not be worth living and want to give up. Do not give up! You are worth everything and you have something to offer the world, state, city, community, family, friends, future mates, and possible future children.

I focus on foster youth as my audience because you all are my inspiration for this book. Also, I know other youth who are experiencing their own difficult situations and can benefit from this book as well as other social workers. Being young is hard and I remember those days. From you (foster youth), I have learned to love unconditionally (which is a constant battle for everyone), respect parenting, value my family, and forgive more often and much quicker. There are so many books for adults and teens but rarely for foster youth that focus on how great and mighty you are. Leadership materials have helped me to enhance my gift of leadership and it is my mission in this book to help you find and enhance your own. This book will be filled with stories, lessons, tips, and Bible teachings to help you find the leader within who is waiting to get out and shine.

Janetta M. Coleman, MS, LSW, CMP

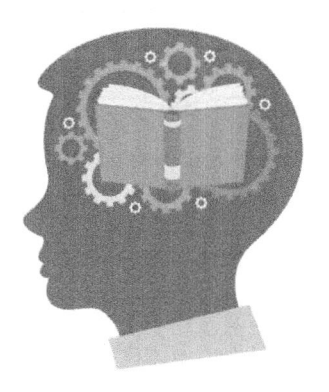

LESSON ONE: EQUIPPED TO LEAD

"For I know the plans I have for you," declares the Lord, "plans to prosper you and not to harm you, plans to give you hope and a future." Jeremiah 29:11 NLV

Did you know that you were born for a purpose? Crazy isn't it! We are all born with a destiny to fulfill. Luke 2:42 states *"blessed is the fruit of thy womb."* God said before you were born you will be blessed because you were formed in the womb and if it were not HIS will, you would not be here on this earth. Have you ever made anyone smile? Smiles are never by accident; they are intentional just like you. When I was a director of a teen parenting residential program, all the young ladies I encountered did not expect to be pregnant, but they were. Some were ready to handle the responsibility; others were willing to learn, while a few were barely coping with their own lives let alone raising someone else. It was always interesting to be around the children because every child born in that program had their own personality that could be seen very early in their development. Each child had a smile that made the staff melt and a certain word they tried to say but could not. What never failed was the children had the capacity to learn. Children have to learn how to grow without understanding why. Children want to do what they cannot and act in ways that adults do. To do that, they have to learn how to walk, talk, and feed themselves. Most children keep on trying until they learn what is needed to mimic the actions of adults. Children do not know that learning at this stage is an innate (meaning it just happens without thinking) behavior with the assistance of adults; children have an internal drive to want to know how to do something. After passing the infancy stage and from a toddler to a pre-adolescent, they learn that they must want to learn, because now you understand you have choices in life. The same still holds true as adults.

God gave children the innate ability to learn and special gifts that can be used for themselves and for others. You can use the power that God has given to reach your goals and He leaves it up to you to keep pushing yourself to learn. Hence, we all started out much the same. Even a person born with a disability has the capacity to learn but may need to learn in a different manner. Essentially, everyone has the capacity to learn. If not, you would not be doing half the physical or mental things you do now. You are equipped to lead because you can learn.

Reflection:

1. What are you good at?
2. What have others said you are good at?
3. What are your best attributes (qualities)?
4. What do you or can you help a friend understand?
5. What did you do when you helped someone understand something you understood or can do?

Janetta M. Coleman, MS, LSW, CMP

LESSON ONE NOTES

Surviving Foster Care: A Journey of Self-Discovery

LESSON ONE NOTES

LESSON ONE NOTES

LESSON ONE NOTES

Janetta M. Coleman, MS, LSW, CMP

LESSON TWO: YOU MUST BE WILLING TO LEARN

"Wisdom is a shelter as money is a shelter, but the advantage of knowledge is this: Wisdom preserves those who have it."
Ecclesiastes 7:12 NLV

If you can learn, you can lead; however, you must choose to keep learning amid every situation. I know you are asking yourself how can that be true of your present situation?

First, you have the ability to speak success over your life. We talk about what we believe, so what is your mouth saying about your life? Are you saying nobody loves me or somebody loves me? Do you think you cannot stand the staff here or that maybe there are one or two things I can learn here? Do you say I cannot wait to get out of here or let me do what I can to positively move things in a better direction? You have all the choices in how you see yourself, but you must be willing to see yourself, flaws, and all. **Second**, make the right attempts. Do not let fear hold you back from trying. Do not let any diagnosis keep you from trying. So, you may have a learning disability but that does not mean you cannot do it. It means you may have to learn the information in a different way. What if you got close to someone and they betrayed your trust? That does not mean you never trust anyone again. So, you did something bad to hurt another person. That does not mean you do not deserve a second chance. You must be willing to put yourself out there and learn over and over again.

Even if you learn, try, and it is not perfect (you will not be perfect all the time), no one can take away from you the fact you tried. Knowing you made the attempt is the success you need over the results. Anything less than success is best seen as feedback to use the next time you attempt something.

I remember when I was an Independent Living Coordinator, I used to take youth for a weekend and simulated living on their own after finishing a few weeks of course work in cooking, shopping, budgeting, and apartment hunting. During that weekend I planned an activity that would leave a lasting impression and happy memories. Horseback riding was usually my surprise activity. There was one particular young lady who had the look of terror on her face when she saw the horse. You would have thought someone threw her in a scene of "Saw" the movie; that is how terrified she looked. I will never forget it because I really thought she was going to freak out. Needless to say, amid her fear she trusted me when I said it would be ok and she would enjoy it. Believe me, I know it is monumental when a foster youth trust the words a person speaks. By the end of the ride, she was smiling from ear to ear! She asked me if we could do it again right away.

I was amazed at not how she trusted me, but how she found just an ounce of strength to push through her fear to try regardless of the results. She did not know what the result would be because it did not matter. All she wanted to do was try. When you try, usually the satisfaction is positive, regardless if the results are good or bad. How can it be positive if it is a bad result? I will explain in Lesson Three.

Reflection:

1. What was the last new thing you experienced?
2. How did you feel after that experience?
3. What holds you back from trying new things?
4. Do you let people talk you out of trying new things? Why?

LESSON TWO NOTES

Surviving Foster Care: A Journey of Self-Discovery

LESSON TWO NOTES

Janetta M. Coleman, MS, LSW, CMP

LESSON TWO NOTES

Surviving Foster Care: A Journey of Self-Discovery

LESSON TWO NOTES

LESSON THREE: MISTAKES AND FAILURES ARE NECESSARY FEEDBACK

"Consider it pure joy, my brothers and sisters, whenever you face trials of many kinds."
James 1:2 NLV

Here is the question…if you were successful at everything how much would you learn about the world or yourself? Let me tell you, not much. Here is what a lot of social workers will not say, being a social worker does not make us perfect, as a matter of fact, we have learned many lessons through the experiences of others. Sure, there are general concepts/theories that can be learned from a book but dealing and connecting with families is something you learn on the job. I know this has been the case for me. Theories are great, but reality is reality. In order to have empathy or the ability to feel and understand someone else's position you must give yourself over to the moment or lesson. Foster youth have a difficult time giving themselves over to the moment because it implies that one must let go, be willing to feel, and trust in someone. I understand an unwillingness to trust people because so many people have let you down. If no one has ever told you, know this now, some people will forever let you down all the way to the grave; however, notice I said some people and not everyone.

Life is a balancing act, like being on ice skates. If you lean too much to the right you lose your balance, if you lean too much to the left you lose your balance, and if someone pulls on you, you may fall. The good thing about ice skates and life is you can always get up and start again. No one keeps you from getting up except you. Someone may be responsible for your fall, to a degree, but only you are responsible for your getting up (recovery) and finding your balance again. Therefore, it is so important to be aware of what direction you are skating in. Sometimes you want to stop and help someone else skate, but if their instability is too much for you to handle; you must learn how to let go and encourage them to keep pushing forward to find their own balance. When you fall on your skates you usually take note of what made you fall and then you begin to avoid it. Then you tell someone else how you avoided the fall to find balance. If you never fall, you will never know how to get up, keep going, nor can you tell someone else how to do it. Falling on skates (in life) is a good thing! It makes you exercise muscles that can help you find balance. The stronger those muscles the better you get when another person tries to pull you down or steer you off course. You quickly learn how to either avoid it or get up faster. I did not say falling would not hurt from time to time, because it will. Hurt is where you learn. You can do one of three things with hurt…face it, avoid it, or dwell in it.

Reflection:

1. What was your last mistake or failure?
2. Why was it a mistake or failure?
3. What was the lesson you learned?
4. What did you learn about yourself in the process?
5. What is an example of feedback you got from a mistake or failure?

Janetta M. Coleman, MS, LSW, CMP

LESSON THREE NOTES

LESSON THREE NOTES

LESSON THREE NOTES

//
LESSON THREE NOTES

Let go of **BLAME** *Let go of* **ANGER**
Let go of **REGRET** *Let go of* **FEAR**

LESSON FOUR: LET THE HURT GO!

"When my spirit grows faint within me, it is you who watch over my way. In the path where I walk people have hidden a snare for me. Look and see, there is no one at my right hand; no one is concerned for me. I have no refuge; no one cares for my life."
Psalms 142:3-4 NLV

Everyone experiences hurt, but I know foster youth often experience an extreme amount of hurt/trauma at such early ages that a person can barely wrap their mind around it. I never wanted to work in a residential facility because I felt the youth and setting would be too chaotic, dramatic, and sad. You cannot feel like it is home because your caregiver changes every 8 to 10 hours, tours are coming through the place you call home, and you cannot come and go as you please. I understand there is no "home" about it. However, I found something else to be more confining than a group home could ever be, and it is your emotions. Emotions are a strong force that can lead you to do and say good and bad things. I have always known this with most of the youth and families I worked with, but for those in residential settings, it was worse. I could see in their eyes the longing for someone and for the pain to disappear.

Hurt can keep you a prisoner for a lifetime if you let it. For some of you, your families will hurt you again and again, which is more painful because you thought they were supposed to love you no matter what. They are supposed to, but some people cannot give it (love) the way you want and need it. I wondered how long it would take for someone to heal from such abuses. The fact is some never heal; unfortunate, but true. That is when you see people repeating the patterns (generational) of their parents or caregivers. This does not have to be your existence. Letting go and forgiving is not for the person who hurt you. It is so you can stop hurting yourself by carrying it around.

There is a song by Erykah Badu called *"Bag Lady"* that says *"One day all them bags gone get in your way. You gonna miss your bus carrying all those bags."* This is so true. Whatever anybody has done to you should not destroy your dreams or the blessings God has for you. The problem with carrying all those bags is they are full of hurt and hopelessness, full of what happened with no action, full of what was said and not what is true about you. Your life is not confined to a diagnosis, court reports, what you did not do in the past, and/or what has happened to you. Letting go will be the most freeing thing you will ever do for yourself. The problem with wanting to heal from abuse and neglect is you want the healing to come from the very person who caused it. **Those who hurt you cannot heal you.** When you are hurt in such a way it leaves baggage that you may carry into future relationships and how you view yourself. Your self-worth does not rest on someone's love or lack of it. You have the power to heal yourself!! You cannot make someone face their mistakes especially if they are still in denial. Do you have time to wait for someone else to heal you? No... *"you gonna miss your bus carrying all those bags."* That bus is your LIFE. Even if someone says sorry, will it give you back what you feel is missing in your heart? In some cases, maybe, and in others, no. The hurt belongs to you and only you know how deep it goes. The person who caused it can never know the depths, which is why your healing is up to you.

I understand wanting the person to recognize what they have done to you, but you cannot stop living while you wait for it. You still have a life to lead. Lead it! Your anger is understandable, but it cannot rule your thoughts, emotions, and actions. Anger can be a destructive emotion and I think you know that. Your goal is to not let hurt penetrate your heart and take up residence. Hurt can and will destroy all hope and leave no room for joy.

Reflection:

1. What hurt are you holding on to?
2. How is this hurt affecting you?
3. What do you need to let go?
4. What's the worst that can happen if you let go of the hurt?

Surviving Foster Care: A Journey of Self-Discovery

LESSON FOUR NOTES

LESSON FOUR NOTES

Janetta M. Coleman, MS, LSW, CMP

LESSON FOUR NOTES

… Surviving Foster Care: A Journey of Self-Discovery

LESSON FOUR NOTES

Janetta M. Coleman, MS, LSW, CMP

LESSON FIVE: WALK A NEW PATH

"You were taught, with regard to your former way of life, to put off your old self, which is being corrupted by its deceitful desires; to be made new in the attitude of your minds, and to put on the new self, created to be like God in true righteousness and holiness".
Ephesians 4:22-24 NLV

Many people will tell you that you need to change and do something different, but they fail to tell you how to do it and what it will really take to change. Changing requires a mind switch to say we are going to x, y, or z. Let us take anger for instance. Some foster youth will suffer from anger. Anger for what your parent/trusted individual did or did not do. Some may resolve that anger by having a direct conversation with that person and in time anger gives way to the ability to move on. What if you cannot get any kind of resolution? What do you do then? The person is unwilling to admit or even discuss the situation with you which fuels more anger. What then? Here is what you need to know about anger and anything else that has an emotional hold over you. Moving on does not require a person to admit their mistake to you. You may have thought that but moving on is the permission you must give to yourself. You decide this emotion will not rule your life, actions, or reactions. Not everything you experience in life will be resolved. Some people will hurt you and keep moving while you are left with the roadkill of emotions. First, ask yourself did you play any role in how the situation unfolded? If so, forgive yourself for your part and admit it to the other person who was involved. If not, then forgive that person for your own peace of mind. Every morning when you wake up forgive yourself and forgive that person. Nothing happens magically overnight. To dwell on something will only stress you out and those around you. It will keep you bound to that moment in time. You are bigger than that moment, your life is bigger than that moment. You have a life to lead, and you do not have time to dwell in self-pity. It will serve you no purpose. The last thing to do is to ask yourself what you learned. There is a lesson in every good and bad situation, and I do mean every situation! Will you know the lesson right away? Maybe and maybe not.

For every successful person you meet ask them how many times life has hurt them and how it has shaped them to be the person they are today. The most hurtful things in life can be the very situations that brings you to the next opportunity waiting on you. Everyone has a purpose in life, and it is your duty to discover what that is. You will never know what it is if you are only focused on your hurt. Everyone is hurt in this life and while it is not fair, you CAN move past it and have a great life. What does a great life look like for you? For many years I was told I did not write professional enough and it became my excuse for not writing this book. The only thing I knew was I wanted to write a book by the age of 35. I am now age 47, but I started putting words to paper at age 35. Not in a way a professional author would, but in the way God would have me to put them. It is never about the messenger, but the message. Unfortunately, I let the world tell me how the message had to be written. I had to learn the message was most important from my work with young people. Over time I had to let saving and inspiring win out over self-doubt. Even in the midst you may still have reservations, but if your motive is right the result will come to be and the rest will take care of itself. Walking a new path does not mean you will be comfortable with or in it. It means you do what you were designed to do.

Reflection:

1. What kind of life do you dream of?
2. What do you feel like you need to have that life?
3. What's stopping you from having that life?
4. What's one thing you can do that can move you closer to what you want?

Janetta M. Coleman, MS, LSW, CMP

LESSON FIVE NOTES

LESSON FIVE NOTES

LESSON FIVE NOTES

LESSON FIVE NOTES

Janetta M. Coleman, MS, LSW, CMP

LET'S DO THIS

LESSON SIX: SAY YES

"Let your eyes look straight ahead; fix your gaze directly before you. Give careful thought to the paths for your feet and be steadfast in all your ways. Do not turn to the right or the left; keep your foot from evil." Proverbs 4:25-27 NLV

There is something positive from within calling you. Have you answered it yet? Only you know what it is. Whatever that something is make room for it in your heart. Believe in your mind, heart, and spirit that you can do it. How many times have you said "no" when someone has told you that you have a gift or simply doubted the gift? Other Godly people can see what we have before we even know it is there. We are all born with talents and a purpose. Life is about discovering them and enjoying the journey and all it has to offer. It is a lot easier to accept the bad when you know there is a purpose for it. Saying "yes" also has consequences. The consequence for saying "yes" is you must be dedicated to the journey. You can no longer sit passively by and have moments or opportunities come to you. You must put in the work to get results. If that means college, then you have to study. If that means having a family, you have to date and marry the right person. If that means finding your mother or father, you must start looking. If that means being wealthy, then you have to start saving. The point is you must do the work to make things move forward. The other consequence is giving up what you think you know and look for what you do not know. We all learn continuously and trust me, there is much to be learned the older you get. Those who have not moved in their life have stopped learning. A boat never fails to move it just fails to move in the intended direction because the captain stopped steering. Even when you steer, waves can change your direction, but you always have the ability to get back on course. As a matter of fact, expect unexpected waves. Where we want to go is not always the direction we should go, so life (hence God) will guide you in the direction you need to go to stay on course. Your only duty is to stay alert and be willing to steer through the wave (life). In the end, you always come out facing the right direction with God at your side. HE is there whether you recognize HIM or not.

A perfect example of this lesson was the tornado I experienced in 2004 at the residential facility for pregnant and parenting teens I mentioned previously. The facility was not appealing to the eye and we wanted to remodel the building. I had plans and came up with something I thought was decent with the money we had. Then the tornado hit on May 30, 2004. While I thought this was the worst thing that could have ever happened it was the best thing that could have ever happened. We moved three times over nine months. At the time of the storm, we had ten young ladies with children, and some were pregnant. As you might imagine it was not a fun time for the staff or the residents. I lost five pounds within the first week of this happening! After those nine months we moved into a newly remodeled home that was much better than I had planned. I would venture to say that this was the best looking residential/group home in the state of Indiana (my opinion of course). This home was colorful, perfectly decorated, and warm. People looked at the home and thought "wow it must be nice," but they had no idea what I and the staff had to endure to receive this blessing. I thought what I wanted was enough, but God stepped in and sent a wave and destroyed my plans. HE took control and the only thing I could do, and was supposed to do, was steer through the wave of events. I came out exactly where I wanted to be, but better! When you experience waves (life) where you get wet and even tossed out of the boat all you have to do is crawl back in and be willing to keep steering even though you have no idea where you are going. God always knew because I had a purpose to fulfill for those I was serving. Even the contractors who worked on the building were inspired to go above and beyond by purchasing items for each room at their expense. The right people always come along when you are on the right path no matter how rocky it may seem.

Question, are you steering through your current situation or are you working against the wave? Perhaps you are thinking about or have already let go of the steering wheel. Keep this in mind, you will say "yes" to something with or without a decision. No decision (or throwing your hands up) IS a decision, and is when you find yourself way off course. As soon as you find yourself in a place where you start thinking and saying "whatever" watch out because you just fired yourself as captain of your ship (life) and there is no telling what is about to happen next.

Take your rightful position and work with what you have.

Reflection:

1. When you think about life's possibilities what makes you smile on the inside?
2. Is the current path you are on leading to your goals?
3. Write down three (3) things you can do to get on the path toward your goals?

Surviving Foster Care: A Journey of Self-Discovery

LESSON SIX NOTES

Surviving Foster Care: A Journey of Self-Discovery

LESSON SIX NOTES

Janetta M. Coleman, MS, LSW, CMP

LESSON SIX NOTES

LESSON SIX NOTES

LESSON SEVEN: ARE YOU WILLING TO STAND ALONE?

"Even youths grow tired and weary, and young men stumble and fall; but those who hope in the LORD will renew their strength. They will soar on wings like eagles; they will run and not grow weary; they will walk and not be faint." Isaiah 40:30-31 NLV

Have you ever heard the phrase "it is lonely at the top?" Many say that when they are successful. It can be lonely because there are not many around you in the same position. This statement can be true at times, but it can also be a lonely road to travel. When you are on your personal path not everyone around you can go along for the ride. Frankly, there are some folks in your life that are not meant to travel with you anywhere! On the other hand, there are new people and situations along the way that are just there for right now and not for the future. Do not get me wrong, you may have a person or two who will always be behind you, but if that person is talking negatively when your back is turned, they may not be the person you want to help steer your ship (life). When you let someone, who was not intended to come along for the ride steer your ship, you allow them to take additional turns that were never intended for your path. The old sayings, *"someone else's problem becomes yours"* or *"be careful of the company you keep"* apply here.

This is not to say you will not have friends or someone to support you because you will. There may be periods in your life when it looks like you cannot find anyone. Usually that means self-reliance is required. Times like this can make you feel extremely lonely, but it is a part of your process and it leads to your purpose. You are to be independent of, not dependent on others and rely on your faith. This is a characteristic of maturing. There may be things that not even your closest friend can help you with, but there is a reason for that. As a part of maturing, you must become comfortable with making decisions and stop looking for someone to give you their approval on all your decisions. The more you look for someone else's approval the more hoops you will find yourself jumping through. Be confident. Own what you decide. A person who is afraid to do something is the worst person to advise you. Advice is good and necessary, but not all your decisions need to be co-signed. Otherwise, that is called co-dependence. Co-dependence means neither party can move without the other and normally co-dependent relationships do not push you toward excellence. It has a crab mentality…if you move up, I am latching on so you cannot move without me or fall back to my level. Either way in the end someone is held back from their full potential.

Reflections:

1. What do you think about when you are alone?
2. How do those thoughts make you feel?
3. Is everyone in your life bringing the best out of you or is it draining you?
4. What do you want or need to change?

LESSON SEVEN NOTES

Surviving Foster Care: A Journey of Self-Discovery

LESSON SEVEN NOTES

LESSON SEVEN NOTES

Surviving Foster Care: A Journey of Self-Discovery

LESSON SEVEN NOTES

Janetta M. Coleman, MS, LSW, CMP

LESSON EIGHT: KNOW THAT YOU ARE STRONG!

"Consider it pure joy, my brothers and sisters, whenever you face trials of many kinds, because you know that the testing of your faith produces perseverance. Let perseverance finish its work so that you may be mature and complete, not lacking anything."
James 1:2-4 NLV

We all have to stand alone for one reason or another. Understand that moments like this will prove to you who YOU are. Digging deep for strength allows you to learn more about your ability to cope, focus, survive, thrive, and/or endure. Take notice of your own coping skills in stressful situations. Here is one question that will never change no matter what you face--are you paying attention? Every situation offers two ways out... the right way and the wrong way. You can keep facing the problem until it is gone, or you can turn away from the problem and let it overtake you. You can keep trying or start drinking. You can keep pushing or start sleeping. You can keep praying or wish for death. You can move mountains or be crushed. Life is hard, but life can also be rewarding.

No matter who you are or where you come from there will be moments when you do not have enough money, reliable transportation, enough education, and/or a caring significant other. You may have broken trust, had traumatic events, and/or unexpected experiences even when everything seemed to be going well. For some this has been their reality before turning eighteen. If that is your life, then you are ahead of the game! You have survived what no one anticipated. I know you might be asking why, but the answer to that is in how you live your life when all the decisions are yours to make. While it is difficult to bear at times; traumatic and painful situations greatly shape your life to a point where you have a great testimony and can help someone else. You do not change when everything is going great; you change when what is happening is not working for your life. You must choose which way to get out. The situation(s) you will have or are currently facing may not be fair and/or warranted, yet and still it is on you. What will you do? Will you survive it or die from it? You can still walk the earth and be dead in your spirit.

What is and will always be true in life is that troubles will come. ALWAYS! You are built for your storm. You think you are not, but you are. In time you will see that. As a young person you do not have enough perspective to see it, but over time you will see that certain troubles bother one person but not the next. The skills, attributes, and gifts you have are exactly what you need to fight the good fight. For some of us, our troubles are rooted in our fears. Which challenges us to take those fears captive by facing them. Do not let them linger.

Reflection:

1. How do you feel about yourself? Why?
2. What is the scariest thought that keeps you up at night?
3. What has kept you going?
4. Take a moment and write to yourself, using your own name, and tell yourself how strong you have been thus far and that you have EXACTLY what it takes to overcome each challenge you have to face.

Janetta M. Coleman, MS, LSW, CMP

LESSON EIGHT NOTES

Surviving Foster Care: A Journey of Self-Discovery

LESSON EIGHT NOTES

LESSON EIGHT NOTES

Surviving Foster Care: A Journey of Self-Discovery

LESSON EIGHT NOTES

LESSON NINE: ENCOURAGE YOURSELF!

"Cast your cares on the Lord and he will sustain you; he will never let the righteous be shaken."
Psalm 55:22 NLV

I have had to encourage myself many times. Just because you have an education, supportive parents, a significant other, a place to live, and a good job does not mean you do not have periods of insecurity and isolation. This kind of isolation is within you and not outwardly. It is an internal struggle. Why do you think stars and athletes, who appear to have it all, still have problems that are documented for our viewing pleasure by TMZ, Facebook, Tik Toc and/or YouTube? You would think with all that money and their material possessions they would not have anything to be sad or angry about. They are human and are not exempt from being hurt, disappointed, taken advantage of, physically hurt, and/or experience pain and death.

Money does not change the individual just the quality of life they have along with enhancing who they REALLY are. However, society continues to tell us that money will give you everything and should be your motivation. Money is not everything and motivation cannot be external. A lot of people told me I would never make any money as a Social Worker? What I told them was, *"I am not doing it for the money."*

My motivation for this was born out of watching the pain the children my parents took care of as foster parents. I also believed the principle of doing the work well and money will come. No, the field of social work will not afford someone a summer home, but it will afford you a summer vacation…every OTHER summer! The other thing I have known since I was a child was that I could be helpful to others. I was gifted to do this work just like you are gifted to do something. Let your gift shine through. Your gift is usually what you do with no effort and might be willing to do for no pay. Do not confuse your gift with passion. I have a passion for traveling, but it is because of my gifts that I get to travel. Passions can be misleading because they are what we like to do, but gifts are to be used in places and situations we do not necessarily want to be involved in. Our gifts are for others. If there is something you want to do, do not let anybody say you cannot, and there will be many who will say that. However, be cognizant that what you want may come in a different package than expected. I could not have written this book without living my life and working in the career I have. Life may cause you to go on an unexpected route, but it may be in preparation for what you ultimately want to do. While you are doing something unexpected, keep encouraging yourself to keep pushing forward. Hard work, diligence, and commitment always pays off.

Encourage yourself to push forward even when you feel like you do not have any more remaining energy. Right when you say, *"I cannot take it anymore"*, is when you must keep pushing, so you do not give up and/or give in to the forces attempting to control you. As long as you keep pushing, you are not giving up, giving in, nor quietly taking it. However, when you stop pushing, you allow those forces to push you in the direction they desire for you to go. Either way, there will be some pushing. Encouraging yourself requires diligence on your part. Watching the company you keep, the decisions you make, how you talk, respond, and walk; all make a difference in how you encourage yourself. The company you keep is critical. I have already talked about how people can have a negative pull in your life; imagine if you had Godly friends in your life, who are with you right now. Godly friends will be honest and say, *"You know that is not right"* or *"What are you thinking?"* If they cannot do anything for you then they can pray for you because sometimes that is all they are meant to do. When someone prays on your behalf, they are asking God to look your way and He does! God never ignores a person praying for someone else. As a matter of fact, He takes great pleasure in seeing us pray for others. The only person who ignores

HIM (God) is the person being prayed for. You want to know why? Because the answer is not what he/she wants to hear, do, or even believe.

I was laid off from a job in 2002 and was upset about it! I did not want anything to do with social services. I applied to any and every job I could find that was not related to social services. I kept praying to God to help me, but I was unwilling to hear His answer. I received unemployment checks for seven months without getting one bite on a job. I would get interviews, but no call backs. During my career I have always managed to keep in contact with some of the youth I worked with. Mary, a youth I met when she was seventeen, and who wrote the Foreword to this book, was doing a presentation with me and I was having somewhat of a pity party. I told her of my plans to leave social services and she let me have it! She said to me, *"What? You are just going to run when it gets tough? Stick with what you know."* Mary basically told me to suck it up, what bus to get off and what bus to get on. She told me what I have told her on many occasions which was to suck it up and keep pushing. I was surprised when she let me have it like she did. She is now thirty something and still present in my life. One of the things I said I would never do in my life was work in a group home. I had no interest in it what-so-ever! Well, that is right where I landed, and this was not just your normal group home. I had teen mothers, pregnant mothers, and a daycare on-site to manage. I started as the House Manager and was promoted within six months to Residential Director. The point of this story is I tried to ignore where I was being called. Had I not answered the call you would not be reading this book. Working with my staff and the young ladies is what helped me to know my next role. That facility was my training ground for my next big thing. When you find yourself in a place you did not expect, be encouraged, because that could be your training ground for exactly where you want to be.

In the midst of your fear, encourage yourself to keep going. Encouraging yourself is really you telling yourself to look past what it looks like and do it anyway! A person must train their mind to stay positive and look for a glimmer of light when everything appears to be dark and negative. It is very easy to be negative. As a matter of fact, it does not take much thought to be negative, but to be positive means you are redirecting your thoughts and feelings to feel a certain way even though it does not look that way now.

We naturally respond to difficult situations with an "eye for an eye" attitude. When someone hurt me, I would cut them out of my life. In some cases, cutting a person out of your life is a good thing because you are not watching the company you kept. In other cases, you might want revenge, however revenge only brings on more problems. Oh yes, the closest person to you will hurt you the most. Why? Because they have more access to you. As individuals we fall short of expectations. We are not perfect, and it is impossible to be perfect. You must be willing to forgive and move forward as many times as it takes. If you are holding a grudge against your mother, father, brother, sister, etc. let it go because the grudge only keeps you from growing personally and from building flourishing relationships. Give yourself permission to forgive so you can continue to encourage yourself.

Reflection:

1. What situation stops you in your tracks every time you think about it?
2. As it relates to the answer you gave for question 1, how do you feel about yourself?
3. What are two things you can do to encourage yourself to move past that moment?
4. What makes you happy and makes your heart smile?

Surviving Foster Care: A Journey of Self-Discovery

Janetta M. Coleman, MS, LSW, CMP

LESSON NINE NOTES

Surviving Foster Care: A Journey of Self-Discovery

LESSON NINE NOTES

LESSON NINE NOTES

LESSON NINE NOTES

Janetta M. Coleman, MS, LSW, CMP

LESSON TEN: STAY ALERT

"You are all children of the light and children of the day. We do not belong to the night or to the darkness. So then, let us not be like others, who are asleep, but let us be awake and sober."
1 Thessalonians 5:5-6 NLV

Pay attention to what is going on around you because staying alert limits some of your surprises. Read the newspaper or watch the news every once in a while. Understand the climate (current events) where you live. It can certainly give you some understanding of why situations are exactly the way they are. You cannot live a sheltered life as if nothing in the news ever affects you. MUCH is going on right now that will affect you as an adult. Knowing what is going on around you is also a way to learn and stretch your mind. If you are not going to school keep learning in this manner so you can round yourself out. Leaders learn and read on their own without being prompted, plus you never know where the next inspiration will come from. Those who get ahead read, think, listen, and plan. Do not talk the game, play the game. Playing is the only way to score and win.

Stay alert in your personal relationships. The condition of your relationships also tells the condition of your heart and mind. Look at how you treat those closest to you and how they treat you. Are they similar or are they different? When it is similar hopefully it means you are going in the same positive direction. When it is different a shift has occurred. Is the shift on your part or their part? Is it a positive or negative shift? The company you keep tells a lot about who you are and what you value. Check out your friends. What does how they live say to the world? Is it the way you want to be perceived and/or live? Now family is a different story because you cannot pick your family and not all the family we have will have our best interests at heart. Put the distance where it needs to be put, and for however long it needs to be there. Be prayerful about it to know exactly what you need to do. The point here is to stay alert and be ready for anything. Also, be willing to try new things, meet new people, do what no one else you know has ever done, and go to new places. All these things add to who you are and add value to your life in ways you never imagined. Step out of your comfort zone and do the things that interest you.

Do not let other's nearsightedness keep you from going to a new level. Do not be the mold, break it and make a new one.

Reflection:

1. As a kid what did you dream about being?
2. Do you believe your dreams are obtainable? Why or why not?
3. How can you put it into action (several small steps lead to giant leaps)?
4. Watch or listen to one news program and talk about how a current event might affect you 10 years from now? Really give it some thought.

LESSON TEN NOTES

Surviving Foster Care: A Journey of Self-Discovery

LESSON TEN NOTES

LESSON TEN NOTES

LESSON TEN NOTES

Janetta M. Coleman, MS, LSW, CMP

CONCLUSION

I often wondered how I would end this book. It has taken me a lifetime of experiences to write the words I have written. Whether someone buys this book or not is not really a big concern because I did something I said I would do since I was a kid which was to write a book by age thirty-five. I am forty-seven now and it is finally finished! I did not know what the book would be about or who I would direct it to. I had to live my life to form the opinions I have. Part of the point is that you should still strive for your goals even if you did not accomplish them when planned. I had a daughter, got divorced and remarried. Of course, that really threw my timeline off. For the young mothers out there-- delay does not mean denied. It just means more time, more effort, and maybe even a better plan than what you had. What we plan for ourselves, is not always what God has planned for us or even the timeline. If I had written this book at age twenty-five, I would not have known or even said half the things I shared in this book. I am not sure what I would have written because the experiences were not there. I had to put my fears aside and do what my heart has always desired and that was to put pen to paper and produce words. As a child, I started out with writing poems and journaling. Then I was given the inspiration and the words from working with youth, such as yourself. I knew it was meant for me to write this book because God put the desire in my heart as a kid. What did I know about helping others and writing a book as an adolescent? I will tell you...not a thing! God was all over this which means HE was all over me before I knew who HE was. HE chose me for this assignment just as you have been chosen to do something, as well.

I want you to know that ANYTHING is possible no matter who you are, regardless of your background, and/or if you have a family or not. Anything is possible if you want it. **First** and foremost, you must believe that you are deserving. If you do not believe you are deserving everything you do will fail because you must be your own biggest cheerleader when no one is rooting for you. Remember whatever you believe about yourself is half the battle. **Second**, I want you to know that you can lead! Keep in mind, not every leader is seen or considered the top person. Sometimes you must play on the team as an equal. Eventually, your leadership skills will be recognized, and you will be moved to the starting line-up. Just like in a starting line-up, the players will eventually change, so do not expect to be the starting player all your life. On the same token, you do not have to be the star to get the star! Oprah said it best when she said, *"Not everyone can be famous, but everyone can be great."* This is so true! **Finally**, turn your circumstances into your platform! Make your survival skills the way you continue to strive and thrive, not just survive. I believe in your potential and capability. I hope in the span of my career I have conveyed this to the youth I have worked with. You are not your hurt; you cannot build your life on or around the hurt you have experienced. You will get past your hurt if you do the work consistently throughout your life. Good luck and start living your INTENDED life!

Janetta

ABOUT THE AUTHOR

Janetta M. Coleman, President of Montrell Partnerships LLC and Genesis Mediation LLC is a licensed Social Worker with 24 years of experience in child welfare. She is also married and is raising two beautiful children.

She holds a Bachelor's degree in Social Work and a Master's of Science. She has served on various boards within the community such as the Indiana Association on Adoption Child Care Services, Nina Mason Pulliam Scholars Program at Ivy Tech College, Youth As Resource (YAR) through United Way, Secretary of the Indiana Association of

Mediators (IAM), Region 7 Representative for the National Association of Social Workers for Indiana, and Chair of the Education Committee for Meeting Planners International, Indiana Chapter. She has presented at the Annual office of Family and Children State Directors Conference, the Indiana Association of Child Advocacy and Resources, and has testified in front of state legislators on behalf of foster youth. She was a Task Instructor for Indiana University School of Social Work, and worked as adjunct Professor at Ivy Tech College and is a former Miss Indiana USA Pageant Delegate of 1999.

As an entrepreneur, she addresses the needs of children and families by planning and coordinating various statewide conference for entities such as the Indiana Department of Child Services and the Indiana University School of Social Work through Montrell Events LLC. She provides project management for health and human services initiatives through Montrell Partnerships LLC. She also offers mediation services as an alternative to adversarial litigation between co-parents through Genesis Mediation LLC. Her personal and business goals are to be a connector of resources, a conduit for change, and a mentor to others.

Surviving Foster Care: A Journey of Self-Discovery is a journey of healing, empowerment, and inspiration. Individuals in foster care, and professionals who work within child welfare, will find tools and tactics to give strength and perseverance in place of trauma. This book will help provide a pathway for those who have experienced foster care to answer questions, discover purpose, and reignite life with a renewed spirit.

MONTRELL PARTNERSHIPS LLC AND GENESIS MEDIATION LLC

Janetta M. Coleman is the President of Montrell Partnerships LLC and Genesis Mediation LLC.

Montrell Partnerships LLC, is headquartered in Indianapolis, specializes in project management for Health and Human Service Programs. Montrell Partnerships is committed towards improving the quality of life of Indiana residents by participating in projects that address the important social issues facing our youth, families, and the general public at large. They partner with organizations that have the same commitment and work with them to implement initiatives and programs that achieve a measurable positive impact.

Genesis Mediation LLC, helps families in conflict, especially those separating or divorcing to arrive at amicable agreements without creating more undo stress. They provide expert, professional family mediation services for Indiana residents. Mediation is more expeditious and cost-effective than traditional court proceedings. Participation in mediation reduces conflict, allows each individual to be equally engaged, and remain in control of arrangements over parenting issues, property and financial decisions.

Surviving Foster Care: A Journey of Self-Discovery

Enhanced DNA
DEVELOP. NURTURE. ACHIEVE.
Publishing Division

Denola M. Burton
www.EnhancedDNAPublishing.com
DenolaBurton@EnhancedDNA1.com

Made in the USA
Coppell, TX
11 August 2021